Holding Down a Cartel King

Holding Down a Cartel King

Tiana

www.urbanbooks.net

Urban Books, LLC
300 Farmingdale Road, N.Y.-Route 109
Farmingdale, NY 11735

Holding Down a Cartel King Copyright © 2025 Tiana

All rights reserved. No part of this book may be reproduced in any form or by any means without prior consent of the Publisher, except brief quotes used in reviews.

To the extent that the image or images on the cover of this book depict a person or persons, such person or persons are merely models, and are not intended to portray any character or characters featured in the book.

ISBN 13: 978-1-64556-705-9

First Trade Paperback Printing August 2025
Printed in the United States of America

10 9 8 7 6 5 4 3 2 1

This is a work of fiction. Any references or similarities to actual events, real people, living or dead, or to real locales are intended to give the novel a sense of reality. Any similarity in other names, characters, places, and incidents is entirely coincidental.

Distributed by Kensington Publishing Corp.
Submit Orders to:
Customer Service
400 Hahn Road
Westminster, MD 21157-4627
Phone: 1-800-733-3000
Fax: 1-800-659-2436

The authorized representative in the EU for product safety and compliance
Is eucomply OU, Parnu mnt 139b-14, Apt 123
Tallinn, Berlin 11317, hello@eucompliancepartner.com

Holding Down a Cartel King

Tiana

Prologue

The large crowd gathered outside of the campaign office on Highland Avenue in East Liberty was a sight to see. Never before had there been such a diverse crowd of young people so enthusiastic about getting a state senator elected to office. It was hard enough to get the youth to care about presidential elections, let alone local and state. But this particular candidate had brought the youth out in droves. Black, white, Hispanic, Asian, gay, straight, handicapped, male, female—it didn't matter who you were or what you believed in. They all loved Khalid King because he got them. He understood them and their plight. It was easy to believe that he cared because he was only a few years older than them. He talked their language. They could relate to him and vice versa.

"He's here! He's here!" the crowd shrieked as a black-on-black Yukon Denali pulled up. Cheers erupted simultaneously.

The back door opened, and out stepped Khalid. He wore a white linen shirt with the collar unbuttoned, tan linen shorts, and tan Sperry shoes on his feet. He wore his hair in long dreadlocks, which were pulled away from his face, showing off his fresh shape-up and full, neatly groomed beard. His milk chocolate skin was free of blemishes. His lips were nice and full and curved into a beautiful smile at the sight of the crowd, showing off his blinding white teeth. As he waved, his smile deepened, giving everyone a view of the two raisin-sized dimples he had on each cheek. If he had not chosen a career in politics, becoming a male model was not a far stretch for him. He was that handsome. Some would even go so far as to call him pretty.

"Mr. King! Mr. King!" reporters cried out as he approached the door. Khalid scanned the crowd and decided he would only speak with one.

"Yes, Mrs. Jones?" he said.

Noelle Jones smiled humbly, although she knew that he would choose to speak to her over the other reporters. His family and her husband were very, very close.

"How do you feel about seeing all these young people out here supporting you and your cause?"

Khalid beamed. "I feel great! We all have the same cause, Noelle, and that's to be treated fairly regardless of race, gender, religion, or sexuality."

"Do you feel as if the lawmakers on Capitol Hill are not aware of that fact?"

He chuckled. "The fact that police gun down black men at an alarming rate and their killers are never apprehended says that no, they are not. The fact that men are sitting there, making choices about what a woman should do with her body and her choice to be on birth control or have a baby says that no, they are not. And the fact that same-sex couples still have to fight tooth and nail for the same rights as heterosexual couples says that no, they are not."

"And you feel as though you can make some changes?"

"We can *all* make a change, Mrs. Jones. Look around here." He waved his hand around Highland Avenue. "They've changed this whole neighborhood. Back when I was younger . . ." His voice trailed off as he noticed a gang of motorcycles coming down the street. Each bike had two passengers, and everyone wore black. It wasn't an unusual sight, especially since it was summertime, and many biker clubs drove around the city wearing the same color or the vests that bore the name of their club. To the normal bystander, nothing was out of the ordinary.

However, Khalid was far from a normal bystander. He was a far cry from the typical politician who ran for office, trying to be a voice of the streets but oblivious to what was really going on.

Khalid was street royalty, and as the bikers approached, he knew that this was a hit. On him.

"Everyone get down!" he yelled out as he pushed Noelle to the ground and covered her with his own body; but it was too late. No one could hear him over the powerful sound of the multiple AK-47s shooting into the crowd. The group of bikers were riding on him straight Nino Brown style, and since Khalid always insisted on making all his campaign stops without a weapon, he was caught out there naked.

"Fuck!" he swore as he watched bodies drop like flies. There was nothing he could do to stop the killing of innocent bystanders, all because they chose to believe a dream he was selling them. They knew nothing about who he really was, his affiliations, or his family. Those were all things Khalid had gone out of his way to conceal from the public eye.

He was smart enough to lie completely still as they rode off, knowing that if they saw any movement from him, they would continue shooting, not caring who they killed as collateral damage to get to the real prize: him. Once he was sure they were gone, he stood up slowly.

Noelle stood on shaky feet as he helped her up. She may have been a reporter, but she was also extremely street savvy, thanks to her husband, Zyaire. He was just glad that nothing had happened to her. The same couldn't be said for the dozen or so bodies that littered the front of his campaign office. All were young. All were either severely injured or dead.

It was a sight that would haunt Khalid for the rest of his life.

Chapter One

Khalia

I thumbed through the stacks of money that had just been dumped on a table in front of me, making sure every bill was accounted for.

"Come on, Khalia. You're insulting me," Grimm spoke up after a few minutes. "It's all there."

I smiled. "Well, if it's all here, then I'm sure you won't mind me taking my time to count this shit. Right?" My tone was friendly, but my smile was anything but. I didn't have to reach for one of the many weapons I had stashed right underneath this table and in my Hermes bag for Grimm to know that I wouldn't hesitate to make his ass a memory.

He nodded, like I knew he would. "No disrespect intended."

With my deadly smile still on my face, I nodded and grinned. "None taken." I shook the uneasy feeling that had been haunting me all day and went back to counting the money. Once I was satisfied it was all there, I tossed the leather bag back to him. "We're all good, Grimm. You can go now."

I didn't miss the way his eyes skimmed my curves as I stood up. My 7 for All Mankind jeans accentuated my small waist, hugged my thighs, and made my fat ass appear even fatter. The six-inch Giuseppe Zanotti stilettos I wore only added to my sexiness, and the red shirt that stopped right before my navel showed off my toned stomach and the diamond stud—which was real——in my belly button.

I would have been flattered to have a nigga like Grimm checking me out under normal circumstances. He wasn't the most handsome man, but his charisma and the fact that he was a boss more than made up for what he lacked in looks. I'd caught him eyeing me a few times, but there was no way I'd fuck with any nigga that worked for me and my family. If I were a normal bitch, looking for a come-up, he'd be perfect. But I *wasn't* a normal bitch. I *was* the come-up. And as such, he had no place in my personal life.

My heels clacked loudly as I stepped across the warehouse floor, Birkin bag in one arm, duffle bag full of cash in the other. When I walked outside, my driver/bodyguard Tookie was walking toward me in a hurry.

"Khalia! I was just about to come in there to get you."

I frowned as I placed the duffle bag in the backseat of my black tinted-out Range Rover he drove. "Come get me for what?"

"It's Khalid."

Hearing him say my twin brother's name put me on high alert. "*What* is Khalid, Tookie? What happened to him?"

"His campaign office in East Liberty was shot up. Ten people killed, five in critical condition."

My jaw dropped. "What the fuck? Where is he?" I yelled.

"He was at the hospital with the victims until your mother told him to leave. Everyone is on their way to her house now."

I hopped in the back seat of the truck like I had on Nikes instead of stilettos. Tookie hopped in the driver's seat and sped off as I called my brother.

He answered on the first ring. "Yo."

I had never been so relieved to hear his voice. "Bro, what happened? What's going on?"

"Shit got crazy, sis. A gang of niggas pulled up on bikes and just started spraying the crowd. So many people got hit, man. Some of them were young teenagers. I'm fucked up about this."

He was going on and on about the innocent lives that were lost, but I honestly couldn't care less about them. I needed more details about the shooters. "So, what else did you see, Khalid?"

"Nothing! Shit, I wasn't looking so one of those bullets could hit me." He sighed. "Look, I just pulled up to Mom's. Kenya and Keon are already here. How close are you?"

"Just left the spot. I'll be there in twenty," I told him before ending the phone call and sliding the phone back into my bag.

"Everything all right, boss?"

I shook my head. "No, everything is not all right, Tookie. Somebody tried to kill my brother. He didn't see shit, so I have no idea about who it could have been."

Tookie caught my eye in the rearview. "If anybody can figure out who was behind this, it's you, boss lady. I put my money on you every time."

"As you should," I responded with a small smile. I leaned back into the seat and tried to relax, but I couldn't. I had three siblings in all: my twin brother Khalid, my older brother Keon, and my younger sister Kenya. Of the four of us, I was the most like our mother, Dutchess, and proud of it. My momma was a natural born hustler and a stone-cold killer, on top of being one of the baddest bitches the entire East Coast had ever seen. My pops, Kelvin, had been by her side for her whole ride to the top, but it was clear as day to anyone who saw them that Momma ran the show.

Tookie pulled up to my parents' home, a gated estate in North Huntington. Every time I came out here, I took a minute to marvel at the sheer opulence of the place. It was so different from the projects up Elmore Square on the Hill, where we'd all been born and spent more than half of our childhood.

Tookie opened the back door for me as I grabbed the duffle bag, then my Birkin, and strutted into my parents' house. Everyone was gathered around Khalid in the family room. He sat on the sofa. The news was on, and although it was on mute, it was showing footage of the shooting that had happened earlier.

"This is all my fault," Khalid said in a soft voice as he looked away from the TV.

I threw the bag on a loveseat, then broke through everyone to reach my twin. I hugged him tightly, the uneasy feeling I'd had all day dying down as we embraced. I knew when something wasn't right with my brother or when he was in danger. He was half of me, so I felt whatever he felt.

"It's not your fault," I told him softly as I let him go.

"Like hell it ain't!" Keon yelled as he looked at the TV. "It's everyone here fault for encouraging this nigga to run for the Senate, like he comes from a normal life and a normal family! We're fucking *drug dealers,* Khalia. All of us! Including him! So why would we even consider letting him run for politics, knowing the kind of spotlight that would bring down on us?"

"Name me one politician that isn't dirty," I snapped back. Keon had a fiery temper that was scary to most, but not to me. I had never been afraid of anyone that bled like me, and that included my hot-tempered older brother. Everyone else walked on eggshells around him, but I refused to.

"We all know why he's running for the Senate, Keon," my mom said. "With his access to that much money and power, it's a pipeline that's untapped, just waiting for us to come in. And since your uncle . . ." Her voice trailed off at the mention of my father's younger brother.

My Uncle Jamar had been a state representative with unlimited political connections for us, until he was convicted of raping and sexually assaulting more than ten young girls during his summer internships for disadvantaged youth. Rather than do his time like a man, he committed suicide after his sentencing, but not before mailing a list of very influential power players to my father, along with the last letter that he wrote him. That list allowed us to take our empire to the next level.

"A legal drug dealer." Keon snorted. "That's never been a good idea to me."

"Well, lucky for you, this ship runs on my ideas and not yours," my mother snapped, staring Keon down before walking to the center of the family room. She waited a second before continuing. "What has happened today was very unfortunate, but we still have business to take care of."

My father spoke up for the first time. "Dutchess, with all the eyes on Khalid right now, is that the smartest thing to do?"

"Of course it's the smartest thing to do," my mother retorted, shooting my father a look of disdain. "It's the *only* thing to do. Dope, pills, and lean won't just sell themselves. We need to just make sure we are smart in how we move. Khalid, you need to lay low."

"I can't, Mom. I have to go to these victims' funerals. I have my out-of-town clients; I have . . ."

My mother raised her hand and cut him off. "We will give the victims' funerals at our funeral home at no charge. I know you feel bad, so it's the least I can do, plus it makes you look good. But that's it. Going OT is out."

Khalid shook his head. "I can't just stop going OT right now. I've made some great connections, and if I don't show my face, my political career might as well be over. Plus, we would lose a lot of ground and business that way."

"I don't give a fuck about none of that when it comes to staying free," my mother snapped. "Now, business will continue here at home as usual, but until we know for sure who planned this attack on you, I can't risk you dealing with those high-profile businessmen and politicians. We don't need the world to find out who you really are."

"I can make the OT pick-ups," Kenya spoke up.

We all looked at her in surprise. Kenya had been quiet the whole time. She had just turned eighteen and had graduated from high school this month. We were all fiercely overprotective of her, Keon more than any of us.

"You're not fucking going," Keon rebuffed.

"He's right, baby girl," my father spoke up. "We have other alternatives. We will just have to utilize them."

"Okay, well, even if you do have an alternative to pick up the money owed in the streets, who else can we trust with all those pick-ups from government officials?" Kenya pointed out. "Only the six of us know how many senators, governors, mayors, and chiefs of police we deal with. Can we really let anyone else in on that?"

Once again, everyone was quiet. My parents were basically retired and didn't make moves anymore; Khalid couldn't go for obvious reasons; I was the enforcer and made sure the streets both respected and feared us; and Keon dealt with nothing but wholesale and weight. Plus, it went without saying that Keon was too hot-headed to deal with any government officials, and I was too cocky. It would never work. But Kenya was more reserved like

Khalid and our father: calm, cool, and level-headed. She was the natural choice.

"She might as well," I said after a few moments of silence. "I mean, she was going to have to get her cherry popped in this business anyway."

"Not if she didn't want to," Keon snapped at me. "We know nothing but this life, but she can be the first one of us to be a civilian and not have to watch over her shoulder all the time."

I waved my hand, dismissing him. "Please. She's a King. she was born with this shit running through her veins."

No one could argue that one.

My mom agreed. "That's true. Plus, it's not like we really have a choice in the matter. She's the only one who can go." She walked over to Kenya. "Baby girl, you ready for this?"

"She will be when I'm done grooming her," I said with a smile.

My mom looked at me proudly and winked. "That's my girl."

My father looked like he wanted to say something but didn't. Instead, he went upstairs.

I watched him go and shook my head. I loved my father to death, but I could never have a man like him. To me, he had no backbone at all. He was weak, always allowing my mom to run the show. I could never have a man like that. In my opinion he wasn't a real man at all.

Chapter Two

Dutchess

I sat on my bed, pretending to scroll through my phone. I was really watching my husband, Kelvin, get dressed. I could tell from how tightly his jaw was clenched that he was pissed off at me—again.

I kept my eyes on him as he slid his black Louis Vuitton wallet in the pocket of his khaki shorts, then grabbed the keys to his Bentley Continental GT. He pulled his phone out and walked out of the bedroom door without a word to me.

No, this mafucka didn't! I fumed to myself. I sat in bed for about three seconds before hopping up and following him.

"Kelvin!" I yelled as I ran down the curved staircase behind him.

"What, Dutchess?" he replied with his back still toward me.

"Don't talk to me with your back turned!" I snapped angrily.

"I'm not talking to you. You're talking to me," he responded without turning around.

I hated it when he acted like a fucking child. I rushed around so we were facing each other and blocked the front door.

Kelvin washed his hand down his face and let a frustrated sigh out. "Move, Dutchess. I got something to do."

"Fuck no," I spat. "Not until you tell me where you're going."

Kelvin laughed, but it wasn't a happy one. It sounded forced and sarcastic. "I don't fucking work for you, Dutchess. I don't have to let you know every got damn move I make. I'm a grown man, something you seem to have forgotten."

"What are you talking about? How could I forget you're a man? I made four babies with you and been married to you for going on thirty years."

"Yet and still, you've forgotten that I am a man." He shook his head. "Dutchess, this game has changed you a lot over the years, but I never said shit to you about it. I figured that you'd remember who you were, who I was, who we became. Instead, all you focused on was making more money."

I held my arms open and gestured around the house. "And you gon' sit here and tell me you don't like the money I've made or the empire I've built?"

He chuckled. "See that? The money *you've* made and the empire *you've* built. You did everything on your own, huh?" He lifted me effortlessly and moved me from the front of the door. Then he opened the door and walked out of it.

I fought the urge to chase my husband and demand that he stay in the house with me. Fuck that. I was Dutchess King, the baddest bitch this city had ever seen. I wasn't going to chase after no man, husband or not. If he couldn't appreciate who I was and get on board with how I did things without always talking shit, there were plenty of others that would.

I walked back upstairs and crawled into my California king-size bed . . . alone.

Chapter Three

Khalid

My cell phones were ringing off the hook. I had put all three of them on vibrate, but the constant buzzing kept waking me up.

It wasn't like I could sleep anyway. Each time I closed my eyes, I saw all those kids standing there, cheering for me, chanting for me as I talked to Noelle. They were so innocent and had their whole lives ahead of them. And now, because of some shit that had nothing to do with them, they were gone.

"Baby, are you okay?"

I turned to face my fiancée, Nisa. She was propped up on one elbow, her expensive bundles of hair flowing onto the bed. Her brown eyes were full of concern.

"No," I admitted with a sigh. "I can't take this shit, man. Today is gonna be a fucking nightmare."

"It is," Nisa agreed. She moved closer to me and laid her head on my chest. "But you got this, baby. If anybody can handle this type of pressure, it's you."

I didn't respond as she ran her fingers down my chest. I already knew where this was headed and wasn't surprised when she started kissing all over my chest before going lower. I bit my lip as she slid my boxers down and then pulled my dick out. I let out a low moan as she kissed and licked all over the head before sliding it into her mouth.

I kept my eyes on her as she worked her magic. Nisa was bad as hell with her bronze-colored skin, hazel eyes, juicy lips that she kept wrapped around my dick at all times, and a body Instagram bitches would pay top dollar for. I had been with her for two years, and she made it a top priority to keep me satisfied.

She slid my dick down her throat with such ease, like she did each and every time. I don't know who taught Nisa how to suck a dick, but whoever he was, I loved that nigga. He had schooled her right. She had me coming in no time at all.

Nisa followed the "spitters are quitters" rule and swallowed every last drop. She got up and went to the bathroom as I sat up and grabbed my business phone first.

"Better now?" she asked as she climbed back into bed.

"Yeah." I looked at all the missed calls, emails,, and texts on my phone and decided that the most important call I needed to return was to Tank, my lawyer.

"Talk to me," he answered the phone.

"Yo, it's Khalid."

"Just the man I've been waiting to hear from. Listen, we gotta do damage control immediately."

"I know man. I know." I closed my eyes and saw all those innocent kids again. I popped my eyes back open. I came from a family that did a lot of dirt. I had done a lot of it myself. I wasn't above killing a nigga, but anytime I was forced to take a life, there had to be a legit reason. My mother, Keon, and Khalia seemed to get a thrill out of it, but I didn't. The fact that all those lives were taken because of me, and I had no idea why, was fucking with me heavy.

"Another victim died this morning," Tank said softly.

My heart sank. Another life lost. I couldn't just sit here hiding out anymore.

"We need a statement from you or something, Khalid," Tank went on.

"I don't want to give a statement."

"But you have to—"

"I'm going over there." I cut him off. "I'm going to the hospital to see the remaining victims. I have to see them myself."

Tank paused before responding. "And that's a good idea. We can get cameras to follow you."

"No." I shook my head like he could see me. "I don't want the world to see me going to see these people that are on their deathbed because of me. I'm not doing it for the publicity. I'm doing it to show that I care. No cameras, no phones."

"I understand that, but you have to say something, Khalid. It's not a good look being quiet about this. Didn't your campaign manager tell you this?"

"I haven't talked to him yet," I admitted, knowing that Larry Price was going to throw a shit fit whenever I did speak to him. I hadn't talked to anyone but my family since this bullshit went down. I had to let them know that we were under attack and that whoever was coming at us was very bold.

Even though my parents had made a fortune from our drug empire, it had never interfered with our legal businesses, especially when it came to politics. We had all that shit locked down. Whenever someone came at us, it was on some street shit. People that weren't connected didn't know the real deal behind us. So, whoever this was knew how we really lived. The only question was, who? It made absolutely no sense to come at us. Because we sold heroin, cocaine, pills, and marijuana, everybody ate with us. As a result, our workers and our customers were happy. Of course, we couldn't please everyone, but beef was never a real concern for me. Anyone that had problems with us had to deal with Khalia and Keon, and no one really wanted to fuck with those two crazy mafuckas.

"Well, can you at least do that before you go to the hospital? Text me after you do, then me and him can figure out how to spin this."

"I got you," I told him before hanging up. I didn't bother to check my personal or trap phones. Neither one of those mattered right now.

"So, you're really going to go to the hospital without cameras?"

I turned around and looked at Nisa. "Yeah. Why would I bring them?"

"You would bring them so people can see how you really are and to sway the voters back to your side."

The voters.

I hadn't forgotten that I needed to win this election to make my family's business quadruple. Our future was on my back. But right now, that seemed insensitive when people were fighting for their lives.

"It would kill two birds with one stone," Nisa went on. "Baby, I know how much you need this win. You need to strategize to get it."

She was right, but she was also wrong.

Most of the women I dealt with knew nothing about how the Kings had really become rich, but Nisa wasn't most women. She was street royalty, just like me. She came from a family full of hitmen. Her father had been my father's bodyguard for years before he killed himself two years ago. I'd known Nisa for years, but it wasn't until after her father's funeral that I began to really get to know her. I embarked on a relationship with her because she knew my world and how to deal with me. Most women knew nothing about who I really was, and if they did know, they wanted something in return. Nisa had her own money and wanted nothing from me but me—but that was something I wasn't quite sure I could give her.

My heart had been closed off to love ever since my first love, Amber, had been killed by a bullet that was meant for Khalia four years ago. She had been five months pregnant with my child at the time, and my son had died too. Ever since that incident, I had let no woman get close to me.

Nisa was different. I was with Nisa because she understood my world, but I was also with her because she was safe. Amber had been a civilian; Nisa was not. She wasn't out there making hits, but she did carry and was trained and ready to go at all times. I could trust her in a gun battle before most niggas. I was almost one hundred percent sure that if Nisa had been there with me yesterday, things would have turned out much differently.

Yeah, Nisa was a good choice for me to be with. She was smart, gorgeous, and had her own dough. She wanted nothing more than for me to love her. I just couldn't love her the way that she wanted. I cared for her deeply, but I would never say that I loved her.

"I'll strategize after I see the victims," I told her as I headed to the shower. "I gotta check on them before I make any moves."

Chapter Four

Toni

I sat in the cramped ICU room at UPMC Presbyterian Hospital beside my little brother's bed and held his hand lovingly as tears streamed down my face. It was so unfair that this had happened to him. He was laid up in this bed with no assurance that he would ever wake up. And if he did wake up, the doctors weren't even sure that he would walk again.

"Tommy, you gotta wake up," I whispered to him as I squeezed his hand. "You can't leave me out here all alone."

The tears were falling down my face so fast that I didn't even bother to wipe them away. There was no point. They would just come right back anyway.

I had been a nervous wreck ever since I got the news of the shooting. I knew that Tommy had planned on being at Khalid King's campaign office. He supported Khalid to the fullest, mainly because of his views on gay rights. Tommy was openly gay. Many women had tried to seduce him because with his light brown skin, deep dark eyes, slightly muscular build, and his slight hood swagger, he was very easy on the eyes. He also wasn't effeminate, so no one knew that he was gay until he disclosed that information.

My brother had struggled with his sexuality for years. He'd always been the most popular boy in school and around the way, on top of being a superstar athlete in both basketball and football. Being gay did not fit into that mold, and when he first became attracted to men, he didn't know what to do. I encouraged him that living his truth would set him free. No one would have anything over him, and he would see who loved him for who he really was. During his senior year of high school, he came out and had been living as openly gay ever since.

"They told me I should still talk to you like I would any other day because you can still hear my voice," I said softly as I held his hand. "Today I woke up, went to work, but couldn't stop thinking about you. There was no way I could pretend to focus on customers at the bank when you were on my mind so heavy. So, I left and came here." I wiped my tears as they continued to fall. "I will sit here every single day until you wake up, Tommy, because I know that you will. You are the strongest person I know. You are not a quitter." I looked at him closely, hoping to see his eyelids flutter, his lips move, something.

Nothing.

I held onto his hand as my head dropped to my chest. I sobbed uncontrollably. My brother was all that I had in this world. I couldn't imagine being here without him. For so long, it had been us against the world. I knew without a doubt that I couldn't be out here, couldn't function, without him by my side. He was my lifeline, and without him, I would surely flatline.

I cried long and hard, never letting go of his hand. We were so connected that I knew he had to feel the anguish I was going through as he lay there in his coma, dangling in the space between life and death. There would be no life without him. There would be no me without him. If his soul decided to leave this earth, he would take mine right along with him, leaving me nothing but a shell.

The sound of someone clearing their throat brought me back to reality. I tried to wipe my face before turning around, but it was pointless. Whoever it was would be able to tell I'd been crying just from looking at me. My eyes were red and puffy from all the tears I'd shed. I turned around, ready to snap on whoever interrupted this private moment between me and my brother.

A tall, extremely handsome, chocolate-colored man with dreadlocks stood there. I immediately recognized him as Khalid King, and my blood began to boil. He was the reason my brother was here in the first place.

"Hi, I'm Khalid King," he said as he walked toward me, his hand extended.

I brushed it away angrily. "I know who the hell you are," I hissed as I turned away from him. "Why the fuck are you here?"

I expected him to have something to say about my angry reaction to him, but he took it in stride and said nothing. Instead, Khalid looked at Tommy. His eyes traveled to each and every machine that he was hooked up to. When his gaze landed back on me, it was full of sorrow. "I had to come," he said softly. "I couldn't take not seeing the survivors from yesterday. I needed to face them."

"For what? A photo op or something?"

He waved his arms around him, then behind him. "Do you see any cameras here with me? I came alone." He looked at Tommy again. "I didn't want the cameras to capture this," he went on in a much softer voice. "This isn't for the public to see."

"Funny you should say that, since my brother was shot in the public eye," I retorted.

His head dropped. "I know."

"You know?" I mocked him. "So, what are you planning to do about it?"

"We're looking for the men responsible as we speak."

I folded my arms. "In other words, you don't know who did it?"

He looked me straight in the eye. "No. We don't. Not yet. But we will."

I scoffed and sat back down beside my brother. "I think you should leave."

He did the opposite as he came and stood behind me. "I'm not ready to leave yet. This man laying here in this bed believed in me. He believed in my cause. I owe it to him to be here for him now."

"Well, I don't want you here," I snapped, my back still toward him.

"I'm sure his parents or other family members may feel differently."

"Ain't no 'parents or no other family members'," I mocked him sarcastically. "All Tommy got is me. All I got is him. And now he may not come back to me because of some bullshit dream you were selling him!" I finally turned to face him, my eyes full of anger. "Do you know that he took bullets to his chest, stomach, and his back? He lost a kidney, his spleen is damaged, he has a punctured a lung, and a bullet missed his heart by inches. He went into shock behind all of the blood that he lost and almost died on the operating table. My brother may never wake up again, and if he does, he may be paralyzed from the bullet in his back. He may never be able to walk again, and you want to come here and do what? Talk? Ease your guilty fucking conscience? 'Cause you don't give a fuck about my brother. And he doesn't need your pity." I turned away from him because I felt the tears threatening to fall again, and I didn't want to share my grief with him. They weren't for him to see. They were for my brother.

Khalid placed his hand on my shoulder. I was surprised by how comforting his touch was.

"I'm going to fix this. I promise. And I keep all of my promises. You said you are his sister? Can I get your name, sister?"

"Toni," I told him reluctantly.

"Okay. Toni, look at me." He turned me toward him. "I feel fucked up about what happened to Tommy. I really do. I can't even sleep. Eleven people lost their lives for no reason, and I have four other people fighting for theirs at this very moment, your brother included. I won't be able to rest until I know they are okay and I get to the bottom of this."

I had to admit, it sounded good, but he was a fucking politician. All they did was lie.

I shook his hand off my shoulder and turned back to my brother. "I think it's best that you go now," I told him as I picked Tommy's hand back up.

I could hear him sigh, but he did back away. Before he walked out the door, he said, "Well Toni, I'm leaving my business card on the counter right here and with the nurses. You run into any trouble, anything at all, you call me."

I waited for him to close the door behind him. Once he did, I walked over to the countertop and picked up his business card.

"Khalid King. Manager of King Enterprises," I read out loud. I scoffed and ripped the card into pieces before tossing it into the garbage can. "Fuck outta here." Then I went to reclaim my seat beside my brother. Nothing had changed in the few minutes my attention had been diverted from him, but still, I shouldn't have been distracted at all.

I leaned over to kiss his forehead. He still felt warm, which was extremely comforting to me. The way he was lying there, motionless, was so unlike him. He was always on the move. Tommy was never this calm, never this still. It was almost as if he *were* dead. My brother was never this quiet.

I had been talking to him since I took vigil at his bedside and really didn't have anything else left to say. So instead, I began to sing a song our grandmother used to sing to us when we were very young. I was six, and Tommy was four when she was taken from us, but I still remembered how calm I felt whenever she would sing this song to us. It was so simple, but the words comforted me more than any others I'd ever heard.

I started singing softly. I didn't want anyone to hear me. My voice wasn't for anyone to hear but my brother.

"Jesus loves me, this I know, for the Bible tells me so. Little ones to him belong. They are weak, but he is strong." I smiled a little as I thought about our grandmother, Pearl, and leaned over to kiss Tommy's forehead again. Then, I continued singing the song that used to soothe our young, troubled souls.

"Yes, Jesus loves me. Yes, Jesus loves me. Yes, Jesus loves me, for the Bible tells me so."

Chapter Five

Keon

I sat at my kitchen counter, watching ESPN and eating the egg white and spinach omelet that my maid/chef Marisol had prepared. It was delicious, but so was everything that she cooked.

I had a lot on my mind on this particular morning. I wasn't sure that ESPN and Marisol's delicious cooking could stop my thoughts from running rampant. Today was my oldest son's graduation from middle school, and while I adored the ground Nahim walked on, I wasn't too excited to go. It had nothing to do with him and everything to do with his mom. Usually, I tried to avoid his mother, Stacy, at all costs. She was a damn drama queen who was intent on making my life a living hell because of what I'd done to her during our tumultuous six-year relationship.

I mean yeah, I cheated on her from time to time. Okay, I cheated on her a lot. Shit, Nahim was my oldest son, but Jordan, Mikey, and my only daughter Keonna all came not too far after him. In my defense, I only made Jordan on her. Mikey was conceived when we were on one of our breaks, and Keonna was just five years old. We'd been split up for years before I had her.

On top of the cheating, we fought a lot. It wasn't always just verbal, either. There were quite a few times our shit got physical. I never beat her like she was a nigga in the street, but I had slapped her ass and pinned her up against the wall more than a few times. I couldn't help it. Her mouth made me want to kill her ass. She just didn't know when to shut the fuck up.

With everything going on with Khalid, and with my mom giving the green light for Khalia's crazy ass to show Kenya how to navigate the streets, the last thing I wanted to do was deal with Stacy and her antics today. But I didn't have a choice. I might have had four kids, but I was here for each and every one of them, regardless of what their mothers tried to say about me.

"You need anything else, sir?" Marisol appeared from what seemed like out of nowhere and took my plate.

"Naw, I'm good," I told her. I stood up and watched as she walked over to the sink. Marisol had to be in her mid-thirties, and with her long, black hair, handful of tits, and fat ass, she could pass for the poor man's version of Jennifer Lopez. Her face was naturally soft and pretty. Under any other circumstances, I would have fucked her already. I'd learned my lesson about fucking my housekeepers, though. The last bitch I'd had working here tried to say I forced myself on her and raped her. In all fairness, I'd had a few drinks before I came in, so I was more aggressive than usual, but she had encouraged me every step of the way. It was only after she sucked my dick so good that I had no choice but to pipe her down that she'd decided I'd raped her. I couldn't believe that shit. I was a lot of things, but a rapist was not one of them. I got pussy much too easily for me to ever have to take it.

I ended up settling out of court, but I never got over the fact that she'd tried to put that shit on me. So, I left my housekeepers alone, no matter how good they looked—and they all looked good. It was a prerequisite to work for me. If I had to look at somebody every day, they had to be sexy as hell.

I watched the basketball highlights as they flashed across the ESPN screen.

"I don't care what they say about KD, he still a bitch for going to the Warriors," I murmured just as my cell phone rang.

"Yo," I answered.

"What's good?" Chuck replied.

"Chillin'," I told him as I kept my eyes on the TV screen. "Just got done eating, 'bout to go to Nahim's graduation and shit."

"Oh, yeah, that is today. Damn, tell my godson I said congratulations."

I nodded. "Will do."

Marisol appeared out of nowhere, yet again, with my protein shake.

"Thanks, Mari." I smiled as I took it from her hands. She really was the best. She anticipated each and every one of my needs.

"Mari? You got a new bitch over there?"

I chuckled and walked to the master bedroom. "Naw, nigga, Marisol. My housekeeper." I clicked on the sixty-inch TV that was mounted on my wall. Of course, it was tuned into ESPN as well.

"Oh, that bitch? You still got her around? I told you I don't trust her."

I went to my walk-in closet and started going through the clothes hanging in there. I shook my head at Chuck's comments. He had been my nigga since we met in the sixth grade at Milliones Middle School. Outside of me, he didn't trust a fucking soul. "Nigga, you don't trust anybody. You worse than me."

"You shouldn't trust anybody either, especially that bitch, fam. She look sneaky."

I shook my head. "Yo, what's up? Any word on that?" I asked, changing the subject away from his constant suspicions about everyone to something much more important. I'd had my best shooters put their ears to the streets to see what came up about that attempted hit on Khalid yesterday. Chuck was the best of the best, second only to me. If niggas were talking, he would hear it. If not, he would torture it out of them.

"Not yet, but you know I got a way of making niggas sing," Chuck responded with a laugh. "I'll have something for you by the end of the day."

I tried to be satisfied with that, but the truth was, I wasn't. I mean, it just didn't make sense to me for niggas to try to hit Khalid. Me and Khalia, yeah, but Khalid was cleaner than us. He wasn't in the streets like we were either. As far as niggas knew, Khalid was a typical college graduate that didn't get his hands dirty at all. That was for me and Khalia to do.

I ended the call with him when I saw Kenya beeping in. "Hey, sis," I answered happily. Out of all my siblings, Kenya was my favorite. I didn't even try to hide it. Khalid was always under Dad, and Khalia was too busy trying to be the next Griselda Blanco for me to really treat her like a baby sister. Shit, we were too much alike. We always ended up arguing. A few times, she even swung on me.

But Kenya was like a breath of fresh air. She still had an air of innocence that none of us possessed. She could be the first one of us to pursue her dreams outside of the drug game, and I was here to encourage her to do it. I didn't give a fuck what Ma and Khalia wanted her to do. Kenya was better than this shit. She was better than us.

"Hey, I'm locked out of my car and Triple A won't be here for another two hours. Is it okay if I ride to Nahim's graduation with you?"

"Of course. I'll be there soon." I hung up the phone and placed it on my dresser. ESPN caught my eye again. They were still showing basketball clips and highlights. I stared at the screen without really watching it. All I could think about was the dream that never became a reality for me.

Being a King meant sacrificing everything you ever wanted for yourself for the sake of the family—which wasn't always a good thing. Kenya still had a chance to make something of herself and be something besides a criminal. I was going to see that she did.

Chapter Six

Kenya

Nahim's graduation was nice, if you didn't count the fact that I had to sit right beside Keon to stop Stacy from starting some shit with him. He had brought my other nephew, Jordan, to the graduation with him. It made sense to bring him. The boys were only a year apart, they were extremely close, and most importantly, they were brothers. We, as Kings, had to stick together, no matter what. It was what my mother had taught us and what we would eventually teach our own kids. So far, Keon was the only one to have children, but we also instilled that valuable lesson in them. Family was all we had.

I personally thought that Stacy was being rather childish when it came to Keon's other children. She barely spoke to them and acted like she didn't want Nahim around them. She was just going to have to get over that. Keon might have been a lot of things, but a deadbeat father wasn't one of them. Even if he were, my family wouldn't have allowed the kids to grow up not knowing each other. Our bloodline was too thick for that.

As Keon was talking to the boys after the graduation, Stacy pulled me aside and stared me up and down so hard that it made me uncomfortable.

"Yes?" I asked her finally.

"You just graduated yourself, didn't you?" she asked me.

"Yes."

"So, what are your plans? You going off to college?"

I hesitated before I answered her question. Stacy had practically watched me grow up. She knew what my family was really about. They said she was even out there busting her guns alongside Keon when he burst his. She was almost like family.

But still.

Being *almost* like family was not even close to actually *being* family. There was no way she could know that I was being groomed to basically take over Khalid's role in the family.

"No, I don't think college is the right step for me right now," I answered politely.

Stacy looked over toward my brother and stared at him for a minute. "Well, make sure whatever you end up doing is something that *you* want to do, not your family. If you don't, you'll end up living a life full of regrets, and it'll change you." She kept her eyes on Keon the entire time she spoke.

I wondered what she meant by that but didn't have the time to ask her. Keon was walking back over with both of his sons.

"Nahim's coming with me and Jordan," he informed Stacy.

Stacy sucked her teeth. "No the fuck he's not."

"Yes, he is. I wasn't *asking* you, Stacy. I don't need to ask you for your permission to take my son. He's coming with me, and that's it."

She rolled her neck. "You crazy as hell if you think I'm gonna let my son come with you after they just shot up Khalid's rally. Y'all got shooters coming for y'all, and my son will not be a casualty of some bullshit y'all got going on."

The vein in Keon's neck throbbed dangerously as he took a few more steps closer to Stacy, closing the distance between them. "I don't know who the *fuck* you think you talking to, but—"

I looked at my nephews, who were both engaged in their phones and not paying them any attention, thank God. I interrupted them. "Stacy, Nahim can come with me," I told her. "I'm going to New York for the weekend, and I'd love to have him."

Stacy kept her hate-filled eyes on Keon before looking back at me. I knew that she really didn't want Nahim to come over because she didn't want him around Jordan, which was absurd. The shootout at Khalid's rally just gave her the perfect excuse to say no.

"As long as he is with Kenya and not you," she spat at Keon.

I shook my head and watched as the vein in my brother's neck throbbed even more. She thrived on pissing Keon off. I remembered some of their knockdown, drag-out fights. The whole family was ecstatic when the two of them finally called it quits. Their relationship was extremely volatile and toxic

"Let's go," he said in a low voice.

Once we all got situated in his truck, a black-on-black-on-black Lincoln Navigator, he turned and looked at me. "What's up? Why you going to New York this weekend?"

"There's a rap concert at the Barclays. It's gone be lit!" I exclaimed. "Fab, French Montana, Cardi B, Meek Mill, Dave East . . . I can't remember who else, but I can't wait to go."

Keon nodded as he drove. "And who you going with?"

"Just me and Dionne as usual." Dionne was my very best friend since the first grade. She was the only female I'd met who didn't try to use me or get close to me because I was a King. She also wasn't on that fake shit trying to be my friend so she could fuck with one of my brothers.

"You can't go alone," he said softly. "So, I'll be coming with you."

"Whaaattt?" I whined. "No!" The last thing I wanted or needed was Keon's overprotective ass watching over me at the concert. I loved New York, Brooklyn in particular. I planned on going to that concert and seeing what niggas I could meet while I was in the city. Keon would ruin all that for me. He was like the fun police when it came to me, and I just didn't understand why. He never tried to be all in Khalia's business or stop her from doing what she wanted, and she was his little sister too. It was like he couldn't care less what Khalia did, but when it came to me, he needed to know every single detail.

"Listen, we are in the middle of some bullshit, and we don't know who is after us. We all need to have extra protection. Just because you'll be out of PA doesn't mean you're safe. The Kings are known up and down the East Coast, li'l sis. We have plenty of enemies, and I'm not letting you go out there without protection. Especially since you'll have my sons with you."

I rolled my eyes. "Keon, how am I supposed to step into Khalid's role and handle his OT business if you don't trust me? I'm a big girl. I can handle myself. I know how to shoot a weapon and spot an opp. Trust me."

Keon shook his head. "You think you know everything, and you don't know shit. Kenya, do you think knowing how to shoot is all there is to keeping you safe and alive in this game? If that were the case, there would never be any casualties because *everyone* has a gun, baby girl." He was quiet for a moment before continuing. "Besides, I don't want you to step into this shit anyway."

"Why not? You, Khalid and Khalia do it. What makes me so special that I shouldn't learn the family business?"

"Because you have a choice," Keon responded firmly. "Me and the twins didn't. We were forced into this shit. We had to give up any dreams we had of our own for the sake of the family. This business is a dirty game, sis. It changes people. It will change who you are, and I don't want that for you. I want you to go to college. Find a lame nigga that will treat you like the queen that you are. Settle down and start a family. Live a normal fucking life."

I hesitated before responding. "Khalia didn't do any of that, and she's good."

"Khalia thinks she's me," he spat. "She ain't nobody to look up to."

"Shit, why not? No one fucks with her."

"Because, Kenya. You don't want to be a woman like that. Yeah, she's feared in these streets. Niggas are just as scared of her as they are of me, and not just because they think she'll come get me. Khalia's ass is crazy. But when she goes home at night, she's alone. Those pistols and all that money can't keep her warm at night. She'll never trust a man, and furthermore, she won't know how to be with one because she thinks she gotta run shit. She's ruthless as hell. Tell me, is that the kind of life you want to live?"

I had never thought of Khalia in the way Keon had just described her. To me, my big sister could do no wrong. She was beautiful and fearless. What was so wrong about that? She was a bad-ass bitch that demanded respect whenever she walked into a room without having to say a word. I loved that about her.

Keon drove in silence as I pondered his question. The truth was, I had no idea what kind of life I wanted to live. I had finished high school with straight *A*s but had no ambitions to do anything. College was naturally the next step, and I applied to many. Whenever I received the responses, though, I didn't even open them. I dumped them in my top drawer and kept it moving.

What would I do in college anyway? What would I major in? The whole point of going to college was to get the kind of money that my family already had. I just didn't see the point in it. I didn't have a passion for anything outside of my family, hip-hop, and fashion. They didn't offer college courses for those things.

It was a natural move for me to step into what we did. We owned the largest chain of funeral parlors in the Northeast, among many other businesses. While they all made us very wealthy, I didn't see myself stepping into any leadership positions for any of them. Dealing with death and destruction all day on that level was nothing I wanted to be a part of.

But Khalid's role in the family wasn't bad at all. He was more on the white-collar side. He wheeled-and-dealed with politicians and law enforcement. High risk, low danger. I didn't see why Keon was making such a big deal about me taking over for Khalid while the heat died down. I was sure that I would do just fine.

Chapter Seven

Khalia

"Mmmm . . ." I moaned as my eyes rolled back into my head.

"You like that,. baby?" the man between my legs murmured as he came up for air.

I didn't bother to respond as I grabbed the back of his head and tried to shove it in my pussy. I received no complaints from him as he started moaning louder than I was. I could feel the nut starting to build up from the tips of my toes. I arched my back and grinded my pussy all over his face.

"Yeah, just like that," I murmured. Something about smearing my juices all over a nigga's face as he gave me some fire head turned me the fuck on in ways I couldn't even begin to explain.

He wrapped his arms around my thighs, trying to force me to lower my back onto the bed, but I refused. Even in a submissive position like this, I still had to be the one in control of the situation. Instead, I spread my legs wider and fed my pussy to him as a nuclear orgasm tore through my body.

"Ohhhh, shiiiiiittt!" I yelled as I held his head with one hand, the sheets with another. Even after I was done coming, I still gave his face two extra humps, just to make sure my juices were all over him.

He kissed the inside of my thighs a few times before standing up. He started to unbuckle his pants, and that's when I had to stop him. "Fuck is you doing?"

His brows narrowed in confusion. "What you mean? I just—"

"You just gave me the best head I had all month," I told him with a smile as I got off the bed. "But I'm a busy woman, as you know, and that's all the time I can give you today."

I felt his eyes on me as I got dressed, but frankly, I didn't give a fuck. Darnell was a young soldier who worked for me. He was very, very easy on the eyes: caramel skin, dark eyes, nice smile, tatted up, and most importantly, nice, sexy, full lips. From the moment I saw him driving one of my lieutenants around, I knew I had to have him. He was too tempting to pass up, and I always got whoever and whatever I wanted.

The thing about messing with a soldier in my crew, though, was that I couldn't fuck him. And man, did I want to. He had earned some of this good pussy the way he made me come all over the bed. But I knew better. The day I fucked one of these niggas was the day my leadership would be questioned because if one of them could sex me, why should the others fall in line and listen to me? I would become nothing more than a piece of ass, and I had worked too damn hard to let that happen.

"You got that for me?" I asked him. Playtime was over. It was back to business.

He bit his lip and nodded before walking to his closet. He returned with a small black duffle bag. I took it off him and unzipped it. The bag contained three pistols, two silencers, and two Perkin hunting knives in their cases. I grinned before zipping it back up.

Darnell was a soldier, but he worked under the man who supplied us with our weapons. He'd been sniffing around me for months, so I told him that if he really wanted to get a whiff of this, he'd come through with some clean guns for me. The knives were a bonus. Everyone knew that I'd rather shoot someone before I'd stab, but there were a few instances where knives were much handier. I could tape a blade to my thigh, and no one would know the difference.

"Thank you, baby," I told him with a small smile. He was still looking rejected, so I walked over to him and pecked him on the cheek. "Remember, if anyone says anything about these or notices that they're missing, tell them I asked for them. They can come talk to me if they don't believe that."

Darnell nodded, but he didn't look too concerned about that. Instead, he looked at me. "When am I going to see you again?"

The thought of dealing with someone who expected more of my time than I was willing to give was such a big turn-off to me that I shuddered. There was a reason I had my sexcapades the way that I did. No commitments and no expectations on my end.

It was time for me to go. I walked out the door of his crib, telling him that I would call him later but knowing that I never would.

Tookie opened the back door of the Range Rover for me. "Where to, Boss Lady?"

I sat in the back seat. "Take me up Northview, Took. A little birdie I been looking for is hiding out up there."

Tookie pulled away from the curb. "Do we need backup, Boss Lady?"

I shook my head as I sorted through the small duffle bag I'd gotten from Darnell. "Do I ever?"

Tookie laughed and kept driving.

I wanted to use a gun. It would be quicker and to the point. However, the person who had been hiding had violated. They didn't deserve to have a quick and easy death.

We rode past the security guard at the front. Tookie knew him, but even if he hadn't, we still wouldn't have stopped. I directed him on which court to go to as I slipped both hunting knives into the sides of my jeans, then reached in the back for a wig I'd stashed there earlier.

"You sure you don't need me?" Tookie asked again as he looked at me through the rearview mirror.

I laughed as I put the curly blonde wig over my black hair. "Took, I'm good. Trust me. But if I ain't outta there in about ten minutes, come get me. Okay?"

"Okay," he replied seriously.

I got out of the truck and walked to the project apartment where I'd been told my bait was hiding. The front door was slightly ajar, just as I'd known it would be. I slid some black leather gloves on, then walked through it just as a young, light-skinned woman made her way down the steps.

"He sleep?" I asked her in a low voice.

She nodded. One look at her wild hair, and I could tell she'd fucked and sucked him to sleep like I'd instructed her to.

"You got that for me?" she asked desperately.

I gave her my award-winning smile, complete with the dimples. "Of course, girl. I always keep my word."

She watched me hungrily as I reached into my bra and pulled out a thick billfold of nothing but big-face hundreds. I handed it to her, along with a small bag from my back pocket that contained Percocet 30s. Her eyes widened at the sight of the pills. I swear she was happier to receive those than she was to get the money.

She snatched the money and the bag, then ripped the bag open. She was so focused on getting high that she paid no attention as I pulled one knife out of its sheath. I slit her throat from ear to ear before she even realized what was going on. When she hit the ground, I politely grabbed the money out of her hand, left the Percs, then made my way upstairs.

Marv was still fast asleep from whatever his young girl had put on him. I walked over to the bed and decided to have a little fun. I pulled the cover back, and sure enough, he was naked. I grinned devilishly as I grabbed my second knife from my hip. I placed that one under his balls and stuck the tip of the first blade to his neck hard enough to draw blood.

He woke up, eyes glazed over with sleep and confusion, but when they settled on me, I could tell he recognized me, even with the wig. Then his eyes filled with the one thing I loved the most: fear. Especially when he realized that I literally had him by the balls.

"Yeah, it's me. The boogeyman—or should I say woman—in the flesh," I told him with a wicked grin.

"Khalia, it don't even have to go down like this," he said in a low voice. He was trying to sound fearless, but the strongest man in the world would be scared when there was a knife held to his nuts.

"See, here's the funny thing. It didn't," I agreed. "You made it like this when you insisted on running off with my product and selling that shit on your own. You been missing for what, a few months now?"

"I . . . I ain't mean to—"

I shook my head. "Ah, ah, ah, Marv. I already know what it is. You thought this shit wouldn't get back to me because Cam was your man. He was supposed to keep covering for you, wasn't he? Only he kept coming up short at count. And when I threatened him—in this same exact way—he said your name."

Tears fell down Marv's face. "I'll pay you back all the money, I swear. Just don't kill me!"

I laughed. "I'm not here to hear that shit," I told him honestly. "The only reason I even woke you up was so that you knew who it was that sent you to meet Satan."

He looked around desperately.

"Who you looking for? Kiya? That little junkie bitch downstairs stinking, B. I mean . . ." I teased his balls with the blade, causing him to jump. "How did you think I knew you were here in the first place?"

His eyes showed his rage at her betrayal. In one last effort to save his life, he lunged at me, but I'd expected him to do so. The moment he moved, I sliced his balls in one quick, fluid motion. He yelled out in excruciating pain.

I knew Tookie would be anxious waiting for me, so I made my next move quickly as he bled out all over the bed. I slit his throat from ear to ear. He held it as blood spouted all over him.

"Never fuck with a King. In this life or the next," I hissed before taking the knife and plunging it into his chest, silencing him for good. Then I took both my blades, wiped them on the sheet, and left as quietly I'd come.

Tookie was still in the driver's seat when I hopped back in the truck. He took in my appearance and grinned as he pulled off.

"How long was that, Took?" I asked him as I pulled the blonde wig off my hair, allowing my silky wrap to fall back into place.

"Seven minutes," he responded.

"I told you I was good," I told him with a laugh.

"Yeah, you did. How you go in there and handle all that, then come out looking like nothing happened?" he asked in amazement. "You don't even have a speck of blood on you."

I smirked. "Because I'm a muthafucking professional, Took. And I'm the best bitch to ever do it."

Chapter Eight

Khalid

I walked into my master bedroom and loosened my tie angrily. My shirt came off next. I had just come from yet another funeral for one of the victims of the shooting, and it was safe to say I was just about over this shit. I just wanted my life back. I wanted to get back on the campaign trail. I wanted to run up and down the East Coast, meeting with the most influential politicians to pick up my money and give them their drugs. I wanted to be getting ready to commute between Pittsburgh and Washington, D.C. This whole shooting had set my life back, and I wasn't happy about it.

Nisa walked into the bedroom. As usual, she had on some lacy lingerie and six-inch heels. She always wore expensive lingerie and heels. I saw her undressed way more than I saw her dressed. Our sex life was amazing. I honestly had nothing to complain about. She kept me pleased and coming back for more. In the few years we'd been together, I'd never been bored with her—sexually, at least.

"Babe, how you feeling?" she asked as she sat on the bed behind me and began to massage my shoulders.

"Stressed the fuck out," I responded truthfully.

"Once these funerals are over, Khalid, we need to strategize your next move."

For some reason, my mind drifted back to the other people that were lying in the hospital, Tommy Moore in particular. While there were other victims in the ICU, he was the only one who had yet to wake up. It was safe to say his injuries were the worst, and I felt like shit. I planned on going back to visit him. I couldn't help but hope that his sister was there.

His sister.

Although Nisa was the one touching me, my mind drifted back to Tommy's sister, Toni. She was beautiful, but in a completely different way than Nisa was. She had smooth brown skin, big dark eyes, full lips, and an air about her that made me just want to wrap my arms around her and protect her. Her body was fuller than Nisa's, but I didn't mind that at all.

I wanted to talk to her again, but it had been a week, and she'd never called me. I'd be lying if I said I wasn't disappointed, but with the press conferences, TV appearances, and funerals for the other victims, I didn't have the time to go back to the hospital. I decided that I would go first thing in the morning.

"Baby, did you hear me?" Nisa asked, still massaging my shoulders. "We need to strategize how we're gonna get you elected."

"I heard you. What you think I been doing all fucking week, Nise? I'm out here doing interviews, TV, calling into radio stations, podcasts. You name it, I'm doing it. Tank and Larry got me out here working my ass off."

She moved in front of me and sat on my lap. "I know you have, baby. And they have you doing all of the obvious things to get the vote, but what about the not-so-obvious? What about the community? What have you done for the people to regain their trust again?"

I looked into her hazel eyes and realized that, as usual, she was right. There were some benefits of having Nisa around besides the way she looked and how good she fucked me. She thought outside the box.

"I can't get back out there until I know who was responsible for this, Nise," I admitted to her. "I can't put more people's lives at risk."

She stroked my cheek slowly. "Remember, at the end of the day, it's not about those people. It's all about you and getting you in the Senate to have access to more money and more power. That's the name of the game, baby. To do that you have to show goodwill. Good faith. You gotta show that you're for the people, Khalid. Now, I know you've been going to all these funerals or whatever, and I know that each victim received a free funeral courtesy of King Funeral Homes, but that's enough. You gotta get back out there."

I knew what she was saying was right, but it felt wrong to be selfish at a time like this.

She could feel how tense I was and wasted no time kissing all over my neck. I cupped her ass and unbuckled my pants. She slid on my dick with a sexy grin. Her box was so wet and warm, ready for me. I popped her breast out the top of her lingerie and sucked on her nipple like a starving newborn as she rode me like a bronco. I slapped her ass hard a few times and felt her walls tighten around my dick as she came. I knew what Nisa liked, just like she knew me. I reached up and squeezed around her neck as she came. The choke wasn't too strong, but strong enough that the pressure turned her the fuck on so much that she was moaning and squirting at the same damn time. I took over, pounding her out as she soaked me up. The shit was lovely and the best stress reliever I could ask for. When I was about to nut, she slid off my lap, dropped to her knees, and popped my dick into her mouth as I came, swallowing every last drop.

"Damn, girl," I said with a grin. "I love it when you do that shit."

"I know," she replied cockily as she stood to her feet, still wearing her six-inch heels.

My phone rang. I answered as I watched Nisa walking into the master bathroom. "Yo."

"Khalid, it's me."

I dumped my clothes in the hamper as I recognized my father's voice. "Hey, wassup, Pops?"

"I'll be there in five minutes."

I heard the shower running in the master bathroom and pictured Nisa with water and soap going down her perfect body. I wanted to go in there and join her for round two, but with my father on his way, I couldn't.

"A'ight," I told him. I hung up the phone and walked in the bathroom to clean myself off. Then I slid on some boxers, hoop shorts, socks, and Gucci slides just as the intercom buzzed. I answered. It was the doorman, letting me know my father was here. I threw a new wife beater over my head and told him to let him up.

As I walked toward the living room, I looked around my condo. It was all high ceilings, floor-to-ceiling windows, marble floors, and expensive furniture. None of it was to my taste. It was a little too high-maintenance and fancy for me. But after I got with Nisa, she took one look at my loft on the South Side Flats and told me it was time to upgrade. I didn't really mind. I had grabbed the place after losing Amber because I couldn't bear to be alone in the place we shared together, but I barely spent any time there. Nisa found this condo in the heart of downtown, hired interior decorators, and went to work. I had to admit it was nice, but not my style.

I opened the door for my father. He gave me a one-armed hug, as we always did when we saw each other.

"Never thought I'd see you living like this," he remarked, looking around as he followed me to my study.

"Yeah? Me either," I agreed as I opened the door to the study and then closed it behind my father. I walked over to the mahogany desk and poured two shots of Remy Martin from my decanter sitting on a silver tray. I handed one to my dad, then sat on the edge of my desk. "What's up?"

My father sat in the chair facing my desk and drank his shot before placing the glass on the desk. Then he leaned back and stared at me for a minute.

Out of all my siblings, I was the closest to my father. Kelvin King was one hell of a man. He was an entrepreneur who saw the drug game as a means to the next level, not a way of life. Once he opened our first funeral home, he'd tried to get my mother to see that there was just as much money in burying men as there was in having them sell our drugs. The plan had been to go legit, outside of our political connections. But my mother was nothing like my father. She was ruthless in her quest for more money and more power. My father fell back from the streets and focused on making King Funeral Homes the top chain of funeral parlors in the Northeast. When he succeeded in doing that, he decided to expand up and down the East Coast. He had a mind for business that very few could rival.

"I wanted to tell you how proud I am of you. Of the way you're handling what went happened."

I pinched the bridge of my nose. "Thanks, Pops. I'd be even happier if I knew who did the shit. That way, I could get back to business without throwing my baby sister out there to the wolves."

My father shook his head. "Even though you ain't on the streets like Keon and Khalia, I don't agree with her taking part in this at all. But you know your mother." A look I couldn't describe came over his face at the mention of her.

"I do." I threw my shot back, picked the decanter up, and poured us two more. "I know her, but I don't understand her," I admitted as I handed him his glass.

Pops looked at his glass for a minute. "Dutchess . . . your mother, she's a very intelligent woman. It goes without saying that without her, I wouldn't be the man that I am today. She had a vision for this family that even I couldn't see."

"So, you're saying she's ambitious?"

"That's one way to describe her." He threw his second shot back. "Listen, son, I didn't come over here to discuss your mother with you. I came over here because I'm going to open a new business, and I wanted to know if you want in."

I was confused. "If I want in? What you mean, Pops? All the businesses we open we always include the whole family in—"

"This ain't for the whole family." My father cut me off. "This ain't no new business venture so we can clean our money. This is something that's going to be clean. Legit. One hundred percent drug-free. None of that shit can touch my place."

I looked at him in surprise. I mean, yeah, we had our funeral homes where we stashed the drugs and were able to move them. Those homes had been very prosperous for us. Even before Uncle Jamar was locked up and doing his thing in Washington, he'd been supplying both the liberals and conservatives with narcotics. Running a business or doing something that wasn't a front was unheard of for the Kings.

"So, you're going completely legit, Pops?" I asked, just to be sure.

"I want to. It's a start for me to head in that direction."

"And you don't want anyone else to do this with you?"

He looked directly into my eyes. "No, I don't. I haven't mentioned it to your brother, your sisters, not even your mother. Just you."

I bit my lip. "What kind of business we talking?"

"Restaurants. Five-star dining only. And I already have a name for it. The King's Club. We make it exclusive. The more people we turn down, the more people with money will want to eat there. We make the shit an experience, too. I'm talking different foods, the best liquor and wines, live bands. There's nothing out there like it."

I watched how his eyes lit up talking about this place. I shouldn't have been surprised that he wanted to open a restaurant. He loved to cook. I don't think I ever saw my mother standing over a stove, but growing up, I'd seen my father do it plenty of times. Once we got too much money to still live in the projects and moved out to North Huntington, we could have hired a full-time chef. Instead, my father cooked, and on the days he didn't, my mom picked up food for us.

"You sound like you've thought this through," I told him honestly.

"I have. Already got a few locations in mind to start." He stared at me seriously. "Me wanting to open this will put a wedge in the family. Your mother, Khalia, and Keon are definitely going to be against running a location that is one hundred percent clean. I don't know which way Kenya will go. But you. Khalid, I know you want more for yourself. Now I know you will get out here and bust your gun when you have to, but you don't thrive on that shit. You always see the bigger picture, a better vision than the rest of us. That's what makes you so perfect to pick up where Jamar fucked up in the political world."

I stroked my chin thoughtfully. He did make some good points; yet at the same time, I was unsure about doing something that wasn't bringing in double profits. My mom might have been ruthless, but she had made us a lot of money by being that way. What Pops was offering sounded good, but would it really be a moneymaker?

Still, at the end of the day, I was close to my father. I trusted his vision. If he believed in The King's Club, then I would too.

"I'm in," I told him.

He grinned. "I knew you would be, son. Let's have another drink."

Chapter Nine

Keon

Going to Brooklyn to keep an eye on my kids, little sister, and her annoying-ass friend at a rap concert wasn't really my idea of a good time. Matter of fact, as we made the drive, I was mad that I hadn't just shut the whole trip down.

When we arrived in Brooklyn, I ignored Kenya's instructions to go to the Tillary Hotel where she had already reserved a room.

"You're not gonna take over this whole trip, Keon," she snapped.

"I don't even wanna be here, so what makes you think I want to take over this fucking trip?" I snapped back.

"Well, you ain't going to our hotel."

"Look, that's a spot you booked when it was just you and Dionne coming up here. I don't know about you, but I don't wanna be in one room with five fucking people, a'ight? So just chill. I made other arrangements."

"Oh." Kenya sat back in her seat.

I shook my head as I thought of how my mother and Khalia really wanted her to run things during Khalid's absence. She was still an immature little girl, and it showed. We had spoiled her, me in particular, and she was in no way ready for the streets.

I pulled up to a brownstone on State Street and killed the engine before hopping out of the truck. When no one else made a move, I stuck my head back in. "Y'all coming or what?" I asked impatiently.

I popped the trunk, and everyone grabbed their bags. As I walked up the steps to the front door, a few people stopped to greet me.

"Ke, how you know all these people up here?" Kenya asked me.

"I'm a king, little sis," I responded cockily. "No matter where I go, everybody knows me." There was no point in being modest about it. She knew that we were known all over Pittsburgh, but it was time for her to see how many people really knew and respected our family.

"Wow," Dionne said in awe as soon as we walked through the door. The place was one of the newly renovated homes on the block, with shiny hardwood floors, airy living spaces, huge floor-to-ceiling windows, granite countertops, and stainless steel appliances. "Whose place did you say this was again?"

"I didn't," I replied shortly as I looked her up and down with a frown. Dionne and Kenya had been best friends since they were little girls. I had practically watched her grow up from a badass child to the teenager she was now. She was a cute girl, with her cocoa complexion, short haircut, and petite frame, but she always asked too many damn questions.

"Dad, how many rooms are here?" Jordan asked excitedly.

"Five," I told them. "One for everybody."

"Let's go pick one!" Nahim exclaimed. They both ran for the stairs.

"What do you need with a five-bedroom house, Keon?" Dionne asked as she looked at me again with a flirty look in her eyes.

My frown deepened. If I didn't know any better, I would have sworn her young ass was flirting with me. "Who said it was my house?"

"Who cares whose house it is? We're here now, and I'm ready to party!" Kenya said excitedly. She smiled then turned and glared at me. "I ain't wit' you stopping all my fun this weekend, Ke. For all that, you could have stayed home."

"Man, I ain't thinking 'bout you. I came to protect you, and that's what I'm gonna do. We in the middle of a war, and all you can think about is having fun," I mumbled as I walked out onto the deck.

I took in the view of the city in hopes of getting myself a little pumped for this concert we were going to tonight. I had always loved NYC, which was why I had purchased this brownstone as soon as it hit the market a few years ago. No one knew that I owned it. It was my little getaway when family business got too hectic or when Stacy and I got into another one of our many fights. It was something of a sanctuary for me, a place to collect my thoughts with no interruptions, and for a man with four kids and just as many baby mamas, on top of family drama, I needed a place like that from time to time.

I reached into my pocket and pulled out a small prescription bottle full of Perc 30s and popped one just as I heard the back door slide open.

"Beautiful view," Dionne said from behind me.

I sighed. "The fuck are you doing out here?" I asked her impatiently, not even bothering to hide the irritation in my tone.

"I just wanted to thank you for bringing us here. Kenya might not like it, but I do," she said boldly as she stood close to me. "This is much better than the hotel we booked."

"Yeah, well, I ain't bring y'all here 'cause I wanted to," I assured her. "So don't think I'm goin' out my way to treat y'all special or some shit."

She took a couple of steps farther onto the deck to get a better view. "Don't worry. I don't think that, Keon." The way she said it and looked at me made me think otherwise, though.

"Can you take a picture for me?" she asked as she walked back toward me, her iPhone in her hand.

"No," I scoffed. "Fuck I look like? Ask Kenya to do it."

"She's in the bathroom right now, and I don't know how long she'll be in there. You know she takes forever."

I couldn't help but laugh at that.

"Please, Keon," Dionne went on. "I need a pic for the 'Gram. This view is dope as fuck."

"Ask Jordan or Nahim."

"Why ask them when you're right here? Damn, you've known me my whole life. You can't take a picture for me?" she said in disbelief.

I sighed impatiently. "Fine, man. Come on. Hurry up," I ordered her as she placed the phone in my hand.

"Make sure you take a few from a few different angles. Get all my good sides."

"I'm not a fucking photographer," I snapped at her. "I'm taking one, and that's it."

She rolled her eyes.

"Or you can get somebody else out here to do it," I suggested.

"A'ight, fine." She did that dumb-ass pose all women did, standing to the side with her hip poked out and one foot on her tiptoes. Then she put her hands to her lips. "I'm ready."

As I snapped the picture, she blew a kiss. Then she walked back over to me. "Let me see it."

"You better like it, 'cause that's all you getting," I told her seriously. I was not there to entertain her or Kenya's bullshit.

She took the phone from me, her fingers lightly grazing mine. She looked at the picture I took and grinned, showing off a deep dimple in each cheek. "Damn, this is nice. Look."

I looked down at the phone and had to admit the picture was dope as fuck. She looked good, and the Brooklyn backdrop was nice as hell.

"Great job. I'm 'bout to post this now," she said excitedly.

"Glad you like it," I said dryly.

She looked up from her phone and locked eyes with me. "I love it," she said boldly. For a moment, I had to wonder once again if her little young ass was hitting on me. I quickly dismissed that thought, though, and blamed it on the Perc I'd just popped. There was no way Dionne would ever think I would look her way.

But as I watched her walk back into the house, her hips had an extra sway to them. And right as she opened the door, she looked back at me to see if I was watching her. Once she realized I was, she grinned and blew me a kiss before disappearing back into the house.

I pinched the bridge of my nose. I already had enough problems. Dionne needed to stay in her lane. I was a grown-ass man, and she was nowhere near ready for me.

Chapter Ten

Toni

For the last two weeks or so, my routine had pretty much been the same. I went to work, called the hospital on my breaks to check on Tommy, went back to work till quitting time, then came over to the hospital. Each day, I was told the same thing: there was no progress being made. He wasn't getting better, but he wasn't getting worse either. I wasn't sure if that was a good or bad thing, especially considering the fact that he may or may not be paralyzed.

I just wanted my brother back. The news coverage had begun to slow down since there were no leads on anyone bold enough to shoot up a Khalid King rally. The man himself had not even bothered to come back, for which I was grateful. I blamed him for what had happened to my brother and the drastic change my life had taken because of it. I was a single woman with no kids who worked and went to school to obtain a degree in finance. I was so determined to make something of myself that I was enrolled in the fast-track program at Point Park University, opting to graduate in three years instead of four. That meant that I had to still attend class during breaks and all. Here I was in my third and final year, and I couldn't bring myself to go to school or study while my brother was in this coma.

I exited the elevator on the ICU floor where Tommy's room was. Before I walked into the ICU, I said a small prayer, although I had doubts that it would work. I wasn't the most religious person. For the majority of my life, I had always felt like God had forgotten about me. Yet going through this alone was killing me. I knew I would need something or someone to help me get through this.

"Hi, Ms. Moore," a perky nurse at the nurse's station greeted me as I walked through the doors of the ICU.

"Hi," I said with a small wave. I couldn't remember her name. They all looked the same to me.

"Your brother has a visitor who has been there with him all afternoon," she told me.

I had already strolled past the nurse's station, but her words made me double back. "Excuse me, what?"

She nodded her head and gave me a sly smile. "Real handsome guy, too. He's been sitting there with him for hours. He had plenty of questions about his condition, but as you know, we couldn't tell him anything without you being here."

A real handsome guy sitting in my brother's room? Only one man came to mind, but I was sure it wasn't him. After all, he was entirely too busy to waste an afternoon at Tommy's bedside.

"But yet you all let him sit there with him," I snapped.

She shrugged. "You don't have any restrictions on who gets to visit him, and he knew the password."

Of course he did. I sighed and fixed my sagging Coach purse on my shoulder as I entered my brother's room. Sitting at his bedside, scrolling his phone, looking like he didn't have a care in the world, was Khalid King. For a moment, I couldn't speak as I looked at him. I had honestly never seen a more perfect man in my life. Of course, I'd seen Khalid speaking on TV when he made history as the youngest congressman in the city of Pittsburgh. Then he was exposed even more during his run for Senate. Everywhere you turned, you saw his smooth skin, long dreads, and dimpled smile as he gave one interview after the other about his family's business or his political aspirations. He was perfect in every sense of the word on TV, but in person, he looked even better. I could not find one flaw. I self-consciously ran my hand over my short haircut before smoothing any wrinkles out of my red button-up shirt. I noticed a stain on it from the tacos I'd eaten for lunch and hoped that he wouldn't notice.

I cleared my throat, and he looked up. "Oh, hey. My fault. I didn't hear you come in," he said as he stood.

"Of course you didn't. You're too busy on your phone."

He slid it into his pocket. "No, it's just I have a lot of things to follow up on, and—"

I held my hand up to cut him off. "Mr. King, why are you here?"

"Well, first of all, you can stop with the 'Mr. King'. I'm not my father," he joked with a grin, showing off those perfect teeth and deep dimples. Again, I wondered how a man could be so damn fine.

"And I'm here because I've followed up with all the victims. It's the least I could do."

I looked at my brother, hooked up to every machine possible and still stiff as a board. Tears filled my eyes the same as they always did every time I saw him. "My brother is not a victim. He is a survivor," I corrected Khalid.

He shoved his hands in his pockets and nodded his head. "That he is. So, what all do you know about his condition and the care he is receiving here? I asked, but they wouldn't tell me anything."

"As they shouldn't," I snapped. "And he is receiving the best care that I can afford, Mr. King. We aren't all filthy rich."

"I've been blessed," he said with a nod of his head. "I would like to share that with him and make sure he gets the best treatment possible."

"I don't need you to do that," I scoffed.

"No, you don't, but I'm offering." He looked back at the bed. I want him to have around-the-clock care from the best healthcare professionals. When he wakes up, they will also assist in his full recovery."

I noticed that he said "when" he woke up instead of "if," and while I appreciated that, I still didn't want to take his offer. "We don't need your charity. He'll be fine here."

Khalid looked back at me. "Will he really be fine here? These nurses have a few patients. He's not their main concern. I'm offering you private healthcare from a team that will be there exclusively for him and specializes in his injuries."

"I don't need you doing anything for him," I snapped at him. "It's because of you that he's here. You've already done quite enough."

A sad look crossed his handsome face as Dr. Harvey walked into the room. "Hello, Ms. Moore," he greeted me as he washed his hands at the small sink. When he turned toward us, he looked at Khalid. "Mr. King, you're still here?"

"He was just leaving," I informed Dr. Harvey.

"Yeah, I am, after you give us an update," he said firmly.

Dr. Harvey looked between the two of us. I reluctantly nodded my head. The doctor walked over to my brother, lifted his eyelids, and looked him over before looking back at me.

"What's new?" I asked him hopefully, the same thing I asked every day.

Dr. Harvey sighed. "I'm gonna be honest, Ms. Moore. It's all up to him now. He has to want to come back to us."

"He *does* want to come back to us!" I insisted.

Dr. Harvey gave me an uninterested look. "We'll see." With that, he washed his hands again and left the room.

Khalid's eyes followed him before landing back on me. "*We'll see*? That's the man you trust with your brother's life right now?"

"Please leave me alone," I said in a low voice as I pulled a chair up next to my brother's bed.

"I'm just saying, why turn down a chance to get him the treatment he deserves? I'm trying to give him the best possible chance at survival."

"Why are you talking like he's already given up? He hasn't!" I yelled as more tears filled my eyes.

He placed his hand on my shoulder. I hadn't been touched or comforted in so long that I was surprised by how much such a small gesture immediately soothed me.

"I didn't say that he did," he said calmly. "I just want to make sure he comes out of this in the best possible condition. You've done all that you can for him. Please let me help."

I shook my head before he could even finish his sentence. My grandmother had always instilled it in me and Tommy to never take handouts. Khalid throwing his money around like he could provide for my brother better than I could was pissing me off. Granted, he might have had access to better healthcare options and physicians, but I would rather work my fingers to the bone to provide that for Tommy myself than take any handout from him.

"You're making a mistake not taking my help," Khalid said with a sigh after a moment of silence. "Can you at least take my number in case you change your mind?"

He was getting on my nerves with his persistence. I let go of my brother's hand and stood up to face him. He returned my stare without flinching, and for a second, I almost forgot what I was going to say. He looked so damn good that I was sure he was used to getting whatever he wanted from whomever he wanted. For some reason, that pissed me off even more.

"I won't need your number, Mr. King," I assured him. "There's really nothing that you can do for me or my brother except leave us alone."

An offended look came into his eyes. "Damn. Well, I'm sorry you feel that way, Ms. . . ." He raised an eyebrow.

"Toni."

"Toni." He nodded his head. "Well, I'm sorry you feel that way, Ms. Toni, but here's the thing. I'm sure if your brother were woke, he would disagree with you and say something very different. Tommy was one of my biggest supporters, if not the biggest, and where I'm from, you don't just turn your back on people who have been down for you. He believes in me and my cause, and because of that, I'm not going to leave him alone. His recovery is very important to me, and once you swallow your pride, you will realize that him getting better is all that matters, and not this independent woman bullshit you're trying to pull." With that, he left the room.

I watched him leave before sitting back down at my brother's bedside. I looked over his complexion, usually so vibrant and smooth. It was now ashen and dry no matter how much I moisturized it. I ran my hand over his hair, which was usually spinning with 360 waves. It was now overgrown and in bad need of a cut and shape-up. He would go crazy if he could see how unkempt he was looking right about now.

I couldn't stop the tears from flowing as my eyes raked over his body. Tommy prided himself on staying fit. He'd been a star athlete all his life and was always muscular. However, he was now looking smaller every day.

I broke down as I realized that he was disappearing right before my very eyes. He was becoming a shell of himself. By rejecting Khalid's help, was I letting this happen? Was I letting my pride get in the way of what was really right for my brother?

I wasn't sure what to do anymore.

Chapter Eleven

Kenya

"Why are we even at the gun range?" I asked Khalia as I walked to the back of the shooting range with her and my mother.

"Well, baby girl, you want to step up, right? How you gonna do that and you don't know how to shoot a gun?" Khalia asked as she strolled ahead of me, confidence dripping with each step. She barely stood at five feet but had the presence of a giant.

"I do know. Daddy taught me," I informed them.

Both my mom and Khalia laughed at that.

"And who do you think taught Kelvin?" my mom asked me with a wink.

I chuckled along with them. My mom and sister were harder than a lot of these niggas.

Khalia put the protective glasses on, cocked the gun, and emptied the clip into the target with no hesitation. Afterward, she stood back and looked at her handiwork with a grin.

My mom stepped up, looked and grinned too before waving me over. "Look at her target. Nothing but head and chest shots," she said proudly.

Khalia shrugged. "Sorry to that man," she joked.

Mom emptied the clip and reloaded before taking her stance. I noticed that she, like Khalia, did not hold the gun with both hands the way that Daddy had instructed me to do when he first taught me. Both of them stood with one arm extended and fired with surprising precision.

"Not bad, old lady," Khalia said when Mom was done. She had also landed nothing but head and chest shots.

They both turned and looked at me when it was my turn. Believe it or not, I was a bit nervous to go around them. They were such professionals, and shooting cans in the woods with my father seemed like amateur work compared to both of them.

"Kenya, would you come on?" Khalia snapped as she tapped the ground impatiently in her YSL heeled sandals. "I have shit to do."

I picked up the gun and held it with both hands, one at the bottom and one on the trigger. I didn't want to disappoint them with my results after they were so happy with each other's.

"Today, please!" Khalia said loudly, letting it be known that I needed to hurry up.

I was about to squeeze the trigger when my mother tapped my shoulder. I looked back at her.

"You might wanna take the safety off first, sweetheart. Just a suggestion," she said sarcastically with a laugh.

Embarrassment flooded through me, and I could feel my cheeks getting warm as I cocked the gun.

"Kelvin never taught you that?" Mom asked, but since I knew she was just being smart, I didn't bother to reply.

"Now, remember, you want to get kill shots," Khalia instructed me. "Let's see what you got, baby girl. Let's go."

I imagined that was how a coach talked to one of his players before a big game. I took a deep breath and fired my first round, which landed on the target's shoulder. The second hit his thigh, the third his hand, and when the fourth hit his kneecap, Khalia was too through. She snatched the gun away and glared at me.

"Why the *fuck* did you lie to us?" she asked angrily.

"I didn't lie. I swear! When I was twelve, Daddy took me to the woods and—"

"Wait one minute." Mom cut me off. "So, you mean to tell me that you haven't fired a pistol since then? *Six years*? Is that what you're telling me right now?"

I started to lie, but the looks on their faces revealed that neither one of them was in the mood for my bullshit. So, I nodded my head.

Khalia threw her hands up in the air. "We're finished!"

"Calm down, Khalia. No, we are not. We will have her ready to do her job in no time," my mom assured her.

Khalia snorted. "Yeah, right. Did you not see what I just saw? She has no fucking aim. She might as well have just closed her eyes and started shooting. Maybe then she would have actually hit a target."

I was getting sick of her mouth. "Well, what do I really need to learn how to shoot a gun for anyway? I'll only be dealing with politicians and high-profile businessmen. They ain't like these niggas on the street."

Mom shook her head. "How are you so green and you're my child?"

"Y'all spoiled her," Khalia answered with a shake of her head.

"Shut up, Khalia," my mom snapped before looking back at me. "Listen to me and don't you ever forget this. Those muthafuckas in those five-thousand-dollar suits are more dangerous than any nigga out here on the corner. They have a lot to lose and won't hesitate to kill you because of that."

"Facts," Khalia agreed.

She stepped in front of me. I took in her whole appearance. From her hair, falling in soft curls around her beautiful face and touching her shoulders, to the red bustier type lace top she had tucked into her skintight jeans and her designer sandals showing off the white polish on her freshly manicured toes, she screamed boss bitch without ever saying a word. I wanted my presence to command a room the same way as hers did, but I wasn't sure if I could do the things she had done to get it.

"You may not be ready, Kenya. If so, that's okay. We can find another way," she told me.

"What other way, Khalia? She's the only person I trust," Mom insisted.

"No, I'm ready. I promise that I am," I told them with much more confidence than I felt. I wasn't at all, but letting my family down when they needed me wasn't even an option for me. They had always had my back and made it so that I never had to worry about a thing. Now that they needed me, I wouldn't hesitate to show that I could be an asset just like them.

"Show me what I need to know. I won't let y'all down," I promised.

I meant that shit, too. Any dreams or ambitions I had for myself would have to take a back burner while I held my family down. I was tired of being the weakest link in the chain.

Chapter Twelve

Dutchess

I pulled up to Pearlie's, an old school bar located in the heart of Bloomfield, and killed the engine of my rose gold Bentley Continental. I flipped the visor down to check my appearance and was satisfied with what I saw. Going on thirty years of marriage, four kids, and being in the dope game, and I still looked like I had barely cracked my thirties. My chocolate skin was flawless, eyes bright, and my long, thick hair that I wore down my back had not a hint of gray. I had added maybe a good twenty pounds to my frame, but it was all in my hips and ass and did nothing but compliment me.

Satisfied that I looked like a million bucks, I reached into my waist and put my pistol under the seat. I knew I would be thoroughly searched here and didn't want any problems, especially since I was on my own. No one would even think to find me here.

I got out of the car, straightened the crisp light pink linen dress I had on, and grabbed the matching Valentino bag. On my face were a pair of huge pair of black Gucci shades and, of course, nothing but Christian Louboutin stilettos graced my feet.

I hit the locks and approached the bar. Upon walking in the front door, one would think that I was severely overdressed for such a dive bar. The place was half lit, with raggedy wooden tables with even more raggedy seats around them. A short, fat woman with short, mousy blond hair was behind the bar. Two white men who looked like truck drivers were sitting at the bar, and one was trying—and failing miserably—to flirt with her. To the naked eye, nothing out of the ordinary was going on here, but I knew better.

I walked over to the bar, pulled out a twenty, and waved the bartender over. She walked over and immediately looked me up and down. I knew why. Black people were not known to frequent this part of town that often, and especially ones dressed to the nines like me.

"What you drinking?" she asked me.

"Let me see your seafood menu," I told her casually. For years, that had been the secret code at this place to see the real bosses.

She raised one eyebrow, undoubtedly surprised that I was there to see a big fish. "Seafood?" she repeated with disbelief lacing her tone.

"Ain't that what I just said?" I replied smartly.

She looked at me with disdain. "I don't know who you think you are, but—"

"Dutchess!" a man's exclaimed happily from behind me, saving the woman from getting cussed out in front of everyone.

I turned around to face none other than Vincent, the head of the Morelli crime family.

"Vinny, you know her?" the disgruntled bartender asked.

"Do I know her? I should be kissing her ring. This right here is the queen of the city," Vincent exclaimed as he wrapped his arms around me for a big hug. I inhaled his familiar scent and smiled before pulling away and looking back at the bartender. Her eyes had been red the whole time I'd been here. She kept twitching her jaw, looking like she had what we liked to call to "coke jaw," and her nose kept running. She made no sign to wipe it or hide the very obvious signs of her addiction.

"You might wanna clean that shit up. You wouldn't all your customers to know just how much coke you snort," I told her with a laugh before Vincent led me to a heavy door located in the back.

"Be nice," he said with a chuckle.

"Fuck her," I responded.

Vincent held the door open and allowed me to walk through, his hand grazing my ass ever so softly as I walked past him. Then he placed his hand on the small of my back as we walked down the narrow hallway and entered the back room, which was completely different from the front of the bar. Back here, they had two huge TVs mounted on the wall, black leather couches, and glass tables with a modern bar stocked with every type of liquor and cigar you could think of.

Vincent's flunkies immediately came to pat me down as he stood to the side.

"We aren't better than this by now?" I asked him with a grin. Inside, I was hoping they didn't find the blade I had taped to my inner thigh. Although I left my gun behind, I would never walk into any establishment unarmed. I needed something to feel protected.

"It's never personal, always business," he told me with the same shit-eating grin he gave me over thirty years ago.

"So, what are you drinking, Dutchess? White wine per usual?" he asked me when his goons walked away.

"No drinks today. I won't be here long," I assured him as I walked over to a loveseat and sat down. I expected Vincent to sit across from me, but I wasn't too surprised when he chose to sit beside me instead.

"What brings you here today?" he asked me, placing one hand on my knee.

I looked directly into his sapphire blue eyes. "I need your help."

"I figured that when I saw your car pull up in front of my bar. I never hear from you unless you need something," he replied smoothly, never taking his hand off my knee.

"So, you knew I was here and still made me talk to that bartender instead of coming to get me right away," I said with a shake of my head. Vincent had always been one to play mind games. He just had to be in control all the time, and my personality just wouldn't allow me to sit back and accept that shit. It was the main reason we'd clashed years ago.

"I decided to humor myself. I knew she would have a fit hearing the secret code come out of your mouth. We don't get your type around here every day," he said as he looked me up and down while biting his lip.

"I'm nobody's type. There's only one of me," I replied cockily.

"I agree."

"Well, now that we finally agree on something, can you help me?" I asked him. "I need answers that I'm sure only you can give me."

"You mean like a line on who shot up your son's political rally, right?"

I nodded my head. The Kings knew about every major crime that happened in this city except this one against us. All of the people Khalia and Keon had combing the streets kept coming back empty-handed, which led me to believe that this was an inside job. Either that, or someone even higher up than us had ordered the hit on my son, which was an egregious act that I took personally.

There was only one crime family with more power than us here, and that was the Morellis. They had been around since the Prohibition era, and the whole bloodline was considered to be legend. They were actually related to Vito Genovese of *the* Genovese crime family, one of the Five Families of the Italian mafia. Their money and power had no limits, and when I began to build the King legacy, I based it on what I had seen the Morellis do. If anyone knew what had happened to my son, it was them.

"I was surprised to hear about that news myself. I know you run a tight ship over there. I taught you well," Vincent went on as his hand crept up my thigh.

I closed my eyes as I tried to ignore the sensation going through my body at his touch. I don't know if it was him or the fact that my husband hadn't bothered to touch me in months. Either way, I was turned the hell on and losing focus.

"You did," I assured him as I removed his hand so I would remember why I was really there. "Which is why I'm surprised something like this could happen."

"I was too. Especially considering the fact that your son is running for office. It was a very public message someone was trying to send. How is my stepson, by the way?" Vincent asked me with a smirk.

I sighed. "Vincent . . ."

"No, no, no. You came here for answers, right? Well, I want some too. You had to know I had a few questions of my own.'"

"Like?" I asked, as if I didn't already know.

"Like how is Keon? I was disappointed when you all didn't let him pursue his dream and play basketball. I would have loved to see him on TV. Hell, who knows? Maybe I might have caught a game or two courtside."

I looked around cautiously at the men who were there before responding. "This isn't the time or place," I hissed at him.

He shrugged. "I guess it's not the time or place to discuss who is coming after your family either."

"Vincent, if you know something, you have to tell me," I pleaded with him, sounding desperate and so unlike myself. I hated it.

"Wrong," he responded, his blue eyes now cold as ice chips. "I don't have to tell you shit. You act like I owe you, but I don't. You took something away from me that was so precious."

"Oh, please. You act like I had a choice. I didn't. I did what was best for the both of us at the time."

He nodded his head. "Okay, so what about what's best for us now? You need to know who has a hit out on your family. I may or may not know the answer to that." He moved even closer to me and tilted my chin up slightly so that I was forced to look him in his eyes again.

"I need to know my son, Dutchess," he said in a low tone. "I've gone twenty-six years and never said a word to you about it. But I think it's time now."

"Why? What would that help? Why can't you just help me out this one time, Vincent?"

He backed away from me with a shrug of his shoulders. "Because I'm all out of favors, Dutchess. I want my son to know where he comes from and who he is."

"Oh. And you think everyone is just going to be accepting of the fact that you have a black son? What would your wife think?"

He shrugged. "She'll think whatever I tell her to think. As far as that other shit, I don't give a damn. It's up to you if you want the truth about what's going on with your family. All you have to do is bring him to me. I'll take care of the rest."

I shook my head. Not many things disturbed me or made me feel all emotional, but this right here was one of them. Fuck the murders I'd committed, the drugs I'd sold, and all the guns I busted. This right here was my biggest secret. I had never wanted anyone to know about me and Vincent, or the fact that Keon belonged to him and not Kelvin. It would stain my reputation, ruin my marriage, and shatter Keon's world as he knew it.

After a few moments of silence, Vincent let out an irritated sigh. "Listen, I never had to ask your permission to meet my son. Out of respect for you and everything you got going on, I never did it on my own. But you have to know that if I choose to go meet him today, there's nothing you or anyone else can do to stop me. I don't need you to bring him to me."

"Vincent, please don't do that," I pleaded with him. "Keon would not take kindly to that, and I still have my marriage—"

"I don't give a fuck about your marriage, and from the way you constantly cut your husband's balls off, I don't think you do either. I'm giving you three days to make up your mind about how you want to play this. If I don't hear from you in that time, I'm meeting him on my own."

"Why is this so important to you now? If I hadn't walked through that door today, would you even be concerned with meeting him?" I asked angrily.

"Actually, I would. I've been thinking about this for a while now, but you never call, so you wouldn't know," he responded sarcastically.

I stood up to leave. I had been sure that I would find the answers I was desperately seeking here, but instead, he threatened to blow the lid off my life. To say I was pissed was an understatement. "Goodbye, Vincent," I said smartly as I turned and walked away.

"Dutchess, wait!" he called after me.

I didn't bother to turn around. I had seen enough of his ass for one day.

"If I were you, I would take a closer look in-house," he said to my back.

A sick feeling settled in the pit of my stomach at the thought of someone that we broke bread with actually being bold enough to betray us. Yet I couldn't rule it out. We had been so successful for so many years and had never had to deal with disloyalty, but I knew better than anyone how greedy and malicious people could be when they wanted to get to the top. I myself had done some dishonorable things to sit on the throne, and I wouldn't hesitate to do so again if it meant I would have the same outcome.

The thought of having to cut the grass to expose the snakes bothered me to my core, yet it had to be done. I would probably have to come out of retirement for this one.

Chapter Thirteen

Khalia

I didn't get much free time to myself. When I got it, one of my favorite things was going to the Farmer's Market. Many people didn't know it, but I could cook my ass off. I'm talking about making everything from soul food to soufflés. I could do it all, and whenever I did, I would only use fresh ingredients. They made the food more colorful and gave it a better taste than any seasoning ever could.

I lived in Plum, an affluent suburb that consisted of soccer moms. These ladies were actually some of my best customers. They were all hooked on opioids. To them, popping pills didn't make them a real junkie since they weren't smoking something or shooting it up. If they had any sense, they would know that opioids carried the same addiction as heroin, but I let them live.

Anyway, even though it was the Kings' drugs that supplied these women, they had no idea who I was. I kind of liked it that way sometimes. I mean, everywhere else I went, I was Khalia King, the most feared bitch in the city. At these markets, I got to shop just like everyone else and discuss the ripeness of vegetables or the prices. In a weird way, it brought me a sense of peace, just like my cooking.

I made my purchase and drove home, playing some old-school Toni Braxton.

"A nigga was always doing Toni's ass wrong," I said out loud with a laugh as I sang along to her classic "Seven Whole Days." I was just in a good-ass mood and couldn't tell anyone why. We were at war with an unknown enemy, and we were about to toss my baby sister out to the wolves when she was nowhere near ready. But for some reason, none of that shit mattered to me at the moment. I just wanted to cook, listen to my oldies, and relax all day.

I pulled my Mercedes G-Wagon into the driveway of my home and just stared at what was in front of me for a moment. My parents had gotten us out of the projects on the Hill when Khalid and I were around eight years old, so even though I had entered puberty rich and privileged, I still had a memory of where we truly came from. Even though we were undoubtedly the most paid family in our projects, I still remembered how others lived and knew we were blessed not to have it like them. So, for me to go from that to a seven-bedroom, six-and-a-half-bathroom home that I could call my own made me feel good about myself and my grind. Yes, I worked for my family, but nothing had been given to me. I had to earn it all.

I grabbed my bags and hopped out of my truck just as the mailman was walking up the path to my mailbox.

"How are you today, Ms. James?" he asked me with a smile.

"Fine, and yourself?"

"I'm doing all right," he responded as he held a stack of mail out to me.

"You can keep all those bills," I told him with a roll of my eyes as I pushed them away.

"Quit playing. You know you want them," he joked, but we both understood the double entendre of his words.

The mailman's name was Drew, and he had no idea who I was. All the mail that came here was addressed to Kyra James, which was an alias I used quite often. The King name was just too notorious to be attached to everything that I did, and with me being the main enforcer for our family, I liked to take extra precautions so that I couldn't be found.

Drew and I had been flirting with each other for probably the last six months. He was fine as fuck to me. I loved me a chocolate nigga, and Drew was special dark with straight white teeth that beamed when he smiled and honey-colored eyes. He probably hit just six feet tall and had a slightly muscular build. Besides his smile, the best thing about him was his full beard. Every time I saw him, I pictured riding his face and drenching it with my juices.

I definitely wanted Drew, but he was a civilian, and as such, he had no place in my world. Besides, I only fucked with bosses. What would I even look like giving a mailman a taste?

"Sometimes I do. Other times I don't," I flirted back.

He handed me the mail with that grin on full display. "Looks like you're 'bout to cook up something good," he remarked as he pointed to the bags I had yet to take into the house.

"Everything I make is good," I boasted.

"You can't cook," he said with his head tilted to the side.

I widened my eyes. "Fuck outta here! I'ma put a plate up for you so you can taste it the next time you come."

He openly looked me up and down and for a moment. I actually felt self-conscious that I had thrown on an old pair of Adidas stretch pants and a fitted tank. My ponytail was hanging down my back out of the blue Adidas "dad hat" I wore. I looked like I had just made a store run.

"So, I can finally taste it, huh?" he said with a lick of his lips.

My pussy jumped involuntarily, but before I could think of anything flirtatious to say back, Tookie's black-on-black Ford F150 turned into my driveway. I shook my head for being so consumed with Drew that I hadn't even noticed him coming down my street. I was slipping by talking to him, and that never happened.

He noticed my demeanor had changed with Tookie pulling into the driveway, and he respectfully walked away.

"What are you doing way out here without calling first, Took?" I asked him as I slid the key into the lock and opened my front door. He followed behind me but didn't close the door. I looked at him like he was crazy. "Bruh, I know we in the suburbs and all, but we still lock all doors around here," I told him.

"We can lock it when we leave back out."

I shook my head. "Nuh-uh, not today. I'm off, and I'm chillin'."

"Khalia, you know better than anyone else ain't no off days in this game. This ain't no Monday-though-Friday job."

I waved him off as I walked toward my kitchen. I could already taste the homemade chicken Alfredo I planned on making with the fresh bell peppers and garlic cloves I had gotten at the farmer's market.

"Whatever it is can wait, or you can call Keon. I'm not doing a damn thing today." I started to unload my food on the island in my kitchen.

"I called him too. Listen to me, Khalia." He came and stood in front of me. "I wanted to be the first person to tell you this. The warehouse burned to the ground last night."

I almost dropped the fresh whipping cream in my hand. "My *main* warehouse?" I asked just to be sure.

"Yes." Tookie washed his hand down his face. "No one knew who it belonged to, of course, so no calls were made. I went there to make sure that the gun delivery would go smoothly today and saw all the fire trucks surrounding it. I don't even know how long they had been there. All I saw was what used to be main hub nothing but ashes."

I damn near hyperventilated at his words. The amount of drugs and guns we kept stashed at the main hub was easily worth millions. I had the resources to bounce back, and taking losses was all part of the game, but this would be the biggest loss I ever took. And the fact that someone had disrespected me on this level had my blood boiling. This was no random act at all. Only those close to my operation knew the location of the warehouses and exactly what was in them. And only someone extremely close to me would know just how much we had in that warehouse.

"Let's go," I barked at Tookie. Cooking and R&B music would just have to wait. There was work to do, and before the day was over, I planned to make sure whoever was responsible for this would bleed. Then I would wipe out their entire family just to make sure niggas remembered why they should think three times before ever fucking with me.

Chapter Fourteen

Keon

I stood in front of what remained of the warehouse and stared at the rubble in disbelief. Smoke was coming out of my ears; I was so pissed.

"Yo, I can't even think of the words to say right now," Chuck said from beside me. I knew he was almost as pissed as I was. He had been with me since day one, when my mom told me to hang up my hoop dreams. We went from balling at the summer leagues together to slinging bricks together.

I said nothing as I stood there. I heard more cars pull up behind me, but I didn't turn to face them. Honestly, I didn't know which one of these niggas I could trust and didn't trust myself to stare at them without pulling my pistol out and letting it do the talking for me.

"Keon," I heard Khalia say as she walked toward me. "How long have you been here?"

"I just got here," I responded. "I came as soon as Tookie called me." I turned to face her and was surprised to see how dressed down she was in leggings and a tank top. Khalia was a queenpin and made sure no one forgot it each and every day. This was the first time in a long time I hadn't seen her in some six-inch heels.

"This has to be connected to Khalid's shooting," she murmured.

"You think?" I snapped at her.

She glared at me. "I was just thinking out loud. You might wanna watch how you talk to me."

"Or else what?" I barked at her. "I ain't one of these niggas walking around here scared of you."

She chuckled and shook her head. "You better be lucky you're my brother. I know you hot right now, so I'ma let you live. Make that the last time you try to come for me, though," she said calmly before walking away.

I glared at her as she walked away. Part of me knew I was wrong for snapping at her, but the other part of me hated how she walked around like her balls were just as big as mine.

"You need to chill, K," Chuck told me. "Li'l sis ain't do nothing but state the obvious. No way Khalid's shit getting hit up and this ain't connected."

I washed my hand down my face. "I know, man. Shit is foul."

We only trusted four people besides ourselves, Tookie, and Chuck with the location of our warehouse. The four lieutenants were standing in front of us now, looking lost.

"I hope y'all niggas saved for a rainy day 'cause it's about to thunderstorm," I told them honestly. "Now, we still got some work in other parts of town, but it's nothing compared to what y'all are used to gettin' hit off with. We gotta rebuild to get back to where we were."

"So, what we supposed to do till then?" Noah asked. I wasn't too fond of him because he had the tendency to keep a little too much drama going in the streets, but Khalia swore he was a moneymaker when she promoted him, and I had to admit that she was right.

"Fuck you mean what you supposed to do till then?" I snapped back.

"Chill, Noah," CJ said calmly. CJ was hand-picked by me. He was low, never wore any flashy jewelry or clothes, and even drove a Ford Escape. No matter how much weight he moved, everyone knew that early mornings were reserved for him dropping his wife and kids off at school, and the afternoons were reserved for picking them up. His family came first, and I could do nothing but respect that.

"K, did we ever get the camera work done?" CJ asked me. He had been telling me that the security cameras worked intermittently, and I was supposed to have them fixed, but it had slipped my mind because I always had someone watching the place. Plus, I had foolishly thought no one would be brave enough to fuck with us.

"Naw," I admitted with a shake of my head.

"So, losing all that work could have been avoided if you fixed the cameras?" Noah said in disbelief. "We're supposed to starve because you were slippin'?"

I pulled my pistol out, aimed it at Noah, and fired, hitting him right in his forehead. He dropped to the ground like a bag of rocks.

"Keon!" Khalia screamed at me. "You didn't have to do that!"

"He talks too fucking much," I snapped back. "Now, y'all can split the weight we got left three ways and make more money. Anyone else have something to say about the way I do shit?"

CJ and the remaining two lieutenants shook their heads.

"Good. Tookie, get rid of the body," I instructed him. He looked at Khalia first, who nodded her head, then went to work. I didn't like that shit but figured I would address it at a later date.

"I'll hit y'all for pick-ups," I told them before walking away.

"You wrong as hell for that shit!" Khalia yelled after me.

I turned around and walked back toward her.

"K, chill," Chuck said, but I ignored him.

"You wanna know what your fucking problem is, Khalia? You walk around here like you a nigga, but you ain't. You're a fucking woman, and you need to remember that shit sometimes. The reason you can't keep a man is because you too busy trying to act like one. Be a lady sometimes."

She laughed in my face. "I'm harder than a lot of these niggas out here. Men wished they had half the heart that I got. Your problem is that you think somebody supposed to be scared of you, and you're pissed because I'm not and never will be. I can't keep a man 'cause I don't want a man, but you got how many kids by how many bitches and *none* of them want you? I mean, what kind of nigga can't go back to any of his baby's moms?" she said with a laugh.

I glared at her.

"Then you kill one of my workers right in front of everyone and think I ain't supposed to say shit? Newsflash, K: I don't work for you, nigga! I say what I want, however I want, and whenever I want to say it! You was wrong for that shit, period! Now, let me go 'cause unlike you, I'm more interested in killing the mafucka's family that did this, not our workers."

She stomped off toward her G-Wagon, and I almost went after her smug ass, but I knew she was right. Lately, I had been more hostile than usual. I guess the life was just getting to me after all these years. I had never wanted to be a part of this shit anyway.

"Let's go throw a few back," Chuck said to me. "Fuck it. We need it after today."

I shook my head as I hopped in my truck, opened my console, and pulled out a bag of Perc 30s.

Chuck frowned. "I wouldn't be a real friend if I ain't tell you that you need to chill with that shit," he advised me.

I shrugged. "You act like I asked you for your advice, nigga." I popped two and took a swig from the water bottle I had in the truck. Even though the pills always made me feel good, I wanted something that would make me feel even better.

I scrolled through my text messages, but none of the women in there had my interest. I had fucked them and never called for a reason. Just as I was about to say fuck it, I came across the text I'd got from Dionne in Brooklyn. It was nothing but her picture, but as I looked at it again, I had to admit she looked good as hell.

I had watched the girl grow up, so I really had no business fucking with her. I told myself that as I stared at the picture. She was eighteen, the same age as Kenya, and I knew I would have a fit if a nigga my age was trying to fuck with my little sister. Still, that didn't stop me from sending **Wyd** to her phone. The text was so dry and random that I ain't even expect her to respond.

But when she replied **wondering what took you so long to hit me up right away**, I said fuck it and threw caution to the wind. I was way out of her league and would probably do her more bad than good, but none of that mattered right now. I needed to feel better, and something told me she would be the one to do it.

Chapter Fifteen

Khalid

"Pops, are you still sure this is a good idea?" I asked him as we walked into the PNC Bank located in East Liberty.

"It was a good idea when I presented it to you. Why isn't it a good idea now?" he asked.

I slid my hands into my khaki cargo shorts pocket and shrugged. "So much is going on right now. It seems like all signs point to us not starting a business now."

My pops looked at me seriously. "Khalid, I came to you because I know in the back of your mind, you're like me. You don't want to live that other life forever like the rest of the family. You're different. Son, your potential for an extremely successful political career is right at your fingertips."

"Yeah, right. I fucked that up," I scoffed.

"No, the assholes who shot those innocent people are fucked up. You, son, are destined to be great. Don't let that setback hold you back."

"I get it, but it ain't just that." I looked around and lowered my voice. "The warehouse is a huge hit for us. I can't sit back and do nothing while our family is attacked from all angles."

"You aren't doing nothing. You're opening a business."

I sighed. Opening a business when our cash flow was about to decrease significantly seemed like the dumbest thing in the world to me. "It just doesn't seem like a smart move, considering the fact that we are about to be pulling in less money than usual."

Pops looked at me seriously. "I know you put a lot of that money up, Khalid. You're not a big spender like your brother and sister. Matter of fact, the most money I've ever seen you spend is on that penthouse when you hooked up with Nisa." He shook his head. "Take it from me, son. A woman who puts money, power, and material things above all else is toxic."

I frowned. "Sounds like you just described Mom."

Before he could respond, a young white man came out to the waiting area to greet us. "Hi, I'm Chad," he said in a way too cheerful tone for my liking.

"I'm Kelvin King, and this is my son, Khalid King," my father introduced us as we shook his hand.

"Nice to meet you. I hear you want to open a joint business account. Is that correct?"

Pops nodded his head.

"Well, follow me right this way." He walked toward one of the glass-enclosed offices. I followed him reluctantly as he and my father talked about sports.

Right before we walked into the office, I caught a glimpse of Toni behind the teller's station. She had a smile on her face as she greeted her next customer, but I could tell that she was truly tired.

For the next fifteen minutes, I let my dad do all the talking as I kept my eyes on Toni. A few times, she looked up and caught me staring at her. Chad's office was directly across from her station, and I didn't even try to hide the fact that I was looking at her.

After we gave Chad the proper identification and the money to deposit into the account, he slid us his business card and two debit cards as well. That was the one thing I loved about PNC Bank; they had the ability to print and activate your debit cards right there in the bank instead of making you wait for a week to receive it.

"Khalid, this is a great step for our future . . ." my father was saying, but I could barely hear him as I watched Toni walk away from her position briskly while talking on her cell phone.

"Pops, go head out to the car. I'll meet you," I told him as I tossed the keys to my Benz to him. Without waiting for a response, I took off in the direction where I saw Toni run. When there was no sign of her, I pushed open the door marked "Employees Only" and walked through it with no hesitation.

And sure enough, there she was, sitting at the table, holding her head in her hands.

"Toni?" I said as I walked toward her.

Her hands dropped from her face, and she looked at me in shock. "What are you doing back here? You can't be in here."

"I know. I just saw you on the phone and figured something was wrong from your body language."

"I'm fine," she said defiantly.

I looked at her seriously. She had on a black button-up shirt with black fitted slacks and flat black shoes. Her short hair wasn't curled as it usually was, but she had made it work for her. She didn't have any expensive bundles in her hair, no designer clothes graced her body, her face wasn't flawlessly made up with the best makeup, and her flat shoes were a far cry from the six-inch red bottoms that stayed on Nisa's feet. And yet, her beauty was far more attractive to me because it was so natural, not forced at all.

"Most times when someone says that they're fine, they aren't," I responded with a shrug of my shoulders. "Tell me what's wrong, and I promise I'll leave."

She was quiet for a moment before letting out a long sigh. "Tommy took a turn for the worse," she said quietly, her voice cracking with each word that she spoke. "They called me to discuss my options."

My heart failed at her words. "What are your options?" I asked her in an even tone.

"Hospice or taking him off the ventilator," she whispered.

Each option spelled death for her brother, and from what I had seen so far, he was not a quitter. They were just giving up on him.

"He's resilient," I told her as I took a step closer to her. "Don't let them determine his fate. They just don't see what I see."

She was quiet again for a while. For a moment, I thought she was contemplating giving in, until she spoke again. "Is your offer to get him the best doctors still open?"

I looked at her in disbelief. "Of course it's still open. Nothing changed about that. Are you ready to take it?"

"Yes. When can you get him moved?" she asked urgently.

I pulled my phone out. "Now."

Chapter Sixteen

Kenya

"Well, look what the wind blew in!" Dionne greeted me as I stepped into the small, two-bedroom apartment she shared with her mother, grandmother, aunt, and three little cousins. I waved at her grandmother, who was on the couch as always, but before I could speak to everyone in the living room, she grabbed my hand.

"Ouch! Girl, you heavy-handed," I complained.

She ignored me, pulled me back to the small bedroom where they all kept their clothes, and slammed the door shut in the face of Boogie, her pre-teen little cousin who wanted to do everything we did.

"You ain't have to slam the door in her face like that," I said with a laugh as I sat on the bed.

"I ain't thinking 'bout her little fast ass," she retorted as she sat next to me. "So, where the hell you been, bitch?"

I shrugged and looked away from her. "Had to lay low for a minute. Shit is crazy with my family right now," I told her. It was a half-truth, half-lie. Ever since the warehouse burned down, I had been laying low, but that wasn't the only reason.

Even though we lost a bunch of product in the fire, our out-of-town needs still had to be met. I soon learned why. All those high-ranking officials and politicians turned a blind eye to the substantial amount of drugs Keon moved all throughout the Northeast in coffins. Hearses loaded with kilos of drugs arrived in Philly, Boston, Newark, Manhattan, and other cities damn near every day. For years, our family had been able to open funeral homes in each of these cities without anyone batting an eye. To the public, the King family ran an extremely successful chain of funeral homes, amongst our other business ventures. They would never know just how many bodies my family got rid of using the crematory in each of our locations.

Anyway, high-profile clients such as politicians, CEOs, and CFOs never got their product off of street niggas. Even our lieutenants couldn't make those deliveries. Their identities had to be kept confidential, and they would only deal with a high-ranking member of the family. Someone like my brothers, sister . . . or me.

My first trip had been to the state capitol building in Harrisburg. I had been under the impression that I would make the trip alone, but Khalid wasn't with none of that. Vick, his driver/bodyguard who made all his OT runs with him, drove me to Harrisburg. At first, I didn't want him to, but at the end of the day, it was comforting having someone with me who already knew exactly where I was supposed to go.

Anyway, it had gone smooth as silk. I met one of the state representatives and made the transaction with no problem. After that, we came straight home. In my opinion, it wasn't nearly as dangerous as they were making it out to be. I could even see myself pursuing my other passions while doing those runs.

"I heard," Dionne remarked. She walked over to the closet and started pulling clothes out. "Anyway, I'm glad you're here. You can help me pack."

"Pack?" I asked with a frown. "Where the hell you going?"

"I am moving out," she replied with a huge grin.

"For real!" I exclaimed happily. I still lived at home and didn't mind at all because all of my siblings were out of the house. My parents didn't bother me much, so I had plenty of privacy, but that wasn't the case for Dionne. She literally had no space. I was happy for her to be moving out.

"Where?" I asked her.

She looked at me slyly. "The Washington."

I paused before saying anything to that one. The Washington was a fancy high-rise condominium complex located right by the PPG Events Center. The rent there had to be sky-high and Dionne had no job. How could she even afford it?

"The Washington?" I repeated. "How are you moving in there?"

She grinned again. "My man got the place for me."

"Your man?" I said with a laugh. We were both single. I had been ever since Chris, my high school boyfriend, got caught getting head from some bitch in the bathroom stall at our homecoming dance. He had broken my heart to the point where I turned guys down for months. Only after graduation did I feel open to looking for love again.

"Yeah, my man, bitch. Why is that funny?"

"'Cause when the hell did you get a man, sis?" I asked between fits of laughter.

She threw her hands on her hips. "It's new."

"Oh, yeah? And who is he?" I pressed.

She went back to the closet. "I can't tell you who he is."

"Oh, so now we keeping secrets? Since when do you keep any nigga you fucking with a secret?" I challenged her. We told each other everything.

"This time. I don't wanna jinx this."

I was still doubtful. "So, you met a nigga with enough money to move you up outta here and into The Washington, but you won't tell me who he is? Wow."

Dionne stopped taking clothes out of the closet and looked at me. "Why can't you just be happy for me? If you finally met a nigga to knock the cobwebs off that pussy. I would be happy for you."

"You would be asking who he is, just like I am," I shot back.

She laughed. "A'ight, I probably would. If I could tell you, I would. But I can't. This is the best way for me to get outta this spot, Kenya. You know I hate it here."

I was silent for a moment. Dionne didn't have a family like me, or money either. She had always wanted to get out of her living conditions but never had the means to do it.

"I'm happy you're getting your own space, girl. And you know my phone been dry as shit lately. Maybe your new nigga got a friend for me," I joked with a smile. I had a few guys I texted every now and then, but no one special since Chris. The homecoming dance had been back in October. It was now the middle of the summer, and I was finally ready to meet someone new.

"We'll see," she said with a dry laugh. "I kinda want to keep this low for a while, see how it goes."

I was about to point out that if he was moving her into her own place, at The Washington no less, their relationship wasn't going to stay low for long. But I didn't. She must have had her reasons for keeping him a secret, the same way I hadn't told her that I was one of the new drug mules for my family. Some things were simply better left unsaid.

Chapter Seventeen

Keon

"Oh, so you finally remembered you got a son over here?" Stacey snapped as she opened the door.

"Fuck is you talkin' 'bout? I just had him in Brooklyn wit' me not too long ago," I reminded her. "And I call him every day. You been bullshittin' when I call you to see him. What's good with that?"

She put her hand out to stop me. "You don't get to just walk up in here anymore. You lost that privilege."

"Well, send my son outside then."

"No," she replied defiantly.

"Fuck you mean, *no*?"

She folded her arms across her chest and glared at me. "It was bad enough that niggas were gunning for you. That, I could deal with. But now you got the mob after you too?"

"The mob?" I repeated.

"Yes, nigga, the muthafuckin' mob. One of them slick bastards came up to me when I was out eating with our son and told me that Vincent Morelli wants a sit-down with the boy's father. So, I said I didn't know who they had me confused with, and that's when he told me to have you contact them directly."

"And he said my name? Keon?" I asked her, just to be sure.

She rolled her eyes dramatically. "Of course he did! I only got one kid by one nigga named Keon. Last time I checked, that was yo' ass."

I stroked my chin thoughtfully. I had never knowingly crossed paths with the Morellis, but then again, I had so many bodies, I could never be too sure.

"Did he leave a way I could reach out to him?"

She shook her head. "Said that Dutchess would know how to get in touch with him."

"And you're just now telling me this?" I snapped at her. "You heard about what the fuck we been goin' through. They could be the people behind it!"

"They could," she agreed with a shrug. "But you been so busy with your little girlfriend and all that I didn't want to interrupt." She looked at me with a smirk that made me want to wring her fucking neck. Out of all my baby's moms, it was always Stacey that gave me the most problems. Somehow, she always knew who I was dealing with and would find a way to ruin it to spite me.

I had no idea how she knew about Dionne, though. I kept everything about her a secret because I knew I had no business fucking wit' her for real. I couldn't help it, though. She adored me. She had wanted me for so long that I could do no wrong in her eyes. I loved that, and after long days of grinding and putting in work, with the occasional body here and there, I needed that adoration. Plus, the sex was crazy. She was young, full of energy, and sexy as hell.

"The concierge at The Washington called to make sure I would be home to get my dry cleaning," she went on when she saw the surprised look on my face. "I told them of course I would, then called the condo, pretending to be the concierge. Your little girlfriend picked up. I told her I needed the correct spelling of her name, so imagine my surprise when she told me it was D–I–O–N–N–E." She looked me up and down, a look of pure hatred on her face. "You moved that little girl into a condo that you bought for *me*?"

I sighed impatiently. I could tell where this conversation was headed, and I wasn't in the mood for it. Plus, she still had me standing outside on her doorstep. "I bought that condo when we were together. When I left yo' ass, it was no longer yours, so whatever I do with it is no longer your concern. Now, where the fuck is my son?" I asked her as I pushed past her and walked into her house.

"Get outta my house, Keon! I don't want you in here!" she yelled at me as she ran up on me.

I pushed her out of my way like she was nothing more than an annoying-ass fly. "I bought you this house. This my shit. Get the fuck out my way," I snapped as I made my way toward the stairs.

"He's not here!"

"Why the fuck didn't you just tell me that then?" I yelled at her. "Got me standing outside for nothing."

"'Cause even if he was here, I wasn't letting you see him. You do too much, and I'm sick of it," she yelled back at me. Tears were in her eyes, and her voice was cracking.

I knew her feelings were hurt because of Dionne, and that was the real reason she had been acting up. Even though I hadn't been with her in years, a part of me still felt bad that she found out the way that she had. She'd watched Dionne grow up right along with Kenya like I had. Stacey could be a bitch, but she didn't deserve that.

"You're right. Sometimes I do shit that ain't right. None of it is intentional or meant to hurt you," I told her honestly.

"You really fucking wit' that little girl? You moved her out her grandmama house." She looked me up and down with a frown. "What is she, your woman or something?"

"Man, she ain't nowhere near that. She'll be at the crib till I'm done with her. You worried about the wrong shit, Stacey. Yo' ass should have called me the moment one of Morelli's men approached you. Fuck was you thinking?"

"I was thinking, out of all the bitches and baby's moms this nigga got, why I always gotta be the one to look out for him and hold him down? He didn't appreciate me when he had me, but I'm supposed to keep looking out for him like I'm his woman? Why should I do that?"

I sighed. "That wouldn't have been just looking out for me, Stacey. It would have been looking out for all of us. You got my son, so you're a target too. You see how easy it was for them to find you."

She was quiet for a moment.

"My family is under attack, and them mafuckas might be the ones behind it," I went on. "You don't think I deserved to know so that I could protect us?"

"You keep shit from me all the time."

Fed up with trying to reason with her, I nodded my head. We were getting nowhere fast. I needed to talk to my mom anyway to see just how she knew Vincent Morelli. "A'ight, man. Tell Jordan to call me when he gets home." I turned to leave, but she grabbed my hand and pulled me back.

"Does she make you feel as good as I did?" she asked in a sexy voice as she licked her lips.

"Stace, you know we don't go there no more," I reminded her. To say our relationship was toxic was putting it nicely. We fought and argued constantly and were no good for each other. Nothing pleasant had come from our time together besides Jordan. Removing myself from such an unhealthy relationship was probably one of the best decisions I had ever made.

"You don't need a little girl, Keon. You need a woman. A real woman that knows what you like," she murmured as she stroked my arm and snaked her hand further down to the front of my pants.

I wanted to back away from her, but my dick had other plans. Sex was the one area where we had always clicked. Shit, the sex was so good between us that it had saved the relationship the last few years. We clicked in the bedroom, but nowhere else.

"He still likes me," she whispered as I started to get harder and harder each time she stroked.

"That was never our problem."

"It wasn't," she agreed. And before I could stop her, she sank to her knees in front of me.

This shit was wrong as hell, and I knew it. I hadn't fucked Stacey in years because of the drama that came along with it. I never even allowed myself to be in a position to fuck her. I dropped my son off at his doorstep and called when I was outside. We were never alone because I didn't want this to happen. Crazy as she was, the sex with Stacey was so good that I knew if it was just the two of us, I would never be able to tell her no.

"Mmmm," she moaned as she slid my gray Nike sweatpants and black Polo boxer briefs down. My dick sprang free and saluted her. "I missed him." She kissed the head and gave it a long lick before looking up at me. "He tastes even better now." She began to give slow sucks, licks, and kisses until her mouth was wet enough to slide all of me in it and down her throat.

Once the tip hit her tonsils, it was a wrap for me. All the reasons I stayed away from her faded to black, and even though I knew I would regret this shit later, all I could think about was how good it would feel to slide up in her again.

Chapter Eighteen

Toni

I allowed Khalid King to move my brother to Silver Lakes, a super exclusive private facility on the North Shore. It was a two-story state-of-the-art building with a maximum of two floors, the first being a nurse's station and a total of six rooms, and the second consisted of offices. I was skeptical at first because the building looked more like a doctor's office than an actual acute care facility, but I saw the difference from the moment Tommy was admitted. The care team immediately gave him proper bathing, trimmed his nails, and groomed his beard and his hair so that he would look somewhat like himself again. The room was huge and more like a suite, with a fancy, large hospital bed, floor-to-ceiling windows, a plush couch and love seat, a glass coffee table, and a big flat-screen TV mounted to the wall. Every single channel I could ever want was available on the TV. The bathroom had a glass-enclosed shower and a whirlpool Jacuzzi tub. I wondered who this facility was equipped for, the patients or the family members?

"Both," Khalid had assured me. "You can come and go here as you please. You can even sleep here on the pull-out bed and go to work. Tommy is in the best of hands. Trust me."

It had been hard to trust him. I hadn't exactly led a life that let me trust many people, but when Tommy began to move his fingers on his own the day after he was admitted, I was glad that I had decided to put my trust in him.

That was a week ago, and ever since then, Tommy had been showing more and more improvements every day. True to Khalid's word, he had a medical team that was there solely to work on him. The team consisted of a doctor, two nurses, two CNAs, and an occupational therapist. All in all, I was pleased with his progress. I still went to see him every day after work. Seeing him get better was the highlight of my day.

Today was an exceptionally nice summer day. Any other time, when my life was normal, I might have made plans with my brother to spend it outside somewhere. This Friday night would still be spent with my brother, just at his bedside. Still, I was in good spirits when I walked through the sliding glass doors of Silver Lake. I waved at the nurses at their station before walking into Tommy's room, which was located directly across from the nurses. To my surprise, Khalid was there, holding a bag of food in one hand and a bottle of wine in the other.

I noticed Tommy's bed was empty and looked at him with questioning eyes. "Where is Tommy?"

"He's with the occupational therapist," he told me.

"Okay..."

"Come have a seat," he said as he waved me over to the couch.

I walked over to him slowly, taking in his appearance of khaki shorts, a white wife beater, and white Gucci sneaks on his feet. With his smooth chocolate skin and long dreads, Khalid made the most simple outfit look like a million dollars. I had worn a pair of fitted jeggings and a white wrap top today but still felt like I didn't compare to him.

"I got your favorite. Thai food," he told me as he pulled containers out of the bag.

"How do you know Thai is my favorite?" I asked him as my stomach growled at the scent of the food.

He smiled, showing off those dimples. "Come on now. How you think? I studied you."

"Studied me?" I repeated.

He nodded as he pulled out paper plates. "Yeah, I noticed this was always the food you had at the hospital and here, too. I figured you wouldn't mind if I brought you some to eat. I knew you would need dinner when you got off work."

I eyed the wine suspiciously as I sat down. "And the wine?"

"You had a long week. Why not have a drink or two? It's Friday. Plus, I thought we would celebrate Tommy being able to speak full sentences again."

My eyes widened in surprise. Tommy had been getting much better but still hadn't been able to fully use his vocal cords again due to all the tubes that had been shoved down his throat. "What? He spoke? When?"

"When I got here to wait on you," he said with a grin. "That's a cause for celebration, right? Thought we might have a toast." He fixed our plates before sliding mine to me.

I looked at him in awe. "Why are you being so nice to me?" I asked him. I had to know. I had Googled him and knew all about his life. He came from a rich family, had a promising career in politics, and was engaged to one of the prettiest women I had ever seen. I had studied her photo a million times and knew that all the fantasies I had about him were pointless. He was way out of my league.

"Why shouldn't I be? Since Tommy's been here, we've gotten pretty close, right? I consider you something like a friend." He smiled and melted my heart once again with those dimples. "You should always be nice to your friends, right?"

I shrugged. I didn't really have friends. The two-faced nature of females made me reluctant to let anyone get too close. All I had was my brother.

"Plus, I feel like you deserve to have someone be nice to you," he went on. "Your dedication to your brother is admirable. You're here for him, but who is here for you?"

"I got me," I said defiantly as I bit into my food.

"Impossible," he replied casually. "You can't lean on your own shoulder."

"I've been doing it all my life. No need to stop now."

He bit into a spring roll and chuckled. "Yo, you got your independent woman thing down pat, and I'm loving it. But it's cool to scoot over every once and a while to let somebody else take the driver's seat."

"And who would that somebody else be?" I inquired. "You?"

He shrugged. "Yeah. I have no problem doing that from time to time if you let me."

"Oh, really? And how would your fiancée feel about that?" I wanted to know.

He looked at me in surprise. I had never brought up the fact that I knew he was engaged before but figured now was as good a time as any.

"She won't mind me helping a friend," he responded.

I snorted. "I doubt that."

"How you know?" he challenged me.

"'Cause if it was me and my man was all of sudden helping some random bitch out, I would have a problem with it," I said flatly.

"Well, for one, you're not no random bitch. And she's not like that. Won't you meet her and see?"

I snorted. "Meet her? For what? I don't need to meet her."

"Yeah, you do. I plan on being very active with both you and Tommy. It seems like it'll make you more comfortable if she knew what I was doing, so come on. My parents' anniversary party is next week. Come party with us."

I looked at him skeptically. I wasn't so sure that any of this was a good idea. After all, I didn't want or need his handouts. And Tommy was his supporter, not me. I didn't need him to do anything for me. But my brother and I were so close that helping him was inevitably helping me, too, one way or the other. And so far, taking his help had done wonders for Tommy. I had to admit that he knew what he was doing.

"I'll come," I said reluctantly. "But the moment I feel like she's about to be on some funny style shit or don't want you around me, I'm leaving."

He smiled, showing off those dimples and bright white teeth, and I swear I could have melted right then and there. "Don't worry about that, Toni. I would never let you leave."

Chapter Nineteen

Dutchess

"I don't understand why you still think it's a good idea to have this party with everything we have going on," Kelvin grumbled as we pulled up to our house. We'd just come from the mall, where I'd picked up matching red Christian Louboutin shoes for both of us.

"Because we already planned it," I said sweetly. "And why shouldn't we celebrate thirty years of marriage?"

Kelvin didn't bother answering. Instead, he went to the trunk of the Maserati we'd been driving and grabbed all the bags from our trip.

My phone rang as we entered the house. I noticed the caller was private and didn't bother to answer it. The last few times I had answered, the caller had been Vinny, wanting to know if I had revealed the truth about Keon's paternity yet. I didn't need that on top of all the other stress I was dealing with, so I didn't bother to pick up.

He was becoming really annoying with that shit. I couldn't understand why, after all these years, he suddenly wanted to claim his illegitimate black son. Everyone knew that Italians didn't care for niggas at all. Plus, we were both married with our own families. What good would it do to tell Keon the truth now? I just didn't get it.

The affair with Vinny had started so innocently. I had always been more ambitious than Kelvin, so it didn't surprise me that he didn't want to make any big moves in the game at the time. Selling pounds of weed had been enough for him, but it was never enough for me. I had bigger dreams.

The Morellis had always been somewhat like royalty in our town. I never dreamt that I would be able to get in bed with them. After all, they were the Mob and kept their businesses completely separate from all of the hustling and street-level shit I was into. But I was growing desperate for a plug to get my hands on some real money, and being a woman trying to move up in the drug game was a difficult task. Niggas were willing to let me be their mule or sell ounces, but that was pretty much it. No matter how much work I put in, no one wanted to connect me with the plug.

I figured if I couldn't get in through the front, I would take the back door. My method was risky, but I figured I didn't have shit else to lose, so I might as well try. Luckily, I didn't have to do no hot shit to get a meet with the Italians. Vinny's most trusted bodyguard was a white boy named Leo who had grown up in the hood around us niggas and was practically one of us. He was cool as fuck and real chill. He was definitely invited to all the cookouts, parties, and holiday dinners. We smoked with him all the time. Matter of fact, he was one of our most loyal customers.

Anyway, I begged Leo to let me meet Vinny one time. I didn't know what I would say to him, but I begged Leo for the chance until he finally agreed. I still had no idea how to approach him, but I figured I would bend his ear and try my luck. Little did I know that I didn't have to twist Leo's arm at all. Come to find out, Italian Vinny was really into black women. He tried his best to fuck me the first time he met me, but I was far from stupid. If he wanted anything from me, he would have to earn it, but only *after* I soaked up the game from him.

Finessing him took a little more work than I thought. I had originally planned on just running game on him until I got what I wanted and then leaving him high and dry, but Vinny wasn't the boss for nothing. There wasn't shit slow about him. I went from pretending like I gave a fuck about him to actually caring more than I wanted to. During that time, he introduced me to some Spanish guys in New York as his protégé. If they were surprised, they didn't bother to show it, and they dealt with me with the utmost respect. They even shaved the price of each kilo I copped for me off the strength that I was with Vinny. He had plugged me in something sweet, and I was forever grateful to him for that. Our business ran smoothly as ever, thanks to all the tips he gave me. Still, it wasn't until we sold enough weight to beat out all the competition that I decided to give him some pussy.

I didn't like white boys. I had never fucked one before Vinny, and never since him. Still, that didn't matter. Vinny happened to be a fine-ass Italian, and he had two things that turned me the fuck on: money and power. Yes, I was married, but Kelvin was so busy trying to build a legit empire from our dirty money that he barely had time for me. Vinny always had the time— and the means.

I wish I could say that I regretted fucking with Vinny, but I didn't. My affair with him had been one of the happiest times of my life. He spoiled me rotten, from penthouse suites at the best hotels to the finest jewels and exclusive trips whenever we could get away. The dick was even better than I ever thought it would be. I was living the life most women could only dream of and probably wouldn't have walked away from him if his wife hadn't turned up pregnant. It was one thing for me to be fucking Vinny, but for me to be doing it while he had a baby on the way just didn't sit right with me. So, as much as I didn't want to, I ended things between us.

Almost immediately after I did so, I discovered I was pregnant too. My intentions had been to abort the baby, but when Kelvin found out, he was ecstatic about being a father, so I decided I would just keep it. I mean, there was a chance the baby was his. I figured if the little mafucka came out light, bright, and damn near white with blue eyes, we would still be good to go since Kelvin was so fair-skinned himself. It was a win-win situation for me.

The moment I laid eyes on Keon, I knew he was Vinny's. He was the color of coffee with just a dab of too much cream and had the prettiest hazel eyes that turned green whenever he was upset. To the naked eye, he was the perfect combination of me and Kelvin, but all of his facial features, from the color of his eyes to the sharpness of his nose and jaw to his lips, were all Vinny. Then, as he got older and I saw just how short his fuse was, that confirmed it for me. Vinny was known for his fiery temper, and Keon had definitely inherited that from him.

Still, it was a secret I would have taken to my grave. Vinny's wife had had several miscarriages over the years before finally giving him a child, but it wasn't the boy he'd always wanted. I never imagined he would wait so long to pop up and decide to be his father, but here he was . . . and I didn't know what to do.

Once we reached our room, I turned to face Kelvin. The years had been so good to him. He looked even better now than ever, and I couldn't stop myself from reaching up to stroke his face gently. It had been so long since he touched me that my body was instantly on fire just from being so close to him.

"You don't wanna celebrate being married to me?" I asked seductively.

He looked at me and bit his lip. "We've grown apart, Dutchess. What is there to celebrate?" he asked, crushing my spirits.

I snatched my hand back like he was on fire. Any tenderness I had just been feeling toward him was gone. "Fuck you mean, what is there to celebrate? The fact that you're married to *me* is a reason to celebrate every fucking day."

"All we do is argue, and I'm over that shit," he responded calmly. "You've treated me as less than a man for years. You know how hard that was for me to accept and still stay?"

I snorted and walked away. "Here we go with this bullshit again."

"Yeah, that's right. What I say is always bullshit. Anything you say, though? Oh, we gotta listen like it's the end of the fucking world."

I put my hand on my hip and glared at him. "Why does it always feel like you're trying to pick a fight with me, Kelvin? What reasons do you have to be unhappy? We have anything that you could possibly want. We're rich with a beautiful family. What more could you fucking want?"

"Respect," he replied simply. "You don't have any for me, and the way you carry on in front of our kids makes them lose respect for me too."

"How?" I asked in disbelief. "They are grown. They make their own decisions. I have no control over that."

"You have plenty of control over that," he spat. "You ever stop to think that you might be the reason none of their relationships work?"

"Really? We're gonna do this now when we should be getting ready to celebrate our marriage?"

"Keon has four different kids by four different women," he went on like I hadn't said a word. "Poor Kenya is scared to date, Khalid is engaged to a woman he doesn't even like, and Khalia acts so much like a man that she will never allow one to come into her life and lead her, kind of like someone else I know."

I snorted. "Now I don't let you lead."

"Are you saying you do?"

"No, I'm saying a real man wouldn't have to *ask* for my permission to lead," I shot back. "He would just do it."

"Now I'm not a real man." He shook his head. "You hear how you talk to me? And I'm supposed to celebrate thirty years of this shit? You're supposed to speak life into me, Dutchess. Instead, all you do is say everything that you *think* I've done wrong."

"So, each year you've been married to me has pretty much been miserable, huh?"

"I never said that."

"You didn't have to say it," I cut him off.

He looked me up and down. "You wanna know what ruined us? This game. This money. That's what fucked us up."

I laughed. "So now being rich is a problem?"

"No, but being in this game is. It's changed you into a person I don't know and haven't known for a long time now. It's never been for me, and I've been telling you for years that I want out. There's other things I want to do with my life, and I never thought it was a good idea for the kids to follow in our footsteps."

"Fuck that. They needed to learn a skill to put food on the table the same as I did," I spat. "We've made them richer than they would have ever been working some fucking desk job and have left a legacy for them, so I really don't see what the problem is."

He was quiet for a moment before responding. "I want us all out. It's no longer safe for us. Somebody is coming for our crown, and I'd rather give it to them than die trying to protect it. Now, I did the math, and with what we bring in from the funeral homes combined with—"

"No, no, no, *hell* no. Are you crazy?" I snapped before he could finish. "First of all, I wipe my ass with that money from the businesses. No way in hell all of us could live off that. Second, why would I let any of our enemies defeat us? If somebody wants the crown that bad, they gone have to see me to get that shit!"

He shook his head. "And that's why we have a problem. You let this street shit become more important than your marriage. I am your husband, and I'm telling you it's time to get out, and instead of even thinking about it, you shut me down real quick. Marriage is about compromise, but you don't know shit about that. Keep working on being the queen of these streets though, baby. I know that's what matters to you the most." He pulled a wad of cash out of his pocket and tossed it on the bed. "Since that means so much to you, I knew it would be the perfect gift. Happy anniversary."

I watched as he walked out of the bedroom without another word. Once he was gone, I picked up the money and flipped through it. A part of me felt like I should have been mad that he didn't get me something more thoughtful, but fuck it. He was right. I did love money.

And I would do whatever it took to keep making it my way.

Chapter Twenty

Khalia

"Boss. Boss, wake up. You're home."

I opened my eyes slowly and looked around. I had been sleeping in the back of Tookie's truck. In my outstretched hand was a 9 mm pistol with the silencer attached.

"Thanks, Took," I said as I yawned and reached for the back door.

"You need to get some rest, boss. You been going hard all week," he said with a hint of worry in his voice.

I shrugged. I hadn't gotten a full night of sleep since the warehouse fire. I couldn't. Niggas were so busy trying to figure out who did it that everyone was slow to react. I wasn't like that. We had no solid clues as to who did the shit, so to me, the only way to answer violence was with even more violence. I told no one but Khalid my plan, and even though he said I was crazy, he was willing to go down whatever road I led him. Together, we rode out on everyone that I *thought* did it. Fuck it. The streets were watching and waiting for us to respond, and I refused to sit by and twiddle my thumbs. Niggas would start to think that we were soft. It was bad enough that no one had paid for shooting up Khalid's rally. Was I supposed to let this go unanswered too?

Hell no.

Over the last seven days, I had been on a warpath. Nobody was safe. Anyone who ever went against the grain, anyone who had ever had any minor beef with me or my family, I killed them on sight. The bodies were piling up so fast that the cops and media couldn't keep up. The news stated that this was the bloodiest week in Pittsburgh's history. This number of bodies had never dropped in such a short period of time. I wouldn't say I was proud, but I would say that niggas got the message loud and clear not to fuck with us anymore.

Still, for all my efforts, I had yet to get a name of who was fucking with our family. With this amount of people getting murked, people usually started talking right away to save their own asses, but I was no closer to finding out who did this than I had been when I started. For that reason, I couldn't help but wonder if this was an inside job.

"Somebody had to do it," I responded, hopping out of his truck. "Listen, it's my parents' anniversary party tonight. You can come as a guest, not security."

He shook his head. "No, boss, if I'm there, it's to protect you."

I smiled at him. Tookie's loyalty was second to none. When all of this was over, I was going to reward him for that. "It's a family party, Took. You can enjoy yourself. I'm sure my mom went all out for security."

This time, it was him who shrugged. "Never can be too careful."

I laughed and slammed the door shut. As soon as I stepped on the porch, I noticed a large bouquet of flowers and a card. Frowning, I looked around before picking them up. These had to be at the wrong house. No one knew my address or even my real name out here.

I pulled the card out as I unlocked my door and walked into my house. Tossing the flowers down on an end table in my living room, I pulled the card out and read it.

Kyra,

I think it should be obvious by now that I like you. I would like to get to know you, maybe take you out to eat somewhere since I never got my Alfredo LOL. Give me a call so I can make you smile.

Your friendly neighborhood mailman, Andrew.

His number was at the bottom of the card.

I read the message a few times and couldn't stop myself from smiling. Andrew was so different from the men I let into my world. Everybody I associated myself with was a hustler, a drug dealer, or a killer just like me. Andrew was not. He worked an honest nine-to-five, and his paycheck probably couldn't cover one of my Chanel handbags. He wasn't a boss, just a regular guy. I had no idea what to do with a regular guy.

But he didn't know who I was. He had no idea that I was one of the deadliest women the East Coast had ever seen. If he knew who I really was, no way would he have come at me with a bouquet of flowers. I doubt he would have even approached me at all.

I looked down at his number again. I felt so conflicted. I was so attracted to him and didn't feel the urge to fuck and dismiss him as I did everyone else. However, other niggas knew who I was and not to expect a damn thing from me. They never asked me out on dates or anything like that, and they certainly never bought me flowers.

I bit my lip and decided fuck it. Why *not* call him? With him, I could be free to be whoever I wanted, not the bad bitch everyone always expected me to be. He could be the perfect thing to take my mind off all the bullshit going on in my life, even if it was just for a little while. I picked up my phone and dialed his number before I could change my mind.

"Hello?" he answered on the second ring.

"My friendly neighborhood mailman. What's up?" I greeted him.

"Kyra?" he asked, and although I couldn't see him, I could tell by his tone that he was smiling.

"Yeah, it's me." I sat down on the couch and kicked off my shoes. I had been so tired in the back of Tookie's truck, but now I was wide awake. "Or were you expecting someone else? I mean, you did say you were the friendly neighborhood mailman."

He laughed. "Naw, I said I was *your* friendly neighborhood mailman," he corrected me.

I laughed, too, and got comfortable. I could tell from the vibe this was going to be one of those nice, long, getting-to-know-you phone conversations. I couldn't remember the last time I had one of those. I deprived myself of all the simple things that made you feel special when you dealt with a man, but I knew with this one I could do things a little differently. I didn't have to be Khalia King. I could be Kyra James, and she could be whoever I wanted her to be.

Chapter Twenty-one

Khalid

I sat at the bar in my penthouse, waiting for Nisa to emerge as I threw back a shot of Remy Martin. I usually wasn't a big drinker, but tonight had me a little on edge. I had a lot on my mind. It had been a while since I had to get my hands dirty and put in work on the streets, but this past week, I had caught more bodies than I had in all the years I'd been in the game. I didn't have a choice. Khalia insisted on getting revenge for our family immediately, even though we had no idea who to go after. I didn't agree with her, but I would never have let her go out in the streets alone like that, so we did what we had to do. I don't know how many niggas we killed or how many we robbed. All I knew was that we had enough money to attempt to get back to where we were before the fire.

Then there was the fact that it felt like I was living a double life. I didn't like to lie or keep secrets, but here I was, lying to my family and Nisa about doing a big business venture with my father that could very well let us retire from the drug game. My family would be against it for obvious reasons, but so would Nisa. A big part of the reason we were together was based on who we were and what I did.

I sighed and was about to pour another shot when I got a text from Toni. Hearing from her excited me more than I was willing to admit.

Toni: Are you sure me coming to the party tonight is a good idea?

I frowned before I responded.

Me: Of course it is. You don't trust me by now?

Toni: I do. I just don't want anyone to get the wrong idea.

Me: How? Everyone knows about you and Tommy. If he would have gotten clearance from the doctors he could have came too. You deserve a night out.

I waited a few minutes for her response. When she didn't, I slid the phone back in the pocket of my tailored Armani slacks, hoping that she wouldn't go back to that stubborn, independent woman bullshit. I loved strong, independent women, but the problem was they sometimes turned down help and preferred to do things the hard way. I could tell Toni had always been like that, and considering how she grew up, it was understandable. Still, I hated that she let it get in the way of making life just a tad bit easier for her.

"Baby, you ready?" I heard Nisa ask. I turned on the bar stool to face her. As usual, Nisa looked fucking gorgeous. Her bright pink, yellow, and orange dress hugged every curve just right and showed off her beautiful body. On her feet, she wore six-inch heels, which she knew I loved. They made her legs and ass stand out even more and appear even sexier. Her face barely had any makeup on it, and her hair had been straightened so that it fell down her back. I always told Nisa that she stood out as the baddest bitch in the room no matter where we went, and she always proved me right when she showed up and showed out like this.

"You look great," I told her as she walked up toward me.

"I know," she replied arrogantly.

I chuckled, stood up, and offered her my arm. "You ready?"

"Yeah." She looked back at the bar. "How much you been drinking?"

"Just had a shot."

She looked at me knowingly. "What's wrong, Khalid? You never drink unless something is bothering you."

"You tryna be my shrink or something?" I asked her with a laugh. "I'm good, baby. It's my parents' anniversary. I want to celebrate. Is that good with you?"

"It's great if that's the only reason why," she shot back as I held the door open for her.

I slapped her on the ass as she walked past me. "Trust me, it is. You'll love it tonight."

"I love it every night," she replied with a grin on her face.

"I know you do," I said with a smile.

We rode the elevator hand in hand and didn't speak another word until we were comfortably seated in the back of my black Maybach Benz.

"I wish we had a whole fleet of these," Nisa said wistfully as Julio, my driver, pulled off.

"Why would we buy a whole fleet of these when there are other options?" I asked her.

She shrugged. "I don't need to keep my options open. I know the only thing that I want."

I frowned. "You still talking about cars?" I asked, knowing that wasn't the case.

Nisa glared at me. "You know I'm not. Khalid, when are we getting married?"

I rubbed my temples. "I can't believe you wanna talk about this shit right now out of all times."

"If not now, then when? You never wanna discuss wedding plans with me. I can't even get you to commit to a date."

"Nisa, you know there are things I want to do and certain political goals I want to reach before I get married. You claimed you understood," I reminded her.

"Well, I thought I did, but now I don't know. Everything is always about what you want, when you want it, and how you want to do it. What about me, Khalid? What about what I want?"

"Now I don't give you what you want?" I asked in disbelief.

She folded her arms. "What do you give me that I can't give myself, Khalid? Dick? That's pretty much it."

I ain't gone sit up here and act like I didn't feel some type of way at her words. They definitely stung. "A'ight then. So, if all I do is fuck you, why you even wanna marry me? I mean, since you do it all and I don't do shit, it seems like we should never get married to me."

"Khalid . . ." she said softly as she reached out to touch me, regret lacing her tone. "That's not what I meant."

"You ain't gotta clean it up, baby. You said it. Own that shit," I told her smoothly as I pushed her hand off my arm. "I don't think you should even wanna touch me right now. I don't want you getting the wrong idea if I try to touch you back since you know all I wanna do is fuck you."

"Oh my God," she snapped. "We are on our way to your parents' house right now. Is this really how you wanna act all night?"

"You said it, not me."

She nodded her head as the driver turned up my parents' street. "I did say it. But that's not the way I meant it. What I meant is the only thing you give me *entirely* is dick. The other parts of you that I really want to reach—your heart, your mind, your soul—are all closed off to me. I feel like you reserved those for Amber, and she's not here. I'm the one with you, but I'm competing with a ghost for your love."

I stared at her in silence for a moment. I never knew she felt like that, but I also knew that she wasn't lying.

At least, not completely. I didn't have my heart, mind, or soul closed off to her intentionally, but she was just so different from Amber that she wasn't able to reach those parts of me. I didn't know how to tell her that without hurting her feelings, though, so instead, I said, "You're not competing with anyone for my love, Nisa. Trust me. If I didn't want to be with you, I wouldn't be with you."

"You don't want to marry me," she mumbled with her lip poked out, pouting like a spoiled brat who didn't get her way.

"I never said that." I kissed her as the car came to a complete stop. "Now, come on. Let's go have a good time."

She smiled at me. "Okay, baby."

The driver opened the back door on my side. I got out, then walked to Nisa's side to help her. As she stood in front of me, smoothing her dress and fixing her hair, I admired her physique. Physically, she was perfect. She was also intelligent as hell and knew the game in and out, but I yearned for something more than that. I didn't need a gangstress like my sister or my mother on my arm. I wanted a true lady that did her own thing outside of me.

As soon as we entered the house, my phone vibrated. I pulled it out of my pocket and saw I had a text from Toni. Nisa had faded into the crowd, so I was safe to open it.

Toni: You did not have to send a limo for me tonight! I could drive my own car

I grinned. I knew if I had told her I was sending a car for her, she would have told me not to, so I did it without her permission. A part of me did because I wanted her to truly relax and worry about nothing that night, but the real reason was that I wanted to be sure she made it. The only time I got to spend with her was in a hospital room. I wanted to see her be free outside of worrying about Tommy, if he would heal, and the rest.

Me: What did I tell you before? If I do something nice for you, just accept it.

Toni: You're right. Thank you so much. I appreciate it! See you soon.

I appreciate it. I couldn't remember the last time Nisa, or anyone, for that matter, said those words to me. I couldn't stop the smile from spreading across my face. I couldn't wait to see her.

Chapter Twenty-two

Kenya

"Bitch, you got inches!" Dionne squealed as I pulled my bonnet off my head.

I laughed as my silky sew-in fell to the small of my back. I hardly wore weaves, and when I did, it was never this long. But tonight was different. It was my parents' anniversary party, and everyone who was anyone would be there. I was tired of being lonely and always playing the background. I wanted someone to notice me.

I mean, yeah, I had niggas in my DMs on IG and Facebook, but I didn't really like meeting guys like that. How are you bold enough to hop in my inbox on social media but when I see you, you're scared to say a word to me? I liked the guys I dealt with to have confidence. I hadn't met anyone worth giving my attention to yet, and I was sick of not having a Good morning, beautiful text to look forward to every day when I woke up.

So, in addition to having hair down to my ass, I had opted to wear this badass strappy black Christian Dior dress. It crisscrossed across my midriff and my back, stopping right before my knee. My titties sat up like two ripe melons. On my feet, I had a pair of black Giuseppe Zanotti high-heeled sandals, and Dionne had done my makeup to perfection. I looked like a fucking bank vault full of money, and I knew it. Only the niggas with the most confidence would even think about stepping to me, and that's what I wanted: someone who didn't care who my family was and only saw me.

"So, you really didn't invite your new man to party with us tonight?" I asked Dionne as we took final looks in my mirror.

She frowned. "Kenya, how many times I gotta tell you we on the low?"

I held my hands up in surrender. "A'ight, I'm sorry, sis." I looked her up and down and nodded my head in approval. "I see he upgraded you, though," I told her as I checked out the new ice shining on her wrists, around her neck, and dripping from her ears.

Dionne smiled and smoothed down the front of her midnight blue Chanel dress. She was finally able to afford all the high-end designers that I wore regularly, and I was happy for her. If anyone deserved to stunt, it was definitely her.

We went downstairs. Unsurprisingly, the party was already crowded. My dad had said that this would be a small gathering of family friends, but I knew better. Dutchess King never missed an opportunity to show off, and her thirtieth wedding anniversary was as good a day as any to show everyone how good life had been to her, despite our few recent unfortunate mishaps.

"This party is lit!" Dionne exclaimed excitedly. No matter how often she visited my family, she was always amazed by how we lived.

"Ain't it?" I said with a grin. The best of the best had shown out to show my parents love.

I took a flute of champagne from a passing waitress and knocked it back before I looked around. The party had drawn a mixed crowd. People of all ages and races were there. My mom didn't really like to deal with people outside of our illegal businesses, but the way my dad kept our legal hustles going meant we got to rub elbows with a little bit of everybody. Mom usually left all that to him, so I was surprised to see her talking to some fine-ass white man who had just walked through the door. He was darker than most of the white guys I saw, leading me to believe he was Italian or maybe even Greek.

"Wow," Dionne murmured next to me. "I don't really fuck with white chocolate, but that mafucka right there would make me reconsider."

I chuckled. He did look good, but white men had never been my style. "I gotta go to the bathroom. I'll be back," I told her as I set my empty flute on a side table. I rushed to the bathroom right between the kitchen and the dining room, knocked twice real fast, and swung the door open. I was surprised by what I saw on the other side.

A man had been standing at the toilet, pulling his pants up, but not before I got a glimpse of the beautiful meat he was packing. It was a nice length and had equal girth, and it was soft. I couldn't imagine how it would look when it was hard.

"Oh, shit!" he exclaimed once he noticed me. I took in his handsome face, from his walnut complexion to the long lashes that framed his almond-shaped, deep brown eyes. He was fine as hell.

"I–I'm sorry. My fault. I guess I didn't knock hard enough," I replied as I continued to check him out. He looked like he might have been six feet tall or close to it, and his hair was spinning in three-sixty waves on his head. He had on tailored black slacks, black Ferragamo loafers, and a black button-down that he tucked back into his slacks. Around his neck, a Cuban link chain shined brightly, and I could tell with my experienced eye it was definitely the real deal. I had never seen his fine ass around, yet here he was in my bathroom like it was nothing. Who the fuck was he?

"I'm sorry. I didn't hear anything," he said apologetically as he flushed the toilet before walking over to the sink to wash his hands.

"It's a lot of noise in here. It's fine," I said with a wave of my hand.

He finished washing his hands, grabbed two paper towels from the sink dispenser, and finally looked at me the same way I had been eyeing him. His eyes lit up, and he smiled, revealing a small dimple in his right cheek.

"Maybe we can find somewhere quiet to go and talk," he suggested.

"I'm sure we can—after I use the bathroom," I responded with a laugh.

"Oh, yeah, my fault," he said with a laugh. "My name is Armani. I'll be waiting outside the door for you, Ms. . . ."

The fact that he was here in my house, at my parents' party and didn't know who the hell I was turned me on slightly. "Kenya. You better not leave," I said with a sexy smile as I pushed him out of the bathroom and shut the door. As I relieved my bladder, I couldn't help but smile a little bit. My goal for the night was to catch, and not even five minutes at the party, I already had a fish on my hook. Tonight was looking to be very promising indeed.

Chapter Twenty-three

Toni

"Tommy, you should see this limo," I told my brother as we talked on FaceTime. "It has everything in here. TVs, ice buckets for champagne, all this room . . ." I flipped the camera so he could see the inside of the Mercedes Benz limo himself. "You see this shit? All this just for me."

"Why not for you?" he asked. He was killing therapy and looking and talking better each day. His recovery was bordering on miraculous. We had thought he would get clearance to go to the party, but he was still under heavy observation from his medical team. They wouldn't let him go anywhere until he was one hundred percent better.

"I mean, I haven't done anything to deserve all this," I responded.

"Sometimes being a good person is all you need to do." He looked at me seriously. "I told you when Khalid King was running his campaign that he was one of the good guys. Do you believe me now?"

"I do." I wasn't that much into politics, so I hadn't followed Khalid's career, but Tommy had, which was why he was one of his biggest supporters.

"By the way, do you know what he's planning on doing about his race for senator? I know he's not going to let them beat him."

I shrugged. I had no idea what he planned to do. It hadn't occurred to me to ask him. All of my available energy had been thrown into Tommy and his well-being.

"Sis, you have to make sure he gets back on the campaign trail," Tommy urged me. "He's one of the good guys. We won't get too many candidates like him."

"How am I supposed to convince him to do that?"

"I saw how he looks at you," Tommy remarked slyly. "He likes you. He'll listen to you."

"Please," I scoffed. "He is fine as hell, plus filthy rich, and he has a fiancée. What would he want with me?"

"I wish you would quit doubting yourself all the time," Tommy snapped. "I wouldn't care who he was engaged to or how much money he has. None of that shit makes him better than you. I'm a man. I know when a man likes a woman. I'm grateful that he does like you too. I would probably be dead right now if he didn't."

I was quiet as the limo pulled to a stop in front of the house.

"But look, don't overthink it. Tonight, you get to mingle with the rich and famous, so get loose and have a good time," he encouraged me as the back door opened.

I stepped out, expecting to see the driver, and was surprised to see Khalid himself. "Speak of the devil," I told Tommy as I flipped the camera around so he could see Khalid.

Khalid grinned and took the phone from me so he could talk to my brother. "Tommy, my man. How you doin'?"

"Great. I was just telling my sister we need you back out there on the campaign trail, fighting the good fight for the people," Tommy told him.

"Yeah, you know I want to get back out there. I just felt so bad for what happened. But there's so much work to do," Khalid said wistfully.

"You can't let them beat you. We need you, brother," Tommy said.

Khalid bit his lip and looked at my brother on my phone screen. "You're right. First thing Monday morning, I'm gonna have a meeting with my team to see what my next steps should be. But I'm not going back out there until I know that you are one hundred percent better. I may even have a job lined up for you. Who knows?"

"For real?" Tommy said excitedly. I knew that getting into politics was a dream come true for him.

"I haven't lied to you before, and I ain't lying now."

Tommy smiled. "A'ight bet. Y'all have fun for me, and bring me a plate."

I snatched my phone back from Khalid. "Bye, Tommy," I said with a chuckle as I ended the call and placed the phone into my black clutch.

Khalid gave me a quick hug. I closed my eyes for the few seconds I was in his embrace, inhaling his scent and loving the safe, protected feeling being in his arms gave me.

"You look amazing," he told me as we walked toward the house, which was really a mansion. I had never seen anything like it or been anywhere close to it. I came from broken sidewalks, projects, and row houses, but the estate before me was anything but that. There were Bentleys, Rolls Royces, and Range Rovers in the winding driveway. A fountain was in front of the house.

"We match," he went on as he looked at me and then back at himself.

I looked down at my black Calvin Klein wrap dress and smiled a little. The dress showed just enough cleavage and was fitted at my waist, then flared out before it ended right before my knees. I wasn't a fan of being uncomfortable in six-inch heels all night, so on my feet were black peep toes that had a slightly clunky heel and stood at about four inches. I had simple gold jewelry and carried a black-and-gold clutch. I had gotten my hair, nails, and toes done earlier. I told myself it was because I wanted to treat myself, but I knew better. Deep down, I wanted to impress him. I was glad that I had.

Khalid, on the other hand, never looked anything less than perfect. Tonight, he had surpassed that with his tailored slacks, Gucci loafers, black Gucci belt, and short-sleeve black Gucci button-up with the red and green stripes down the sleeve to match the loafers. He had a simple gold chain with a cross dangling from it, and his dreads were long and wavy, like he had just taken them out of braids that same day. As usual, they were shaped up nicely. He looked so damn good that my pussy did a little jump, reminding me that I had been neglecting her.

"We do," I said to him with a smile. "And how did you know I was already here?"

"I had the driver text me," he told me as we walked toward the front door. "I knew you were feeling a little doubtful about coming here, so I wanted to be the first face you saw to make you feel comfortable."

He was always so thoughtful. I smiled again. "Thank you."

"No, thank you for coming."

The front door opened, and I walked into the most beautiful home I had ever seen. We were in the foyer, which had marble floors and a crystal chandelier. To my left was a living room with large bay windows, expensive furniture, and a white grand piano, and to my right was yet another room that I wanted to call the living room, though it wasn't as big. There were still couches in there as well. Two winding staircases led the way upstairs.

"You grew up here?" I asked, amazed.

Before he could answer, a gorgeous woman wearing a brightly colored dress marched over to us. "Khalid, where have you been?" she asked him, one hand on her hip.

"Chill, Nisa. I met Toni outside. This is her first time here. I didn't want her to come in by herself," Khalid explained. He shook his head impatiently. "Toni, this is my fiancée, Nisa. Nisa, this is Toni, Tommy's sister and my friend."

She shot him a surprised glance at the introduction and tried to change her facial expression before extending her hand to me, but I noticed everything. Growing up the way I did, I had no choice. Nothing got past me. I knew that she wasn't too thrilled to have him introduce me as his friend. On the other hand, I was surprised that he did. I mean, we definitely talked and connected on a level that made me more than just Tommy's sister, but I knew how niggas liked to downplay shit, especially to their women. Khalid didn't, and I respected him for that.

"Hi, friend," Nisa said with a fake smile as we shook hands. "I'm Nisa, his fiancée."

"He's talked so much about you," I lied with ease. He rarely mentioned her.

She looked at him and smiled. "He better."

"Listen. Nisa, I want to take her to meet everyone—"

"Oh, no, you don't have to do that," I cut him off.

"Are you sure?" he asked me in that concerned tone that always let me know that he genuinely cared about my well-being.

"Absolutely," I assured him. "I don't need you to babysit me."

"Stop acting like her daddy, Khalid. She's a big girl. She can watch herself," Nisa said as she gave me another fake smile. I knew that big-girl comment was a jab at my weight, and while I did feel slightly self-conscious about my appearance around her, all I had to do was remember how adoringly her own man had looked at me not even five minutes before. He clearly had no problem with my weight.

Khalid glared at her. "Nisa . . ."

"It's cool. Go head. I'll call you when I need you." My words were for Khalid, but I was looking right at Nisa when I said them. Any other time, I wouldn't have dared to say those words to another woman's man right in front of her, but she had started it, so I would finish it. I wanted her to know that I could call her nigga, and he would come running to me.

I felt her eyes burning a hole in my back as I walked away, but I didn't care. I decided to take my brother's advice and enjoy the night, and for the most part, I did just that. I met a whole lot of different people who became interested in me looking over their portfolios once they learned that I worked in finance and went to school for it as well. Khalid hadn't told me that tonight would be a great networking opportunity for me. I was pleased as ever and riding high on my wave when I exited the bathroom and literally ran into Nisa.

She made no secret about looking me up and down before finally settling on my face. Her lip curled in disgust. "Do you really think you can have my man?" she asked me. I could tell from the way she was talking that she was a little tipsy, and I tried to push past her a little bit, but she moved right with me.

"I don't want your man," I lied.

"Bullshit! Everybody wants Khalid," she snapped.

"But you got him, so what the fuck are you bothering me for?" I asked as I threw my hands up.

"'Cause I know all my man's *friends,* and never has he ever gone out his way so much for one of them as he does for you." She looked at me snickered. "I think it's 'cause he feels sorry for you, to be honest. I mean, why would he even waste so much time on you if he didn't when he has me at home?"

This time it was my turn to laugh. "Well, why don't you ask him that, sis? I damn sure never have to beg him for his time. He gives it voluntarily. I've never asked him to do anything. He just does it."

She sneered at me. "Don't get used to it. I'll be putting a stop to that shit real soon." She flashed the huge diamond on her ring finger. "You see this here? He put it on my finger. He wants to marry me, and when I tell him how much I don't like him being around you after I met you, he'll stop y'all little 'friendship' real quick," she said, using air quotes around the word *friendship*.

"I doubt it," I told her with the utmost confidence. One thing I was certain of was how much respect Khalid had for our friendship. He would never let anyone ruin it, least of all her.

She just laughed and shook her head. "See, here's the thing. You don't know how hard I worked to get him, or what I had to do to make sure I had him to myself. I'm not willing to share him, especially not with you. You ain't even his type. Out of all the years I've known him, I've never seen Khalid with a fat girl before."

This time it was my turn to laugh. "Is that all you can do, boo? Make comments about my weight? You gotta do better than that, sis. I can pull the same niggas you do looking the way I do. It's nothing. You need to worry about keeping your man happy 'cause if you were, he wouldn't have to spend so much time with me." With that, I walked away. I knew she was probably thinking we had fucked from my comments, but honestly, I couldn't care less. She should have never stepped to me like I was doing something to her relationship by being close with Khalid.

If anything, I was helping it by not acting on how I really felt about him. In the back of my mind, I knew that if I did, he would have no problem reciprocating. Instead of going off on me, Nisa should have been thanking her lucky stars that I wasn't willing to go there with him because he would have no problem taking it to the next level with me.

Chapter Twenty-four

Khalid

"Oooh, shiiiiiit . . ." Dionne moaned as she threw her ass back.

I smacked one ass cheek so hard that my hand stung. She loved that shit and threw it back so hard the bathroom sink began to shake a little.

"Chill," I told her, but I really loved the fact that she was just as aggressive as me when it came to sex.

"You chill," she shot back before making her ass cheeks vibrate all over my dick.

I usually liked to be in control, but I bit my lip and enjoyed the view for a minute until she started to feel too damn good. Then I grabbed her by the waist and gave her long, hard strokes until her juices were dripping down my balls. When I felt my nut starting to build, I pulled out, ready to bust on her ass; but she sank to her knees and took me in her mouth while massaging my nuts at the same damn time. I swear to God, she made me bust the best nut of my life. I damn near screamed like a bitch as she swallowed every drop with no problem.

"Damn, girl," I murmured as I helped her to her feet. "You the best, baby."

She grabbed a paper towel from the dispenser on the sink and smiled at me. "You bring it out of me," she said with a wink as she wiped the corners of her mouth. She smoothed her dress and looked at me. "Do I look a'ight? Or can you tell I was in the bathroom on my knees?"

I laughed and reached out to stroke her pretty face. "You look fine. Go head. Walk out first."

"A'ight. I'll see you later?" she asked hopefully.

"Hell yeah. Tonight is all about you, baby," I promised her.

She grinned and put some lip gloss on her lips. "I can't wait." She opened the bathroom door, stuck her head out cautiously, and walked out. I adjusted my pants, waited a couple of minutes, and walked out of the bathroom as well.

We had been in a small bathroom in the back of the house, but the sound of the party was still going strong as soon as I stepped out. I made my way to the front to rejoin the party.

"Keon!" My mom appeared from out of nowhere. "I been looking all over for you. Where have you been?"

I had a feeling she wouldn't want to hear that I had snuck to the bathroom with someone I had no business fucking and bent her over the sink right in the middle of her anniversary party. "Enjoying the party, Ma. What's up? Ain't y'all supposed to do a toast soon or something?"

"Later for that." She grabbed my hand and started to pull me toward my father's study, which was in the opposite direction of the party.

"Ma, what's up?" I asked her, confused. I walked around her and headed back toward the front. I wanted to keep an eye on anyone and everyone there. I didn't trust a soul, family party or not. None of us was safe until we figured out who was behind the attacks on our family.

"There's something I wanted to talk to you about, Keon. It's important."

"Can't be more important than me keeping an eye on this party," I said as we walked into the dining room.

I took a glass of champagne from a passing waitress and surveyed the crowd. I saw Dionne across the room talking to Kenya and almost smiled, until I noticed the nigga that was all in her face.

"Aye, yo, who is that talking to Kenya?" I asked with a frown.

My mom shrugged without even looking. "I don't know."

"Well, don't you think you should know?" I snapped at her.

"No, I don't, Keon. Kenya is a grown woman, whether you want to accept that or not. She can talk to whoever she wants."

"No the fuck she can't," I said seriously. I meant that shit too. Out of all of us, Kenya was the one who was the most green. I didn't want no nigga coming in and taking advantage of her because of who she was.

"Listen, we can worry about that later," my mom said impatiently. "Right now—"

One of the servants walked up to us. "Mrs. King, we're about to make the toast."

Mom looked a little confused. "Already?"

"Yes. One of your old friends wants to make the toast, and Mr. King said it was okay. Everyone has champagne, so we're all moving to the front. We want you and the kids to be right there." She started to walk away, but my mom stopped her.

"Kathy, who is making the toast?"

Kathy shrugged. "Said he was an old friend and it was a surprise." She continued to walk.

"An old friend?" I said to my mom as we followed her. I noticed my mom didn't look as excited as I thought she should be. Instead, she looked nervous as she trailed behind me.

There were so many people in attendance that the crowd filled up the dining room and the foyer. Kathy made sure that my family was right in front.

"What's going on?" Khalia asked me as I stood next to her. "Who is making the toast?"

I shrugged. "They said it was a surprise friend."

"Bullshit," Khalid spat from the other side of Khalia. "They don't have no friends that we don't know. So, who could it be?"

"Exactly." I folded my arms across my chest as Kenya came and stood next to me.

"Do we know who is making the toast?" she asked me.

I looked her up and down with a frown. She had on a black dress that showed damn near everything and a weave down to her ass. "The fuck you got on?"

She looked down at her dress and then back at me. "A dress, Keon. What's the problem?"

"The problem is that dress makes you look cheap."

"Please," she snorted. "This is a Christian Dior dress. I could never look cheap in it."

"Doesn't matter who the designer is. What matters is how you wearing it. Why do you feel the need to show everything? Do you know who the fuck you are? You are Kenya muthafuckin' King, baby sis. You don't gotta look like the rest of these bitches out here."

"You mean the same kind of bitches you fuck with?" she shot back.

"Exactly," I responded with no hesitation. "Come on, man. You could present yourself better than that."

"Well, maybe I like this dress and the way people look at me when I wear it," she shot back. "Nobody is scared to talk to me."

"That's just it. Niggas *need* to be scared to talk to you. They need to know they shit gotta be correct before even saying a word to you. Dressing like that, you attract the type of niggas you were talking to tonight."

"You don't even know him," she defended him.

Just as I was about to tell her I didn't want to know that nigga, a white man came from the center of the crowd and stood in the middle of the floor.

"What is Vincent Morelli doing here?" Khalid murmured.

"Right," I said, surprised at his presence as well. It was a well-known fact that the Italian Mob didn't fuck with black people all like that.

"I know he ain't giving the speech," Khalia added as we all stood there trying to figure out why the famous mobster was there. Only Kenya seemed oblivious to who he really was.

"Good evening, ladies and gentlemen," Vincent greeted the crowd. He had on a tailored black tux with shiny shoes that I could tell he spent a nice penny on. A diamond pinky ring blinged on his pinky finger, and I couldn't help but wonder where he had gotten one with such clarity.

"May come as a surprise most of you, but I've known Kelvin and Dutchess here for a long time. Matter of fact, the first time I heard they were going out, I said that they would be married because then Dutchess's name would sound like she belonged in a royal family. Dutchess King," he said with a wide smile.

I looked over at my parents. My pops had a small smile on his face, but Mom's looked forced.

"Yeah, I've known Dutchess and Kelvin before they had their first kid or funeral home. Back then, they were just trying to make it, and I admired them for it. I watched Kelvin work himself to death doing just about anything to keep Dutchess happy. And I knew Dutchess before I met Kelvin. Let me tell ya, she loved her some Kelvin. Never shut up about him. It used to get to the point where I started to admire Kelvin for having a woman love him as much as Dutchess did."

Pops looked over at my mom with an affectionate expression for the first time in a long time. I knew they'd been having their ups and downs lately and was glad to see that they might be ready to get their relationship back on track.

"Yeah, I envied him for the way Dutchess loved him, but then she gave birth to her first son, and I was really jealous. They seemed to have it all."

At that moment, my mom walked to the middle of the room to join Vincent. "Thank you for your lovely speech," she said in an attempt to cut him off, but Vincent wasn't done yet.

"You remember me telling you how envious I was that you all had a son, don't you?" he asked her in what seemed to me to be a condescending tone.

I looked at Khalia and Khalid and noticed that the expressions on their faces were questioning as well. Something wasn't right about his speech; I just couldn't put my finger on it.

He turned back to face us. "My wife had a few miscarriages before we had our daughter. We had three more girls after that. And while I love my daughters with everything in me, I still wanted a son. Every man wants a son. Am I right, men?" he asked as he looked around the room before settling his gaze back on me.

"Vinny . . ." Mom said softly. "Let's toast. The people didn't come here to hear us talk, right?" she asked the crowd with a laugh.

He looked at my mom for a long time before looking at my pops. "You're a good man, Kelvin," he said. "I can't think of a man who deserves to celebrate thirty years of marriage more than you. You have it all: success, a gorgeous wife, a beautiful family, three lovely children . . ."

"Three?" Pops echoed as he stepped forward from the crowd. A low buzz circulated as everyone murmured to each other about what they had just heard.

"Dutchess, what the fuck is he talking about, saying I got *three* fucking kids?" he yelled at my mom. I don't think I'd ever heard my father even raise his voice at her in all the years that they had been married. He was always so calm, cool, and collected. It seemed like my mom wore the pants, to be honest.

"Keon." Kenya touched my arm slightly. "What is going on? What is that man talking about?"

"I don't know," I told her. If he was saying that one of us weren't my pops', I would bet it was her. It only made sense. She was the youngest, after all. It couldn't have been the twins, since they were basically two-for-one.

"Dutchess, should you tell him, or you want me to do it?" Vincent asked her.

She glared at him. "You's a dirty mafucka to come here and do this on my anniversary, Vinny."

He shrugged. "I told you if you didn't tell him in a week, I would tell him myself. Even reached out to his son's mother to get him to contact me, but still nothing. I see he's stubborn, just like you."

Even reached out to his son's mother . . .

The words danced in my head over and over again. Was this the reason he had one of his henchmen following Stacey? Did this muthafucka wanna tell me that he was my father?

"Fuck is he talking about, Dutchess?" my pops repeated as he grabbed her arm hard. He was so mad that the veins in his head were bulging, and he was damn near foaming at the mouth. I had never seen him so pissed off.

Khalid and I ran over to pull him off of her. He let her go but still stared in her face. "Answer me! Tell me the fucking truth!"

Tears were spilling down my mother's face. I had never seen her cry before and was shocked. "I wanted to tell you, Kelvin. I promise I did," she sobbed. "I just didn't know how to tell you." She broke down crying.

"How to tell me what?" he screamed at her. "Quit talking in fucking riddles and just tell me the fucking truth. Which one of my kids is he talking about?"

It seemed like she took forever to finally respond. "Keon. He is Keon's father, Kelvin."

The crowd gasped in shock and started buzzing again.

Vincent put his hand on my shoulder. "Hi, son."

I shook his hand off me just as my father let out a roar of anger. Before anyone knew what was happening, he had his hands wrapped around my mother's neck and was choking her like she was a rag doll.

"Fuck! Pops, get off her!" I screamed. It took me, Khalid, Tookie, and the nigga that had been all up in Kenya's face to pull him off her. She fell to the ground, and Kenya went over to tend to her.

Even after we pulled him off of my mother, my pops was still angry as hell, so it seemed like he had the rage of ten men. He broke free from us like it was nothing and rushed Vincent, delivering blow after vicious blow to his face and abdomen. He was throwing punches that would have made Mike Tyson proud. Vincent tried to defend himself, but he had nothing against the anger that took over my pops. It was clear to see that my pops would beat him to death with his bare hands if we didn't stop him quick. Even after Vinny doubled over and fell to the ground, he delivered vicious kicks in his wing-tipped shoes before pulling out a chrome Glock and aiming it at his head.

"No!" I shouted as I went to stand in front of him.

"All right, the muthafuckin' party is over!" Khalia yelled to the crowd. "Get the fuck out!"

Usually, I talked shit about my sister, but at that moment, I was happy as hell she was such a boss bitch. People knew not to question her and did what she commanded without her having to raise her voice.

"Keon, move," my pops said as he tried to go around me to get to Vincent. The partygoers all looked at us as they walked out, but no one said a word.

"Pops, I can't let you do this," I told him honestly.

"This pasta-eating muthafucka just ruined my party. Shit, he just ruined my marriage, ruined my life! Don't try to protect him."

"He's a Mob boss," I reminded him. "He needed his ass kicked, and you did that. But if he comes up missing, the Mob ain't gone rest until somebody answers for that shit. We already fighting two wars with enemies we didn't even know that we had. The last thing we need is to go to war with the Italians."

Pops looked at me with hurt in his eyes. "You ain't never cared about going to war before, Keon, no matter who it's with. Matter of fact, you love that shit. You tryin' to protect this mafucka because—" He stopped as he looked from me down at Vincent and finally back to me.

"Naw, that ain't it. I don't know that mafucka. He don't mean shit to me. I want to protect our family, that's it," I swore, but to my ears, it sounded weak, so I knew it sounded the same to him.

The anger was starting to leave his face. Slowly, a look of pain began to replace it. "Tell yourself that. I raised you. I know you better than you know yourself."

Khalia walked over to us as the last party guest walked out the door. "Niggas is nosy as hell," she mumbled. She looked at Pops, who was still holding the gun but had lowered it to his side. "He don't deserve a bullet, Pops. That's too good for a dirty bastard like him. Tie him up and let me take care of him. I'll send his family a different body part every week," she said with a glint in her eye.

I had killed my fair share of people, but when it came time to really put in work, nobody in the family was a more qualified killer than Khalia. She would shoot niggas, but she also tortured people too. I guess it all depended on how she felt that day. It was impossible to count just how many bodies she had. Letting her deal with Vincent was far worse than Pops just shooting him.

"No, Khalia. He doesn't die." Pops nodded his head toward me. "Keon wants to keep him alive."

My mother, Khalid, and Kenya had walked over in time to hear that last part.

"Keep him alive?" Khalia repeated in disbelief. "After what he just did? Are you fucking kidding me?"

"I don't think we should kill him either," Kenya spoke up.

Khalia snorted. "You wouldn't."

"We don't have to kill him today," Khalid added. "It's too risky. We just had a fight with him in front of an entire party. It'll point right back to us."

"Exactly," Kenya agreed.

"Do y'all realize who the fuck this man is?" Khalia snapped. "We won't have a better time to do it than right now. This mafucka is heavily protected at all times. We won't get a better shot than this."

"Don't do it," Mom said softly. "He's been telling people about Keon. Who knows how many of them knew he was coming here tonight? We have enough going on with an enemy we can't see. Last thing we want is for the Italians to come after us."

"I don't give a fuck about them. None of that shit matters right now. Do you see what you did to my father by allowing this man in here?" Khalia screamed. It was the first time any of us ever heard her go against Mom and stand up for Pops.

"How could you do this? How could you let him come here?"

"I swear I didn't know—"

"Just like you didn't know he was Keon's father, right?" Khalia spat in disgust.

The whole room was quiet.

Mom walked up to Khalia until they were standing eye-to-eye. They were definitely two pit bulls in skirts facing off with each other. If they weren't family, this confrontation between the two of them would have been very volatile. Even now, the tension between the two of them was super thick.

"Never in your life will it ever be okay for you to disrespect me," she told her through clenched teeth.

"I don't have to disrespect you. The moment you decided running around with another man was more important than being a wife to your husband, you disrespected yourself. Look at you, protecting your boyfriend and picking him over my father. There should be no question about bodying this mafucka from you out of all people, but you choosing to protect him instead, and for that, I have no respect for you," Khalia spat in disgust before turning and walking away.

Vincent began to moan on the ground as he regained consciousness. Pops looked at him one more time before looking back at me. I swear his eyes were wet with tears, but to his credit, he didn't let one fall. Then he looked over at my mom.

"Happy anniversary, Dutchess," he told her before walking out as well.

"Kelvin, wait," she called after him. I waited for her to chase after him, beg him to stay, or something. It's the least she could have done after turning his life upside down. But she didn't. Instead, she let a few tears fall down her face before turning back around to look at Vincent, who was sitting up.

And that's when it hit me. Like, really fucking hit me. My mom had been married to my pops for thirty years today, and not once had I ever seen her look at that man the way she was gazing at Vincent. Her look was full of love, and I wanna say lust too, even with his face bruised and bloody as hell from that ass-whooping.

She had never been in love with my pops, but she was clearly still in love with Vincent. It was all over her face. I looked over at Khalid and could tell that he saw it too.

Vincent stood to his feet, straightened his shoulders, and looked me straight in the eye. "How you been, son?" he asked.

For once, I was speechless.

Chapter Twenty-five

Kenya

"So, tell me a little about yourself."

I leaned back in the plush leather seats of the black Lincoln Navigator I was riding in and smiled at the man's face taking up my phone screen as we FaceTimed. "What do you want to know?"

Armani shrugged and flashed a smile. "What do you want to tell me?"

This time it was my turn to shrug. "There's not really a lot to tell."

"I find that hard to believe. A beautiful girl like you?"

I felt myself blushing slightly. "Thank you, but there's not a lot to tell. I'm boring for real."

"You keep saying that, but I don't believe you." He stood up, and I had to stop myself from drooling at the sight of him. He had on a wife beater and some hoop shorts, and I couldn't keep my eyes from wandering all over his body. The nigga was damn near perfect, from his handsome face to his muscular build.

Armani was about to enter his second year of college at the University of Pittsburgh, and he was the star wide receiver on their football team. He told me he played college football the night I met him at my parents' anniversary party but tried to downplay it. Dionne and I Googled him and found out right away that not only did he play football, but he was the star of the team. NFL teams were already looking to draft him as soon as he became eligible.

I couldn't believe my luck when I saw that. Here I was, just wanting to meet a guy to text and hook up with sometimes, and instead, I met a future NFL superstar. On top of that, he looked good as fuck.

"Believe it, boo," I told him. "Nothing interesting to see here."

"See, now that's where you wrong. I see nothing but interesting things when I look at you."

I couldn't stop the smile that spread across my face.

"Like that smile," Armani said with a grin of his own. "And the fact that you're so caring when it comes to your family is dope. I wish I had a family like yours."

I snorted. "No, you don't," slipped out of my mouth before I even realized what I was saying.

He looked confused. "Why did you say that, babe? Every family has their issues, but y'all are still close. I like that. My family is nothing like that."

I wanted to tell him that when you come from a drug-dealing, murdering family, you have no choice but to remain close. We risked losing our entire empire if we drifted away from each other.

Still, my family had been nothing but a shit show since the party. After Mom refused to let Khalia kill Vincent, she had been keeping her distance from the house. It was kind of sad because I loved it when my big sister came over. She was fly and funny as hell, plus she always had some advice to give me whenever I saw her. I knew she thought I wasn't listening to her, but she was wrong. I admired how great she was and hung on to her every word.

Daddy hadn't returned since he walked out of the house, and I didn't blame him. The party had been a disaster, and then to learn your firstborn son wasn't actually your son . . . man. I don't know how he didn't lose it completely. I called him every day. He was staying with Khalid for now, but I was sure he would eventually get his own place.

Keon tried to go on every day like nothing had happened, but I knew my big brother was hurting. I couldn't imagine learning that the man I thought was my father was not in the way he had. Then, learning the identity of who his father really was had to be another issue altogether.

So, listening to Armani say he wished his family was more like mine was hilarious to me. "Hopefully you're right."

"I am. So, where are you on your way to again?"

"Philadelphia," I lied smoothly. I was actually on my way to Harrisburg for the third time in two months and felt like I was getting the hang of my new position.

"Oh, yeah? What's there?"

"One of my old friends from school is having her baby shower this weekend." I never used to lie about where I was going and what I did, but now that it was a part of my everyday life, I was surprised at how easy it was for me to do it.

"Oh, yeah? That's what's up. I hope you have a good time. Her baby shower ain't gone have shit on ours, though."

I couldn't stop myself from laughing. "Our baby shower, though? You funny as hell for that one. We ain't even been on our first date yet."

"I know, and I can already tell I'm trappin' yo' ass."

"Already?" I asked between laughter.

"Hell yeah. I can't let you get away from me."

I tilted my head to the side. "You could always just cuff me," I suggested.

"I could, but what if you try to leave me over some bullshit how y'all do? You know how y'all get. Gotta trap you, baby. Don't act like you don't wanna see me in the Burberry button-up at our baby shower."

I laughed again. "First of all, you ain't wearing that shit. Second, I ain't tryna have no kids no time soon. I gotta figure my life out first."

"It ain't gotta be soon, long as you have my baby," he joked. "And I know you just graduated from high school, so that's a scary time for people who aren't sure exactly what they want to do. I had it easy. I've always loved football since I was a little boy. It was only natural for that to be my passion. What about you?"

I shrugged. "I love clothes. The fabrics, the cut, all that."

"So, become a designer." He scooped a water bottle up and grabbed his keys. "I'm going for my run, baby. I'll talk to you later."

"Okay, be safe," I told him with a smile. His timing couldn't have been more perfect as we were just pulling up to the capitol building. I checked my waist to make sure my gun was secure before I grabbed the briefcase full of designer pills and heroin next to me.

Anyone I was coming to meet always sent a minion to come down and get me. Because the person was always a high-ranking official, my bodyguard and I were always allowed to go with them without having to go through any detectors or get patted down by security. We took different elevators, where I was escorted to the office of either one or two of the senators I was there to see.

Today was Rod Collins, a high-ranking Democrat who had just tossed his hat in the ring to run for President. He was extremely high profile—and had a huge crush on me.

"You look more beautiful each time I see you." He greeted me with a quick hug.

"Thank you, Rod," I said with a sweet smile. With his blond hair and blue eyes, he had the Democratic party fooled into thinking he was just this wholesome man from Central Pennsylvania looking to make a change, but I knew better. He was really from Berks County, where his family ran a huge meth farm. The money they had made from that very lucrative operation had paid for his Ivy League education, but he still wasn't flying all the way straight. He supplied his family with the pills and dope he copped from us and made more money than he would ever see as a state senator.

"Why are you involved in this dirty business?" he asked as we exchanged briefcases.

"Family values, I guess. The same reason you are."

He chuckled. "Touché."

I smiled. "Nice doing business with you, Rod."

"Always a pleasure, Kenya. You'll find an envelope with a little something extra in there. Don't show your family. That's strictly for you. Think of it as a bonus for having to come way out here."

I smiled and walked out. Once I got back in the truck,, I popped the briefcase open. Rows and rows of hundred-dollar bills greeted me. Tucked in the top of the briefcase was a manila envelope. I opened it cautiously and was surprised to see a thick stack of bills inside, along with a small card that read: *Just for being you.*

I bit my lip as I stared at it. Something told me I shouldn't accept the money, but fuck it. It wasn't part of his re-up money. This was free and clear of that. It would be nice to stack something on the side that was all my own. After all, I wouldn't be doing this for very long. Eventually, Khalid would come back, and when that happened, how would I make money?

I slid the envelope into the Birkin bag on my seat and closed my eyes to take a nap on the long ride home.

Chapter Twenty-six

Khalia

"Mmm," Andrew murmured as he took a bite of the shrimp and grits I had prepared for him.

"Good, ain't it?" I bragged as I slid him a mimosa across the bar.

"Hell yeah, girl!" he said with a grin. "Where you learn how to cook like this? You gone make me fat!"

"You get plenty exercise delivering these rich people's mail," I joked. "You'll be fine."

"Oh, I'll be fine? Come here," he commanded, taking another bite of his food before pushing the bowl away.

He walked around the bar and stood in front of me. He pushed a strand of my curly hair that had fallen out of my bun away from my face before staring me directly into my eyes. "Fucking gorgeous," he murmured before kissing me.

Now, I'm usually not a soft bitch. At least Khalia wasn't. I wasn't romantic, I didn't kiss niggas, I didn't press them. I used them for sex and dismissed them. In my position, I had no choice. Show any kind of emotion, and you were automatically labeled as weak. It was bad enough that I was a woman who sat high on the food chain in a game that was destined for men. I couldn't let anyone think I didn't belong there. My ass had never even been in love before. But when it came to Andrew, I was starting to feel things I had never felt before. I smiled down at my phone whenever his name appeared. I found myself missing him when we weren't together. I loved how soft he was with me, how he complimented me, how he always stared deeply into my eyes whenever we were together.

On top of all that, the sex we had was some shit I had never opened myself up to experiencing before. I figured it was because I had never let myself truly care about any man I laid down with. I fucked them and kept it moving. With Drew, I learned that it was so much better when you actually liked a person and had chemistry with them. Plus, on top of that, he had a big dick and knew how to use it. He got me wetter than any nigga I had ever laid down with in my life.

"Thank you," I whispered as I felt my heartbeat speed up just from being so close to him.

He stroked my cheek before kissing me. Our tongues did a dance as he slid his hand down to cuff my ass, which had been jiggling freely under the long tank that I wore. I moaned at his touch but never broke our kiss.

He pulled away from me slightly and lifted my tank top over my head. My titties bounced free as I did a slow turn so that he could fully appreciate what was in front of him. There was no need for me to be modest; I was the shit from my head down to my manicured toes, and I knew it. I wanted to be sure that he knew it too.

He bit his lip before picking me up and placing me on my marble countertop. I gazed at him through lust-filled eyes. Drew was really into being fit. He got up at five every morning religiously to work out. The results showed in his rock-solid chest, six-pack, and that V shape that led right to all that good dick he was packing.

He picked up his mimosa then took a sip before tipping the glass over and letting some of it spill over my titties and down my stomach.

"Drew," I started but stopped when he leaned down and began to lick every bit of it off of me. I closed my eyes and enjoyed the strokes of his long tongue tracing a trail over my body. My pussy began to tingle in anticipation at what was next, and Drew didn't disappoint as he pushed me further on the countertop before picking up the mimosa glass again.

Watching him pour the rest of the cool mimosa on my pussy before diving in face first turned me on to the fullest. I lost myself in the moment completely as he kissed, licked, and sucked on me like I was the best thing he had ever tasted in his life. I had never felt like this before and wasn't sure if I ever wanted to go through life *not* feeling like this again.

I knew one thing for sure: I loved it here.

Chapter Twenty-seven

Dutchess

I sat on the deck outside my bedroom drinking a glass of white wine. It was my third of the day, and it wasn't even noon yet, but I didn't care. Life as I knew it was over anyway.

Kelvin was gone. He had really walked out on me and refused to answer any of my phone calls. The anniversary disaster was weeks ago. I thought that he had calmed down enough for us to try to work through this latest issue, but it turned out I underestimated him. He probably hated me, and rightfully so, but I didn't want to just throw the towel in. I had spent more than half my life with that man. I wasn't ready to just throw that away.

I had found out from Kenya that he was staying with Khalid. She talked to him every day, as did the other kids. She and Khalid were the only ones still speaking to me. Keon, predictably, didn't have a word to say to me. I had expected that, but I was shocked when Khalia followed his lead and shut me out too. Khalia wasn't the Daddy's girl; that had always been Kenya's role. Matter of fact, I was closer to Khalia than I was to the rest of the kids. I had molded her from my image. She was truly a young me. Khalia turning her back on me hurt almost as much as Kelvin walking out on me. Khalid told me he had asked his twin why she wasn't speaking to me, and she had given him a fairly simple answer: "It's not what she did; it's how she did it. You don't treat the people you claim you love like shit, and you damn sure don't embarrass them like that."

It made sense in a way, but it also pissed me off. If it wasn't for me creeping with Vincent, we wouldn't have half of what we had now. I saw my opportunity, and I took it. It just so happened that Keon was a product of that. None of them realized that had I told Kelvin about Vinny, he would have probably left me. Then, none of their little ungrateful asses would be here.

"Beautiful morning, isn't it?" Vincent asked as he walked out onto the deck to join me.

"I was wondering when you were going to wake up," I murmured as he dropped a kiss on my forehead before sitting in the chair beside me.

"I would have stayed sleeping if you were still there," he said with a grin. "It's so peaceful here. No little kids running around, no dogs barking, none of that shit that breaks my sleep every day."

I shook my head and sipped my wine.

The news of what had gone down at the party had spread like wildfire, as we all expected. There was no way anyone could have kept quiet about that. Vinny's wife had done the predictable thing and tossed him out on his ass, although I don't think she would have done that if the side baby she had found out about wasn't black.

Vinny didn't seem to mind that she had put him out. He never seemed too interested in anything his wife did. "You know we could have had some life together, right?" he said as he leaned back in the chair and took my hand.

My body still reacted to his touch, the same as it always had. "We wouldn't be the people we are now. We wouldn't have the children we have now. No one would have stood for us being together, and you know it."

He shrugged. "Eventually, they wouldn't have had a choice."

"Even if that were true, it still wouldn't have worked. I am not housewife material. Sitting at home having your babies would have never worked for me, and you know there's no place for me inside the Italian Mob."

He laughed and continued to stroke my hand. "Dutchess, you wanna know why it would have worked? Because you are the female version of me. We would have figured it out. You don't get it by now? We're soul mates."

I looked over at him, but he was already gazing at me. Kelvin had kicked his ass pretty bad, but he had already healed from most of the bruises, and the black eyes were gone. Unlike many white men, Vinny was aging gracefully. He looked even better to me than he did all those years ago.

A small part of me knew that the reason I never chased Kelvin or gave my marriage a hundred percent like I should have was because my heart belonged to the Mob boss. It was just a hard truth for me to admit. After all, where I'm from, we just didn't deal with white men at all, or worse, fall in love with them. But I had. And I always had it bad for Vincent. I never fully let him go.

I was never ashamed that Keon was his son, more so happy that I would always have a piece of him with me. He had shaped me into the woman I had become. I had learned so much from him. I had gained so much from him. Plus, we shared a child. That was why, no matter how wrong he was for blowing up my spot at the party, I couldn't let them kill him. My heart wouldn't have been able to take it. It was also the reason why I couldn't turn him away when he came back the next day after his wife put him out. Sure, he had family, friends, or even workers he could have stayed with, but he had chosen to come to me. Deep down, I was glad that he had.

Being with Vinny again was refreshing. It was like we never lost a beat. Still, I knew that it was only temporary. His wife was already telling him she had thought it over and was ready to deal with it. His family ties were telling him that it was time to go home. I really had no place in his world, and truthfully, he had none in mine. We were a love story destined for failure.

"I love you," he said simply before leaning over, cupping my face, and kissing me. We shared a long, sensual kiss before he pulled away and gazed at me again. "I always loved you, Dutchess. Remember that." He stood up.

"Where are you going?" flew out of my mouth before I realized it.

"I gotta get my life back on track. There's work to be done and business to be handled. It was nice hiding out here with you, blocking the world out. I wish I could always live like this."

I nodded. I couldn't speak over the lump that had formed in my throat.

"My kids are begging me to come home," he went on. "They're all still too young to be as mad as your children are. All they know is that they aren't waking up to me every day."

"And Angie?" I asked quietly.

He looked me straight in the eye. "We both know she wasn't going to really leave me. She doesn't have anything going for herself outside of being Mrs. Morelli. Outside of me, she's nothing. She's not you."

I nodded again.

"Keon finally agreed to meet up with me," he went on. "I'll let you know how that goes too."

I really didn't have anything to say. It seemed like everyone was winning in this situation besides me. Vinny got his family back, and Keon would finally get to know his real father, but what about me? I had lost everyone. My own kids wouldn't even talk to me.

"Hey, don't look so sad. We still have us," he said as he came to grab my hand. "We will always have us."

I stood up too. "Do I look like I want to play mistress again, Vinny? I'm too old for that shit. Back in the day, I went along with it because I was married, and you were schooling me on the game. I was learning everything I needed to know from you, and I got the pleasure of actually being with you too. This time it's different. I don't have a man to go home to when I'm done with you. Before, it was cool cause we were both married, but now . . ." My voice trailed off.

"I don't want to lose you again, Dutchess. I can't." He grabbed my other hand and stared deeply into my eyes. "We can make it work. I'll spend half my time there with my kids and the other half with you, and—"

I shook my head. "I don't want half a man. Even with this situation being what it is, I'm worth more than that. Let's just say our goodbyes again."

"No," he replied simply. "I got shit to handle in my personal life, but I'm not forgetting about you or us. We can make this work. I promise." He kissed me again before walking back into the bedroom.

I looked at the bed I had been sharing with him for the last couple of weeks—the same bed I had shared with my husband for years. I should have felt bad about that, and if it were any other man, I probably would, but the truth was I just didn't. I loved Vincent. I always would.

Chapter Twenty-eight

Keon

I sat in the back office of our Eastside King Funeral Home location and tapped my foot impatiently. Against my better judgment, I had agreed to meet with Vincent today. I hadn't seen him since the party, although he had been contacting me nonstop ever since.

I had talked to Pops every single day since the party. In that short period of time, it seemed like we had grown closer than we had been in years, and I was so grateful for that. He told me endlessly that it didn't matter whose blood ran through my veins; I would always be his son, and I believed him.

Things with Dionne were going good, too. I hadn't expected to like her as much as I did. We did everything together. I was slowly starting to cut all of my other women off for her. Ever since I started fucking with her, I didn't feel the need to pop any pills or snort any lines of coke. It was almost like she saved me without even realizing it. She soothed the beast in me so that I was able to concentrate solely on building our business back to what it was before the warehouse fire. It was no easy task, but with Kenya going out of town every week the way that she was, and the money Khalia snatched from all the bodies she'd dropped and all the dope houses she and Khalid robbed, we were getting back to where we once were.

Plus, her dropping the hammer like that let everyone know once again that we were stronger than ever and not to be fucked with. The surprise attacks on us stopped almost as quickly as they had started. I figured Khalia had murked them niggas out during her murdering spree and went back to business as usual.

The only thorn in my side right about now was Stacey. I should have known better than to give her any dick, but I had a weak moment and fell for her. Now she wouldn't leave me the fuck alone. I couldn't completely ignore her since my son was there, but I was sick of her constant threats.

My phone rang just as I pulled it out to check the time. I had about five minutes before Vincent pulled up. I had been dodging his requests to meet with me because he stayed talking like he wanted to make up all the years he'd missed with me, but when he said he had some information to share with me about a snake in our camp, I told him to meet me here.

It was Jordan calling, so I answered. "Wassup, son? I'm on my way to a very important meeting. I'll call you back as soon as I walk out."

"It's not Jordan. It's me."

I closed my eyes in annoyance at the sound of Stacey's voice. "This the oldest trick in the book, Stace. Calling me from our son's phone."

"And yet you still answered, so what does that make you?" she snapped.

"Man, what the fuck do you want?" I asked her impatiently. "Unlike you, I have things to do. I don't got time for this bullshit."

"Well, you better make time, nigga 'cause I'm pregnant."

I damn near dropped the phone. "What the fuck did you just say?"

"I'm pregnant. You knocked me up again. Congrats!" she said sarcastically.

I wiped my hand down my face. This couldn't have come at a worse time. For the first time ever, I was genuinely happy with the woman in my life. I barely stepped out on her or lied to her. I had something real that I was actually afraid of losing.

"Right now ain't the time to play, man," I told her, still refusing to believe it. "You just want my fucking attention, but that ain't the way to get it."

"Nigga, who the fuck you think you are that I gotta lie to get your attention?"

"That nigga," I replied with no hesitation. "You see you had to call me from my son's phone. I don't want shit to do with you and you know it."

"It don't matter if you want anything to do with me. You gone have to take care of this baby."

"I don't even know if you're really pregnant, and if you are, who's to say it's mine?" I shot back. I really didn't have shit else to say simply because I knew there was a good opportunity for it to be my baby if she really was knocked up.

"Wow. That little bitch got your nose so wide open that you would do *me* like this, Keon?" she said after a moment of silence. Her voice was filled with pain, but I didn't feel bad for her at all. She knew what it was when she plotted to fuck me.

"Look, if you are, I'll drop some bread off to you later today to take care of that," I told her as the door to the office opened.

"I ain't getting no fucking abortion!" she screamed just as I hung up the phone.

Vincent walked into my office. I took note of his long, confident stride. I walked the same exact way.

"How you doin'?" he greeted me as he held his hand out.

I looked at it reluctantly before taking it. "I'm a'ight."

"I'm glad you finally agreed to meet with me," he said as he leaned back in his chair and made himself comfortable before I said he could. That was some shit that I would have done. The man dripped confidence . . . the same way I did.

After finding out that Vincent Morelli was my father, I did my homework and was shocked by what I found. He was a Mob boss and a made man, but he was also one of the best basketball players the state of Pennsylvania had ever seen. He broke all records and was heavily recruited but had turned all the offers down when he decided that working for his family was a better career path than trying to make it to the NBA . . . almost the same as I had. I had always wondered where I got the skills. My pops wasn't the most athletic nigga. He was very smart and clever, but no athlete. Vincent was.

Vincent also had a legendary temper that made mafuckas respect him no matter what. They either got wit' him or got rolled over. He could be very violent. Under his regime, the Morelli family was making more money than ever, but it was also the bloodiest reign for the Mob family. His short fuse had made doing business with him bittersweet . . . kind of like me.

And when I saw the pictures of him in his younger days, I had almost dropped my phone. I had his same form in basketball, his same height, and damn near his face. The nose, eyes, smile, jaw structure, all that shit came from him. I was like the black version of him. The shit was mind-blowing to say the least. Finding out that I was half Italian didn't bother me at all. Knowing that I shared blood with some of the most infamous guys the Mob had ever seen, dating back to the Five Families of New York, made me a King on both sides.

Looking into his face now, I saw that he had healed up fast from the fight at the party. Without looking at him all bloody and bruised up, the resemblance was crazy.

"I know," Vincent said as if he could read my mind. It was then that I noticed I had just been staring at him. "I thought the same thing the first time I saw you. You looked just like me. And when I followed you, I noticed that not only did you look like me, you *were* me."

I couldn't argue with that, but I also didn't want to discuss that shit right now. I had already learned from Kenya that he had always known who I was. I had no beef with him never saying shit to me. After all, it wasn't like I grew up fatherless, broke, poor, or in a family that didn't love me. Plus, I was grown. I understood the situation loud and clear. He was married, and so was my mom. My only problem with them was that they kept the lie going for as long as they did, and of course, the way he had let it out.

"What you got for me?" I asked him, getting straight to the point.

He grinned. "A man that's about his business. I can respect that."

I didn't respond.

"Your mother came to me a while ago asking for my help with the attacks that were happening against your organization. I told her to take a closer look in-house. When I said that, I wanted her to take a closer look at the people she lives with."

I frowned. "That doesn't make any sense, though. Nobody lives there anymore but her, my pops, and Kenya. Kenya is just a kid. Mom wouldn't try to chop down the organization she built from the ground up, and Pops . . ."

Vincent smirked slightly.

"Naw. Pops wouldn't do none of this shit," I said out loud, more to myself than to him.

"How can you be so sure?" he asked me.

"'Cause he ain't built like that. That's how," I snapped at him. "He was tryin' to get out the game for the longest. Why the fuck would he attack us and start a war that would keep him in it? Khalid could have gotten killed at that rally. Shit, my sister and me could have been at the warehouse when it burned down. He would never hurt us."

"He wouldn't," Vincent agreed. "But what if he knew that the only way for him to get out the game would be for him to make it seem like you all had an enemy that you couldn't see? We already know Dutchess is never leaving willingly and wouldn't allow him to retire either. What if he figured there had to be another way?"

"One of those bullets could have killed Khalid. He would never risk that."

"Or that plan went astray," Vincent said with a shrug.

I glared at him. "Where's your proof? You come up in here outta nowhere talking this bullshit when it would make perfect sense for you to blame everything on my pops. He got the woman you wanted and the family you wanted, right? So now you tryna turn us against him."

He laughed for a moment before speaking again. "I like how your mind works. That was smart of you to think that, but no, son. I don't have to hate or lie on any man to get whatever it is that I want. That's for cowards, pussies, and rats. I'm none of those."

I couldn't help but smile at that one. No lie, that sounded like some shit I would say. Still, I wasn't about to just take his word for it. "Proof," I repeated. "I need proof before I believe any of this shit you're saying."

"Got it right here," he replied as he pulled out his phone and leaned across the desk. "I have eyes everywhere on you at all times, Keon. It's the reason you've escaped some pretty sticky situations. Anyway, I had eyes trailing the truck your brother rode in on the day of his rally simply because that's your vehicle."

"We switched that day so I could drop his at the shop while he went to his rally," I said softly.

"Exactly, but my men were still there. When they saw Khalid get out of the truck, they were about to pull off, and then the shooting happened." He went to a video on his phone. "I have cameras installed in all my vehicles and homes. Can never be too careful. Anyway, they started to follow the bikers, but they all split up. At the last minute, they decided to keep trailing the one in the front, who was clearly the leader. He drove directly to some small alley in Lawrenceville, dropped a gun off to Kelvin, and sped off."

My stomach was sick as I watched everything he said transpire on his cell phone screen. Sure enough, there was the end of the shooting, with bodies dropping everywhere and the biker gang splitting up. When I saw my pops take the gun from the lead biker, I felt my anger increase.

"Where is the biker?" I asked between clenched teeth.

"Come on," Vincent said with a smug grin. "You really think I let him get away with that shit? It could have been you in that truck. I had my men kidnap him and was just waiting for the day I could tell you the truth. He's yours. You can do what you want with him. Consider it one of my ways to make up for the lost time."

I grinned. I might actually like this guy after all. "And the fire?"

"Well, after I saw that Kelvin was behind the shooting at the rally, I kept close eyes on him, too. He had the schedule down pat when you and your sister would run in and out of there. He broke the cameras on the warehouse himself. The night one of your men left early . . ." He showed me another video. There was my pops, clear as day, going into the warehouse with a can of gasoline. No lie, it broke my heart to see his betrayal. He was inside for a few moments before rushing back out. A huge fire broke out just as he was speeding away in the Porsche that I had copped him for his birthday a few years back. If anything, that made the betrayal even more painful.

"Thanks for sharing that with me," I told Vincent in a low voice. "I need you to send both of those to me, a'ight? I know my brother and sisters won't believe me if I just told them that you're the one who told me."

"No problem. Sending them now."

"Cool." I stood up, pulled a nine out of the desk drawer, and put it in my waistband. "Wherever you got that biker, bring that nigga here. I got plans for him and my pops."

Vincent stood up and looked at me with a hint of excitement in eyes. "What are you going to do?" he asked me.

I smirked as I texted Khalia to meet me at the funeral home and to bring her "tools." Then I texted my pops to meet me there to go over the books. He responded that he would be there right away, just as I knew he would.

"This here is a funeral home, Vincent. We can do whatever we want to whoever we want to here, and the best part about that is we have a crematory to burn them when we're done. Or we can just burn them alive. It doesn't matter." I patted him on the shoulder. "Thanks for your help."

Khalia rushed into the back office just as Vincent was getting ready to leave. She frowned at him and then looked at me. "I was in the area, so I didn't have time to grab my tools. What's going on? Everything all right?"

"Oh, yeah," I told her as I showed her the videos on my phone. "Everything is 'bout to be just fine."

I watched as she looked at both the videos. Instead of her eyes welling with tears or flipping out in hysterics like most females would have done, her face took on an angry expression I had seen countless times. It was the mask she wore when she was ready to put in work.

"Let's do this," she said calmly as she pulled her hair back into a ponytail and removed all her jewelry.

"You're like a young Dutchess," Vincent said in awe as he watched her.

"Yeah, I am. I just don't like white boys," she shot back.

"Chill, Khalia," I told her with a chuckle. "If it wasn't for him, we would have never known the truth."

She shrugged.

Vincent left. Khalia and I sat in silence for about ten minutes before Pops arrived. He walked in smiling, oblivious to what was about to take place.

"Hey, baby girl," he greeted Khalia, who hugged him back stiffly. He looked at her strangely but didn't dwell on it. Instead, he walked over to me to greet me. "What's up, son? What you need me to help you with?"

"It'll be here soon," I responded.

He looked at me in confusion. "What will be here soon, Keon? The books should be right there on the computer."

I looked down at my phone at the text I'd just received from Vincent, announcing they were out front with the biker. I grinned and said, "It's coming through the door now."

Pops looked at me, his expression even more confused. "What?"

Vincent walked through the door. Two of his henchmen walked behind him, holding the arm of a blindfolded man.

"Take that shit off him," Khalia ordered them. They did as they were told and stood back.

I watched the color drain from my father's face as he looked at his partner in crime. They both looked scared as hell.

I walked up to the both of them and cocked my gun. "Now, we can make this real easy or real hard. I know the truth; I'm just waiting on you muthafuckas to confirm it. Be honest, I'll give you a bullet. Lie, and you'll have to deal with her, and let me tell y'all, you really, really don't want to have to deal with her."

Khalia blew them a kiss, which I knew was the kiss of death.

I stood by the biker, held the gun to his head, and glared at my pops. I was so angry at his actions that I didn't see the man who had raised me, just a traitor who had betrayed us.

"Are you working with him to bring us down?" I asked him in a calm tone.

Before he could even answer, I heard a loud boom followed by screams of, "FBI! Get down on the ground! Get down on the ground!"

They hadn't reached the office yet. I dropped the gun and kicked it under the desk before putting my hands up and looking around the room cautiously. Khalia looked just as confused as I was, and so did everyone else, but when my eyes landed on my pops, I saw that he didn't look surprised at all.

As the agents swarmed the office, I vowed to kill him if it was the last thing that I did.

Holding Down a Cartel King

Part 2

Prologue...

"Hey, Kelvin!" Ms. White, a teacher at Kelvin's little brother's after-school program, greeted him as he walked through the door.

"Hey, Ms. White. How was he today?" Kelvin asked her with a grin.

She looked at him and shook her head. "He's back to bothering the little girls again. For whatever reason, he just doesn't understand to back off when they tell him no." She shot him a concerned look. "This is something I really need to discuss with your mother."

Kelvin sighed and shrugged his shoulders. "She don't have the time to come down here, ma'am."

"What about your father? We only see him when it's time to drop the checks off, but this is equally important." She gazed over to her office, where Jamar sat with his arms folded. "We want to nip this type of behavior in the bud now. Once he's older, this kind of things can turn into serious charges against him."

"I know. I'll talk to him today and see if he can make it down a'ight?" Kelvin said just to shut her up. At fourteen years old, he had no idea how troubling his younger brother's behavior truly was. He figured he would talk to him on the way home once again and repeat the "no means no" speech to him for the millionth time. How hard could it be for him to understand that?

Ms. White gave him a doubtful look before going back to her office and getting Jamar. Kelvin signed him out, and they began the walk home.

"Yo, what I tell you about those little girls?" Kelvin asked him seriously.

Jamar shrugged. "If they say no, just leave them alone."

"A'ight, so since you know that, why you keep fucking with them?"

Ten-year-old Jamar shrugged his shoulders. "'Cause I like touching on them. It's fun."

That statement right there should have been a sign to let Kelvin know the type of behavior his brother would embark on later in life, but he brushed it off. After all, he was still a kid himself. It was bad enough that he was mostly responsible for Jamar as it was. Their mother, Crystal, had Kelvin when she was sixteen and Jamar when she was twenty. Having two children under five before she turned twenty-one should have meant that Crystal matured faster than most, but instead, she did the opposite. She wasn't quite ready to settle down and be a mother. After she left her children with multiple relatives for days on end, their father did what most wouldn't at his age and took full responsibility for them.

Victor, or Big Vic as he was known in the streets, had been an amateur boxer at the time. He had dreams of going pro, and if he had the time and dedication, there was a good chance that he might have been able to make a lucrative career out of it. Unfortunately, his dreams were derailed like a lot of young people in the hood. There was no way he could train for the ring and travel the way he needed to get his name out there with two young mouths to feed. His sons didn't have anyone but him, so instead of pursuing his dreams, his reality forced him to hit the block, which he did with a vengeance.

Big Vic put all the energy he had for boxing into his hustle, and it ended up turning out lovely for him. He was able to provide a good life for his sons. They still lived in the hood, but their house was the best one in their hood.

All three of them had multiple closets full of clothes and shoes. Any jewelry he got, he copped them smaller pieces. He was doing so good that Crystal tried to get back with him, but he wanted no part of her. He allowed her to stop by and see the boys occasionally, but that was it. She wasn't even allowed to take them anywhere.

The downside to making so much money was that he had to be gone constantly to do it. The older Kelvin got, the more it fell on him to take care of himself and his brother. He was the one who made sure they got to school on time every day. He checked homework, he cooked, and he cleaned. Jamar depended on him more than he did Big Vic. As for Kelvin, he loved the life his father was able to provide for them but hated that he was gone all the time. He missed everything. Kelvin was a straight-A student. He had skipped a grade, so instead of being the freshman that he was supposed to be, he was a sophomore in high school. Even still, he was taking college courses in calculus, trigonometry, and business. He had a 140 IQ and was considered a genius. Everyone told him that with his brain, he was destined for great things. He believed it. Hustling and drug dealing had been his father's way out and the only way he could provide for them, but Kelvin knew it would be different for him. He was an innovator and had dreams of owning a game-changing corporation like Apple or Microsoft. The route he was taking would allow him to follow his dreams of becoming the next Steve Jobs or Bill Gates—until that fateful day.

The minute he and Jamar turned down their street, he saw various police cars and undercover trucks. Men and women wearing blue windbreakers with the words FBI across the back in yellow were leaving the house with bags.

"Kelvin, what's going on? Where's Dad?" Jamar asked in a panicked tone as his brother grabbed his hand and began to run toward their house.

Kelvin ignored his brother as he tried to cut through all the people to make it inside their home.

"Young man, you can't go in there," one of the agents said when Kelvin tried to move past him. He was a very young black man with a baby face.

"This is my house. I live here," Kelvin exclaimed. He knew what his father was into, and although he had tried to prepare his son for this moment, nothing could have really had him ready for the possibility of losing Big Vic.

The young agent looked at him sympathetically. "I understand that, but we have a job to do. I can't allow you to go in there right now."

"I gotta see if my dad is okay!" Kelvin yelled, although deep down he already knew what it was.

The agent bit his lip and shook his head. Big Vic was one of the many men arrested in a city-wide raid that was supposed to have taken place at the crack of dawn weeks ago. However, the raid had been derailed when his team underwent a few personnel changes. It almost wouldn't have happened if it weren't for the agent's insistence that these violent criminals needed to be taken off the streets.

"Maybe you can go to a neighbor's house and call your mom to come get you and your little brother," the agent suggested in a kind voice.

"We ain't got no mom," Jamar spat at him angrily. Crystal's abandonment had deeply affected both of her children, but it was Jamar who was hurt the most by it.

The agent raised his eyebrow. "No mom? Well, how about your grandma or—"

"I ain't going nowhere until I see my father," Kelvin said flatly. He knew that the agent was trying to prevent them from seeing what was really going on. He also knew that there was no way he could go anywhere before he laid eyes on Big Vic.

"There he go, Kelvin," Jamar said sadly. Both boys watched as two federal agents led Big Vic out of the house in cuffs. He had on a white T-shirt with some basic black sweats but still walked like he had on a tailored tuxedo. It wasn't until his gaze landed on his children that he faltered slightly.

"Dad!" Kelvin yelled and tried to run to him, but the young agent gripped him up quickly.

The boys had never seen Big Vic have a weak moment. He was always so strong. He was a superhero to them. But at that moment, they both saw his eyes well with tears as he realized that he was leaving his boys alone out in the world. Their mother wasn't shit, and their grandmother was sick and aging. She was in no condition to care for them. They literally had no one but him, and he failed them. At that moment, he wished he had continued pursuing boxing. He might have had to travel a lot with that, but it beat being away from his kids for good.

"Don't ever end up like me," Big Vic yelled to his boys as they put him in the back of an undercover car. "Y'all hear me? Don't y'all ever end up like me!" he screamed repeatedly. Even when the car pulled off, the boys could still hear him yelling those words at them.

The agent looked at both boys and felt a pain in his heart for them. His job was to put away criminals, but it wasn't until now that he was able to feel for those families that lost the guys they were locking up. Big Vic wasn't a notorious drug dealer to them; he was simply their father who took care of them. He was all that they had, and they had taken that from them. He felt some sort of responsibility toward the kids that he had just met.

"I'm Agent Keith Davis," he introduced himself. "I'm gonna take care of you guys and make sure you're good."

Kelvin had no way of knowing it then, but his relationship with the young FBI agent would shape the way that he moved for the rest of his life.

Chapter One

Rallo

I sat on the orange crate in front of a raggedy wood table in the trap, counting the crumpled bills in front of me, smoking a blunt. It wasn't filled with the best green to smoke at all, but it was all I could afford, and smoking something was better than nothing.

Rick, my little cousin, walked through the door and looked down at the table before grinning. "That's our take for the whole day?" he asked excitedly.

I looked at him in disgust. "Yeah. You impressed by this bullshit?"

He shrugged. "Money is money."

"This ain't no fucking money," I scoffed. "This ain't shit."

Rick pulled another crate up to the table. "It's the best we can do for now. You know, since the Kings came back up, shit been dry for us."

I took another hit of my blunt and didn't respond right away. I was tired of smoking this bullshit. Tired of hustling for years with no real come up. Tired of all the bills I had piling up with no way to pay them. Tired of hustling backward. Tired of being broke, period.

"Fuck them niggas," I said as I exhaled the smoke.

Rick looked at me sideways. "I told you years ago we should have got on with them."

"Why? So I could work for another mafucka?" I snapped angrily, cutting him off. "Them niggas over there running shit like they the Mob or some shit. Can't nobody make a move unless they all agree to it. I don't move like that. I'm cut from a different cloth. Leo taught me better than that."

Rick shrugged his shoulders. "And that's cool, but with all due respect, where has it gotten us? Our whole crew barely making it out here. We all got mouths to feed. Mr. Leo was a goon, God rest his soul, but you see where it got him."

"Watch ya mouth, fam," I warned him.

"I'm just speaking facts," he responded, refusing to back down. "Mr. Leo put you on the game and taught you how to bust a nigga's head wide open, but hustling was never his sport. He was a gambler and a stick-up kid. He didn't have to work for nobody."

"And you saying that I do?" I snapped at him.

"Where has working for yourself gotten you?" he shot back. Rick was my little cousin, but his temper was almost as bad as mine. We had gotten into plenty of fights over the years. He refused to back down from anyone, which made him a great asset to my team, but he also tended to overthink things, and that made him a big pain in my ass.

"I ain't taking orders from no man. Now, I already told you how I think we can come up," I started, but Rick cut me off again.

"And I already told *you* that I think it's a suicide mission. You tryna go at it with the Kings, and that ain't the right move to make. They're too strong, Rallo. You can't take their organization down. You see what they just overcame."

I snorted. "What they just bounced back from is minor. Look, I don't know about you, but I'm sick of eating other niggas' leftovers. I'm ready to make my own plate, and

I don't need to ask no man's permission to eat. I don't wanna join them. I wanna beat them."

"And how you plan on doing that? You been saying it so much lately that I know word done probably leaked back to them."

I smiled. "Good. I want them muthafuckas to see me coming. They been making so much money for so long that they think shit's sweet. Got the whole city scared to make a move against them. Everybody except for me. They don't like to share, so I'm gone have to take over the whole thing."

I saw Rick look at me with an expression full of doubt, but I didn't give a fuck. I was sick of waiting for my turn at the table. It was time for me to take the whole fucking thing.

Chapter Two

Kelvin

"Your men fucked everything up!" I yelled as soon as I walked into Keith's office.

He was sitting on the edge of his desk with one leg propped up, sipping from a glass full of brown liquor. I knew that it was the Torres 30 brand of brandy. That shit cost over a hundred dollars a bottle and was the only thing that Keith drank.

"I heard," he said calmly.

"You *heard*?" I repeated in disbelief. "Keith, my children think that I'm a snitch now."

He nodded. "I know. I'm sorry about that. For the record, I told you that there was a better way to get Vincent Morelli, but you insisted on having him followed."

I paced his office back and forth, stroking my beard. "I can't be the one to kill him, and you know that. My son will hate me for it, and Dutchess—"

"Dutchess." Keith spat her name as if it tasted nasty rolling off his tongue. "I told you to stay away from that treacherous bitch, and now look at you. Look what she's done to your life, to your family."

I sighed. I wanted to be mad at his statement, but it was straight facts. My life was falling apart at the seams, and everything I had worked so hard for was slowly turning to shit.

After my father was arrested, Jamar and I were sent to live with my grandmother. She wasn't the best guardian for two rowdy boys. She was blind in one eye and had too many other health issues to keep up with Jamar and me. Her house was basically a roof for us. I made sure we had everything else—well, me and Keith, I should say.

True to his word, he had taken care of us after they arrested my father. They hadn't found any drugs or guns in the house when they took him to jail, but they didn't need to. They had the word of a snitch and plenty of wiretaps with my father incriminating himself in multiple crimes. Even with the best lawyers, he was still given twenty-five years. He never made it that far. Five years into his sentence, he had a brain aneurysm and died.

I was devastated by the loss of my father. My mother showed up long enough for us to put him in the ground, but she disappeared once she learned that there was no money left for her. I didn't understand why she thought there would be. All of his legal accounts had been seized and frozen when he caught his case, and all of his safes had been confiscated during the raids. He only had one that no one knew of, located right in my grandmother's house. No one thought he would put anything there since she was so sick, but he had, and once I discovered it, I confided in Keith, the only person I felt I could trust.

For the most part, Keith had tried to be a clean agent, but watching how the bureau targeted people of color instead of helping us had made him see both sides of the law. He didn't necessarily take bribes or work for the drug dealers at first. And to his credit, he didn't put a pistol or a package in my hands. Instead, he gave me a book. When he saw how much I loved to read and how good I was with numbers, he encouraged me to go into business for myself and even turned me on to a few books that would help me achieve those goals. My favorites

Holding Down a Cartel King: Part 2

were *Rich Dad, Poor Dad* by Robert Kiyosaki and *The 48 Laws of Power* by Robert Greene. I had the money from my pops that Keith had told me not to touch until I was sure of what I wanted to invest in. I figured I was in a good space to build whatever business I wanted.

And then I got sidetracked when I met my wife.

Dutchess Samuels was the baddest bitch in the city. Unlike most, she didn't just go for the niggas with the most money. She was interested in building an empire of her own. That's what turned me on the most about her. At the time, I didn't know she meant an illegal one. After what had happened to my father, I wanted no part in any illegal activity. Getting locked up, taken away from my kids, and dying in jail wasn't appealing to me at all. But she was determined to be the queen of the streets, and I loved her too much to just walk away from her. Instead, I married her and invested some of the money my father left behind into the very same thing I swore I would stay away from: drugs.

Keith warned me not to do it, but I couldn't see the forest for the trees when it came to Dutchess. Once he saw he couldn't talk any sense to me, Keith decided the best thing he could do was help me stay free. He was moving up in the ranks at the FBI and had a lot of power and clout. Thanks to him, we had never been on anyone's radar. He rarely came around the house because he couldn't stand Dutchess, but he was something like an uncle to my kids.

"You need to leave that dirty bitch once and for all," Keith went on.

"Watch ya mouth. She's still my wife," I warned him.

"A wife who lied to you about your oldest son. A son, I might add, that would have killed you had we not intervened."

I bit my lip as I thought about the meeting I'd been in with Keon, my oldest son; Khalia, my oldest daughter; and Vincent Morelli, my wife's lover. Somehow, Vincent had found out it was me orchestrating the hits on my family's dirty business, and he had shown the evidence to Keon. I had never intended to hurt anyone. I only wanted out of a business I'd never wanted to be in to begin with. My kids didn't look at it that way, though. Father or not, I had betrayed them and their trust. The two of them were cold-hearted enough to kill me because of it. They were just like Dutchess.

"I know you're concerned, and you have every right to be," I told Keith. "But those are still my kids. I owe them my life, so if they chose to take it, then that would be on them. I would have been perfectly fine with that."

"I'm not." Keith poured me a drink and handed it to me. "Kelvin, you're much too good of a guy to be caught up in all the bullshit your family had gotten you wrapped up in. I know you love them, but you aren't anything like them. You need to make a clean break and get away."

I sipped my drink slowly before replying. "I could never do to my kids what Crystal did to me. You know that. I don't have anybody but them. I'm gonna make them see that going legit with me is the only way out. Everything I did for them is because I love them. They will see."

"And what if they don't? I don't mean to point out the obvious, but Dutchess raised a group of killers," Keith said bluntly. "They aren't as compassionate as you. They won't understand that you just want what's best for them."

"I'll make them understand," I insisted. "Just make sure this all goes away without a trace."

"Don't I always?" Keith said with a laugh. "You don't have a thing to worry about, li'l bro. All those agents are on my special team. They all know what's up."

Chapter Three

Khalia

I sat in the back of the undercover FBI truck, seething. I had never been arrested, never had so much as a parking ticket. I couldn't believe that the first time I was in cuffs was because of my own father.

"He's a dead man," Keon said from his seat across from me.

I nodded my head in agreement. It sounded nice, and I knew that was the plan, but I wasn't sure *how* to feel. Keon had just shown me proof that Daddy had planned the shootout at my twin brother Khalid's political rally. He was also responsible for setting fire to our main warehouse and destroying hundreds of thousands of dollars' worth of drugs. The punishment for these actions was undoubtedly death, and when Keon told me he needed my special skill set, I was all for it. I had no problem torturing anyone until I got what I needed, then killing them. It didn't matter who it was.

I had never been a Daddy's girl, but something about the way he looked at me when Keon demanded the truth from him tugged at my heart. He wasn't scared or begging for his life. It was almost a look of relief, like he wanted to be free. That look told me all that I needed to know and everything that I had always suspected about him from jump. Daddy wasn't cut out for this game and wanted out. I guess he had taken drastic measures to make it happen. Honestly, I couldn't blame him. If the shoe were on the other foot and I was told I couldn't live my life the way I wanted to, I would not stop until I was out either.

The back doors to the van opened, and to my surprise, the same agents who had arrested us were standing there. "You're free to go," one of them said as the other helped us out. Once we were standing there, they unlocked the cuffs from around our wrists.

I looked at them in complete disbelief. "What?"

"Free to go home," he repeated. "Raided the wrong address. The warrant said 4517 Thomas Ave, not 4571 Thomas Ave. It was our mistake."

"Damn right it's your mistake," Keon snapped. I already knew his temper was on go. "Who the fuck will be paying for the damages done to my place of business?"

I placed my hand on his arm. "Chill, bro," I warned him. They may have come to the wrong place, but in no way were we innocent. We needed to thank our lucky stars that we were able to walk free.

"Naw, they can just tear a man's business apart for nothing, and all we get is a simple-ass *I'm sorry*?" Keon yelled, his voice rising more with each word that he spoke. The fact that he was even yelling at them like we weren't a family full of murdering drug dealers was beyond me. We had to keep a very low profile.

The agent shrugged. "That's all we got." They got into their vans and sped off.

"Fucking pigs," Keon said angrily.

"Chill out," I said to him. I watched as the other agents let Vincent, his men, and the guy they kidnapped out of the van across from us. Vincent looked smug, but the poor man who had been their victim looked anything but that.

"Hey there, fellas." I greeted them with a smile. "Now that that's out the way, let's get down to business."

"Wait. Where did Pops go?" Keon asked as he looked around. There had only been two vans, and the occupants of both were standing right there. We had all been escorted out at the same time.

I shrugged. It was possible that he had run off, or maybe he was just hiding somewhere. Now that I knew it wasn't a real raid and that he hadn't snitched on us, I honestly didn't care either way. They had nothing on us, the same as always.

"He got the hell away from us," I snapped. "And can you blame him? His own kids were ready to turn on him."

"I'm not his fucking son," Keon reminded me.

I snickered. "I don't give a fuck whose blood you got pumping through ya veins. Kelvin King raised your black ass from birth. He is your father. You ready to turn on him for a mafucka you don't even know."

Vincent chuckled. "I didn't know any of you, but I made it my business to look out for your business."

I shook my head. "Keon may trust you over my father, but I don't," I said bluntly. Then I looked at the man who had been my pops' accomplice. He was nothing more than a pawn in all of this, but that didn't matter to me. Pawns got sacrificed every day.

"Throw his ass in my trunk," I told them.

After they did, I hopped in my Range Rover and texted my bodyguard/driver, Tookie, to meet me behind one of our smaller warehouses. As soon as I pulled up, my phone rang with a FaceTime alert from Drew. I debated for a second if I should answer it, but the smile that spread across my face involuntarily at the sight of his name let me know that I would.

"Hey, boo," I answered.

"Tell me, is it crazy that I just left you, but I miss you already?" he asked with a wide grin that melted my fucking heart.

"No. Who wouldn't miss me?" I asked cockily.

He laughed. "Talk that shit, baby. What you 'bout to get into?" he asked as he got out of his car.

I watched as Tookie pulled into the lot. "'Bout to go over this business plan with my cousin," I lied easily.

He nodded his head as he grabbed a gym bag out of the trunk. "That's what I like about you, Kyra. You're already successful but never stop looking for more ways to grow. You're inspiring me to be a better man, you know?"

I swear his words tugged at my heart. I loved who I was when I was with him. I wasn't Khalia King, a murdering, drug-dealing gangstress. I was free to be Kyra James, an Internet boutique owner who was looking to expand her portfolio. I could be soft and vulnerable. I could act and feel like a woman and not some killer who always had to go the extra mile to prove herself in a game meant for men.

"You make me better too," I murmured as I looked at his handsome face.

"That's what I'm supposed to do, baby. I'm 'bout to head into this gym. We grabbing dinner later?"

"Okay," I agreed. I blew him a kiss and hung up just as Tookie knocked on my window. I slid my phone into my pocket and hopped out.

If Tookie had seen me on FaceTime, he didn't say a word. That's what I loved about him. He was extremely professional and didn't pry at all.

"Wassup, Took?" I greeted him as I walked around to the trunk. I popped it open and looked down at the quivering man who was lying in my trunk.

"Boss Lady, is that Prime? Leader of the Black Angels bike club?" he asked me, sounding a little shocked.

I shrugged. "Is it? I don't know, Took. Only thing I know is this nigga violated. This mafucka was the main shooter at the shootout at Khalid's campaign rally."

For once, Tookie looked surprised. "Really? This nigga been missing for weeks. How you find him?"

"Long story. Get him out my trunk," I said as I moved out of the way.

Tookie threw Prime over his shoulder like a sack of potatoes and took him to the wall behind the warehouse. I pulled my pistol from my waist. I had planned on torturing him, but I did have a dinner date to get ready for, so lucky for him, I didn't have that kind of time.

I walked up to him and pulled the scarf out of his mouth.

"You don't gotta do this!" he pleaded.

"Oh, but I do," I said matter-of-factly. "You almost killed my brother."

"That bullet wasn't from my gun. We were only supposed to ride past and shoot our guns in the air to scare them."

"And yet somehow, a dozen innocent people lost their lives. More were injured. How do you explain that?"

"Niggas don't listen! I didn't shoot a single soul." He broke down in tears. "Please don't do this to me. I just had a baby. I have a family. I'm all they got. Please."

I shrugged. "Don't worry. Your girl will move on and find your baby a new daddy to take care of both of them in no time," I assured him before firing six bullets into him. He was dead before he hit the ground.

I looked at Tookie. "I don't have the time to do what I wanted to him, but I still want the message to be clear.

Hang this nigga off the light pole at the top of Brushton. They never fixed the lights up there. I want this shit to be breaking news in the morning."

Tookie nodded. "Sure thing, Boss Lady."

"I'm headed out. I'll talk to you later," I told him before hopping back into my Range. As I drove to my home, Prime was already forgotten. The only thing on my mind was what I should wear for my date.

Chapter Four

Khalid

I sat in my car outside my new campaign headquarters. I was afraid to admit it, but I was nervous as hell. Still, I had to get back out there. I was ahead in all the polls before the shooting happened. Since then, my numbers had dropped drastically, but only because I had been out of the spotlight. So many lives had been lost and ruined that I felt like I didn't deserve to piece my life back together while everyone else was mourning because of me.

Then there was the fact that my family had been taking hits since the shooting too. I wasn't in the streets anymore like Khalia and Keon. I handled our family business with politicians and chief of police; however, when it was time for me to tote a pistol again, I was back on the grind like I never left. Robbing dope boys' houses and killing whoever was there with Khalia made me feel like I was taking a step backward instead of forward. That wasn't to talk down on my twin. She was the best enforcer this city had ever seen, even better than our mother. Khalia could kill a nigga and then go order lunch like nothing had ever happened. She had mastered it. I did it, but not nearly as much as her. That was her calling. Politics was mine.

"You know you don't have a reason to be nervous," Nisa said from beside me. "Everyone knows once you get back on your game your numbers will rise again."

I looked at her with a small smile. "You're right. I know they will." I leaned over to give her a kiss before getting out of the Bentley. I went to open her door and nodded my head in approval at her outfit. Nisa was a bad bitch. She had the smoothest brown skin, pretty-ass hazel eyes, and got her bundles done at least five times a month. She was the shit like that.

Her body was perfect from her C-cup breasts to her round hips and fat, plump ass that shook whenever I smacked it. She usually wore something sexy to show it off, but today, she had on fitted black trousers with a thin belt and a short-sleeved ruffled white blouse. Her hair was up in a bun. She carried a tan Valentino clutch to match the Valentino heels on her feet. She looked every bit of the politician's wife—or should I say, fiancée.

"We should have come in the Maybach," she mumbled as she grabbed my arm.

I led the way into the campaign office and shook my head. Nisa came from one of the most notorious families in the city, just like me. For the life of me, I could never understand how someone who was raised in a family of killers acted like a snob. Her peoples had brought her up in money but never hid what they did from her or how they did it, either. The Kings had money, but my parents made sure we didn't act like we forgot where we came from. Shit, we spent half our young childhood in the projects before we moved out to the mansion.

As soon as we entered the office, my campaign manager, Larry, and my lawyer, Tank, were there to greet me.

"Ready to take back what's yours?" Tank asked me with a shit-eating grin. He didn't really have to be there, but I never made moves without him. He was the best criminal defense attorney in the Tri-State area because he understood criminals, having been one for years before finally going legit after he graduated from law school.

Holding Down a Cartel King: Part 2

"Been ready," I assured him.

"Are you sure?" Larry pressed. "Because even though your numbers may have dropped, that's only due to you not being in the public eye. As soon as you get back out there, you'll lock that number one spot down in no time."

"I know," I replied. I wasn't on any cocky shit. I just knew what the people wanted. Everyone had a different agenda for a different group of people: the LGBTQ community, blacks, Hispanics, elders, middle-class, blue-collar workers, the one percent. I had an agenda that worked for everybody, and that's why people fucked with me. I needed them to. As long as I was in office, I could continue to push our drugs through this country's fine political system.

"Okay, so here's the plan. We have a press conference scheduled for six this evening. I gave the reporters that list of preapproved questions so they shouldn't hit you with anything that you don't want to answer," Larry told me. "But just in case they do . . ."

As I watched the next two people come through the campaign office's door, I was no longer listening as my eyes followed Toni and her brother Tommy as they entered the office.

"I'll be right back," I told Larry before going over to them.

"Khalid this is important!" he yelled to my back.

"Tommy! What's up, bro?" I said happily as he reached out to slap palms with me.

"Shit, I can't call it. Just happy to be here and ready to go to work," he responded.

I nodded my head. As I looked at the wheelchair he was sitting in, I couldn't help but feel guilty. He was in that wheelchair because of bullets that were meant for me.

I cleared my throat to stop myself from going on yet another guilt trip. "Well, we got your desk ready for you to go. My first press conference is today, and Larry told me they have a list of approved questions, but I need you to go over them for me again. After that, I need you to go to my website and business pages on social media and let them know I'm back."

"Sure thing. I can also go into all the diverse groups I'm in, let them know you'll be speaking today and have them send questions. That way, they will really feel like you're talking to them and not just reporters."

I grinned. "I knew I did the right thing bringing you on board. Come on. Let me show you to your desk."

Larry appeared by our side from out of nowhere. "I'll take him to his desk. Tommy, right?" he asked him with a grin a mile wide.

As they went to his desk, I turned to look at Toni. She looked like the complete opposite of Nisa in a pair of form-fitting black stretch pants that hugged her full curves, a fitted black Nike T-shirt, and matching black Nikes on her feet. She had begun to let her short hair grow out a little, and it was curled to perfection. Huge blacked-out sunglasses covered her face, but even still, no one could miss how beautiful she was. I felt like a kid with a crush in her presence.

"I'm glad you're here," I told her honestly.

"Of course I'm here," she responded. "Once you told Tommy he had a job when the office opened back up, he bugged me day and night. He would never let me get out of bringing him here."

"You know I could have picked him up," I told her as I reached out for her hand.

She pulled her hand back and pushed her glasses on top of her head so that I could stare into her eyes. "Oh, really? And what would Nisa think about that?"

I had completely forgotten about her just that fast. "She wouldn't mind."

"Please. Your girl don't fuck with me," she scoffed.

I tried to reach for her hand again. I didn't want to talk about Nisa. I just loved being in her presence. "Well, I do."

She tilted her head to the side and pulled her hand back yet again. "And what am I supposed to do with that information?"

"Khalid!"

The sound of Nisa's voice brought me down off the cloud I had been riding on. I took a deep breath as she came and stood directly between us with her back facing Toni.

"What's up? You see I'm talking," I told her impatiently.

She turned, looked at Toni, and rolled her eyes. "It can't be that important. Tank is looking for you."

"Tank could have come and got me," I snapped at her. "Tell him I'll be there in a minute."

She looked back and forth between Toni and me. "I'm sure your little friend won't mind, although I'm not sure if *little* is the word I would use to describe her."

That was a dig at Toni's weight, and I knew it. She was full-figured but curvy as hell with it. I loved it. "Nisa, cut it the fuck out," I warned her.

Toni chuckled. "Girl, keep making little slick comments about my weight. I'll show you what a bitch my size can do." With that, she walked away, and I couldn't stop myself from looking after her.

"So that's what you want?" Nisa snapped at me.

I looked at her in disbelief. "Fuck is you talking 'bout? I'm here trying to get my career back on track."

"And get with that fat bitch too," she spat.

I glared at her. "Let that be the last time you disrespect her to me."

She folded her arms across her chest. "Or *what*?" she asked as she snaked her neck.

"Try it and find out. Now, I'm here to work and get my life back on track. If you got a problem with that, then you can leave. I'll find my way home."

She stood there staring at me, anger flashing in her hazel eyes. Nisa was far from stupid. She didn't want to be there with Toni, but she wouldn't leave so I could be alone with her. Even though we hadn't done anything, the chemistry between us was obvious.

"Go to work. I'll be sitting right here," she told me after a few minutes of silence.

I gave her a half smile and turned to go back to my office to talk to Larry and Tank. As I made my way to the back, Toni looked up from Tommy's desk and caught my eye. The little smile she gave me before going back to help him made my heart jump a little bit.

I wanted her and knew that sooner rather than later, I would have to have her.

Chapter Five

Keon

I walked around our new warehouse slowly, a smile tugging at my lips at the sight of all the bricks of cocaine and heroin. We were slowly but surely getting back to where we had been before, thanks to the twins riding out on the whole city and taking what was ours.

With Khalid going away to college and entering politics, I gotta admit that I thought the nigga had lost it. He gained my respect once again by picking up his pistols and going to work like he never left for the sake of our family. To be honest, our hits had probably hurt him the most. His image definitely took a few negative hits after the shooting, but it was the innocent lives that were lost that hurt him the most. A bunch of young people were killed or severely injured, and since Khalid had such a huge heart, he felt the pain behind each person affected.

But now we were slowly rising back to prominence. And Kenya's OT trips were bringing in more money than anyone suspected. Baby sister was moving that weight like a pro, and I wasn't so sure how I felt about that. I had high hopes for her to be the only King to go legit. I should have known better. Dutchess King found a way to ruin everyone that she touched.

"Damn! Y'all wasn't playin'!" Chuck exclaimed as he followed me around the warehouse. Chuck had been my right-hand man since we were young niggas. We had come up together, and we both excelled at basketball, although I was the more recruited player. Still, Chuck was nice. So, when Dutchess told me it was time to throw my hoop dreams away to come learn the family business, I fully expected him to cash in on all of my offers. Instead, he threw the game away as well. He told me that he only enjoyed playing when we played together, and it wasn't fun without me. So, instead of doing what he needed to do in school, he jumped off the porch with me. Ever since then, I made sure he was straight. Chuck turned into a goon for my family. We couldn't have succeeded without him.

"The twins weren't playing," I corrected him. "They did all this."

Chuck chuckled. "You mean it was Khalia's idea, and Khalid went along for the ride." He knew my family just as well as I did.

I laughed too. "So, what's up? Why you wanna meet before everyone else got here?"

Chuck looked at me seriously. "You know niggas thought we were soft out here 'cause we was laying low."

"Niggas kill me, man. We had to get our weight back up. We ain't no nickel-and-dime operation like the rest of these broke mafuckas walking around here calling themselves hustlers," I spat angrily.

"Indeed," Chuck agreed with a nod of his head. "But the streets are talking. And they screaming Rallo's name right now."

I laughed so hard that my stomach hurt. "Rallo? That nigga sell ounces at the most, yo. He don't have the money or the soldiers to come after us."

Chuck looked doubtful. "He might not have the money, but he got a group of young niggas ready to ride for him."

"Who?" I asked, still laughing. "Their little weak-ass clique? They call themselves the MMC right? The Money Murder Crew who don't get no money and ain't murdering shit? Them niggas?"

Chuck chuckled a little, but not for long. "Never underestimate your enemies, Keon. We're Goliath in this situation, and they're David. And you see what happened with them."

"Man, the Bible been rewritten so many times that we don't know what the fuck happened," I shot back. "Who was even there to witness and write the shit anyway?"

Chuck shook his head. "Man, you goin' to hell."

"I am," I agreed, "but not for that. I can't believe you letting some little no-name, off-brand niggas scare you."

Chuck glared at me. I could tell from the fire in his eyes that I had crossed the line. If I were anyone else, there was no doubt in my mind that he would have resorted to violence with me.

"No fear pumps in my blood. You know that better than anyone," he responded calmly. "I'm saying let's be smart. Young niggas eventually get tired of eating crumbs."

I shrugged. "Everybody knows if you ain't eating with us, then you against us. I don't give a fuck about some broke niggas calling themselves the Money Murder Crew when they ain't dropping no bodies or making no money."

Chuck shook his head slightly. "I don't think it's a smart idea to just brush them off. Rallo been talking real reckless lately."

"Until he say the shit to my face or attempt to knock me off my throne, I don't give a fuck what he say. Niggas already know what it is. Eat with the Kings, or starve like a peasant. And Kings don't address peasants." I looked down at the Presidential Rolex on my wrist to check the time. Those no-names were already a distant memory. "Let's get ready for this meeting."

Chapter Six

Kenya

I walked into the UPMC Rooney Sports Complex, holding a bag of delicious-smelling Jamaican food. I had never been here before to watch the Pitt Panthers football team practice and hoped that I wouldn't be turned away from my surprise visit.

I let the guard know where I was going. I expected him to say I wasn't allowed back, but his eyes were too busy roaming the cleavage poking out of my tight white tank and my thick bronze-colored thighs that were exposed in the cheeky denim shorts I had on to say anything to me. The red Prada stilettos I wore with a matching red clutch completed the outfit.

I made my way back toward the indoor turf field the Panthers practiced on. I had never been there before but navigated my way like I had been there a million times.

Practice was just ending as I walked on the field. I felt the eyes of his teammates and trainers looking me up and down hungrily as they walked past me. A few of them even called out to me, but I ignored them.

Armani was the last to leave the field. He had been running extra routes with the quarterback after everyone else was done for the day. That was something else I admired about him, his will and determination to always do better and be better than the next man. He was being scouted as one of the top receivers in college football, and after this year, he was eligible for the NFL Draft, which he already told me he was entering.

I started to walk toward him, but some high-yellow chick ran onto the field and hugged him. I frowned at the sight of her. We had yet to make anything that we were doing official, but he had assured me time and time again I was the only female who had his attention. I should have known better, though. He was a college athlete. Females lined up around the block to be with guys like him.

A small part of me wanted to turn and leave at the sight of high-yellow all in his face, but an even bigger part of me, perhaps that King pride that we all had, insisted that I stay and let my presence be known. I walked right over to them, where they were still hugging, and cleared my throat loudly.

Armani saw me first and instantly pulled away from the girl. "Kenya! Hey, boo, you ain't tell me you were coming past." He opened his arms to hug me, but I stepped back.

"I know. I grabbed some Jamaican food from Mama Rose, since that's your favorite, and came past to surprise you. Looks like I'm the one who ended up getting surprised instead," I said as I looked the chick up and down. She was taller than me and slim like a model.

Armani laughed as he grabbed the bag from me and put his arm around my shoulders. I expected him to stink since he had just finished practicing, but to my surprise, he still smelled quite clean. "Babe, that's my friend Ashlei. She writes for the school newspaper and just wanted a few quotes from me for the story she's doing on the team."

I didn't miss the hurt that flashed in her eyes briefly at his introduction. "I didn't get everything that I needed," she snapped at him, barely able to keep the anger out of her voice. From the way she looked and her tone, I knew she wasn't talking about no damn article.

"I'll give you some more later," Armani told her before looking down at me. "Damn, you look, good, baby. I missed you," he said as he kissed my forehead and led me away from Ashlei.

I didn't say a word until we got out front. When we reached my car, a royal blue BMW 745, I just looked at him.

"What's wrong? What I do?" he asked as he gave me the smile that made my knees weak the day that I met him.

"You used to fuck with Ashlei, didn't you?" I asked him bluntly.

Armani looked at me in surprise. "Where that come from?"

"It came from the way she looked at me when she saw that I was here for you," I responded with my arms folded.

"Is my boo a little jealous?" he asked with a chuckle. Something was always funny to him. Usually, I didn't mind, but at that moment, I wasn't in a laughing mood.

"I just wanna know what I'm up against."

He lifted the lid on the food, smelled it, and closed his eyes. "Mmm. I can't wait to fire on this. Babe, open your car, I gotta toss this in there before one of the coaches see me with it. You know they got me on a strict meal plan and will kick my ass if they catch me with this"

I rolled my eyes but popped the locks anyway. He slid the food on the back seat before closing the door and leaning against it. Then he held his arms open for me.

I bit my lip before walking over to him.

He wrapped his arms around my waist then tilted my chin so I could look directly into his eyes. "When it comes to me, there is no competition, baby. There's only you."

I raised an eyebrow. "Not even groupies?"

"Especially not groupies," he said with a laugh. "I'm too close to getting my dream and everything that I worked hard for. I can't afford to lose it all over some bullshit."

I remained quiet. We liked each other a lot but had never put a title on what we were doing. I knew a lot of that had to do with me. Armani practiced and trained a lot, but when he did have free time, all he wanted to do was be with me. I was so busy supplying powerful politicians, businessmen, and chiefs of police with my family's drugs across the state that I rarely had any spare time. I was gone at least three days out of the week. The only reason I had decided to come and surprise Armani at practice today was because I had to leave the very next day.

I wasn't the average eighteen-year-old, but I did know what I wanted. I had never had anyone make me feel the way Armani did with just one simple look at me. It had nothing to do with who he was or what he did and everything to do with how happy I was whenever I talked to him or got to be around him.

"Listen to me, Kenya. You don't have nothing to worry about," he told me as he stroked my hair. "You got me."

I cocked my head to the side. "Do I? We ain't even together," slipped out of my mouth before I could help it.

He laughed and pulled away from me slightly. "Is that what you want? For us to be together? You want a title? Will that make you feel like what I'm saying is real?"

"I didn't mean it like—" I started, but he cut me off.

"Naw, you said what you meant. I can respect that. I'm telling you all this shit, but I ain't showing you. So, how 'bout this? I don't want nobody else, and you better not either," he joked.

"You already know I don't," I assured him.

"Cool. So, from now on, you're my woman, and I'm your man. We together together."

My heart skipped a beat as I laughed at him. "Together together? For real?"

"Straight like that. Matter of fact . . ." He pulled away from me and slid his phone out of his pocket.

"What you doin'?" I asked him curiously.

"Let me get a picture of you," he said.

I grinned, fixed my hair, and got my angles just right as he clicked away. When he was done, he showed me the pictures and let me pick which one was my favorite. He looked it over with a nod before saying, "I'm posting this one on the Gram."

I raised my eyebrow. Saying we were together was one thing, but to make it social-media official was another. Armani Collins had a verified Instagram account that already had over one hundred thousand followers. He was something like a celebrity. Was I really ready to be scrutinized by that many people?

"Okay," I said with a shrug like it didn't bother me one way or the other if he posted me.

He posted the picture with the simple caption "MINE" and slid the phone back in his pocket. Then he pulled me back into him. "It's 'bout to be me and you against the world, baby."

Indeed, it was. He was on his way to NFL stardom shortly. Meanwhile, I was transporting drugs across state lines and pushing my own dreams to the back for the sake of the family. I finally understood why Keon was so against me getting into the game. I had a passion for clothes that was unmatched. Everyone always told me I should consider owning a boutique, or at least starting my own clothing line. I wasn't sure which one would be the best for me. Ever since I started to make these runs, going after what I wanted became less important. But now that I was officially with Armani, who was undoubtedly set to be super successful, I decided that I had to figure out what I was doing with my life.

Chapter Seven

Dutchess

I sat on my deck, sipping white wine as I watched the sunset. My eyes traveled along each luxury car parked in my circular driveway. From Maseratis to Bentleys, I had 'em all. I switched vehicles the same way people switched drawers. I lived in a mansion, and my bank account had so many zeros that my grandkids' grandkids were set. I had it all—but it had come at a hell of a price.

I looked down at the furry Chanel slippers on my feet. They had been a gift from Vincent, one of the many he'd sent me as a thank-you for letting him stay with me when his wife put him out. I knew it was really his way of trying to get me to answer at least one of his phone calls, but I just couldn't do it.

I took another sip of wine as Mother Nature painted the sky different pink, purple and orange hues. Ironically, I found myself missing Kelvin. We had shared plenty of sunsets on this very deck in this house built on blood money. He would stroke my hand and tell me that the only thing more beautiful than the sunset was my smile. I used to love the time we spent together until the demands of the game pulled me further and further away from my husband. I didn't have the time to appreciate the kind of man he was trying to be for me or our children. In all honesty, I wanted a man to be rougher around the edges, more street, and have more of a killer instinct . . . more like Vincent. Now, I was beginning to realize what a mistake that was.

I looked down at the divorce papers in my lap. Instead of celebrating our thirty years together, Kelvin wanted to separate permanently. I should have expected this to happen, considering the fact that he had not only found out that I had an affair with an Italian Mob boss, but also that our oldest child was not his. Still, I couldn't bring myself to believe that he would actually file for divorce. I wasn't sure if I was ready to work through this, but I knew that I didn't want a divorce.

My phone rang, disrupting my peace and quiet. I didn't recognize the number but decided to answer anyway. "Hello?"

"Dutchess, it's me."

The sound of Kelvin's voice soothed me. "Hey, how you been?"

"I've had better days," he said flatly. "Have you talked to the kids?"

I shook my head like he could see me. "No, but that's not unusual lately. You know none of them are speaking to me right now besides Kenya, and that's only because she still lives at home."

He sighed. "I wish everything hadn't come to this."

"It doesn't have to be this way," I said to him. "We can fix this, fix our family."

"Fix our family?" he repeated in disbelief. "Why would I wanna do that? I already know you had that white man laid up in the bed I bought the second I walked out the door."

I almost dropped the phone at his words. I was so shocked.

"What? You thought I didn't know? That's always been your problem, Dutchess. You continue to underestimate me."

"Listen, that was nothing. I want our family back. I miss the kids, and I miss—"

He cut me off. "You don't miss me, and you know it. I was never who you wanted, and I see that now. The least you could do is stop lying to me."

"I never lied to you."

He laughed. "Not even when you said Keon was my son? Or that you were faithful to me? If those weren't lies, what were they, Dutchess?"

"So, we gonna sit here and act like I never caught you doing your fair share of dirt over the years?" I shot back. It was a sad defense, and I knew it, but it was all that I had. "I had to cut plenty of bitches over you."

"You did," he admitted. "But the difference between me and you is that was *before* we got married. Once we got married, I stopped all the bullshit. I made a promise to you and God that I would be the best man I could be, and I held up my end of that promise."

I bit my lip as tears welled in my eyes. Still, I didn't let one fall. "I'm human. I made a few mistakes. That doesn't mean I want this."

"I don't give a fuck what you want, Dutchess. These last thirty years have been about what you want, and I went along for the ride because I wanted to keep you happy. The kids are grown and doing what they want, so it's time for me to do the same. Since you haven't heard from them, there's nothing else you can do for me besides sign those papers that I know you got today."

I laughed. "Yeah, I got them. I'll think about signing them."

"Dutchess—"

I hung up before he could finish his sentence. Then I looked down at those papers again. Signing them would signal the end of an era of life as I knew it. I wasn't ready to give that up and wouldn't be signing shit until I felt like it.

I picked the papers up and ripped them to shreds. Then I picked up my wine glass and sipped some more. Everyone seemed to forget who really ran shit. I would remind them soon.

Chapter Eight

Keon

"Dad, Coach Baker loves that jumper you taught me," Nahim said excitedly as we talked on FaceTime.

I grinned as I got off the elevator at The Washington, an upscale condominium complex less than a block from downtown. "I told you that I was a beast in basketball, son. Where you think you get it from?"

He laughed. "I don't know. I guess from you. Can we go to the park to hoop this weekend?"

"Of course. I'll grab your brothers, and we can all go."

"A'ight. And you're coming to my game tomorrow. Right, Dad?" he asked pointedly.

I paused before I answered. I made it a habit to make it to all of his games, but since I had been ducking his mom heavy the last few weeks, I had missed a few, and he wouldn't let me forget it.

"Dad?"

"Yeah, son. I'll be there," I finally told him. I was about to tell him to make sure he finished his homework before playing Fortnite or Madden, until I heard Stacey's voice in the background. "I'll hit you tomorrow, son. Love you," I told him in a rush just as Stacey yelled, "Nahim, don't hang up the phone with your father!"

I ended the call before she could take the phone and laughed a little, although the situation with her was not funny at all. She claimed she was pregnant with my baby. I hadn't touched Stacey in years before slipping up recently, so I wasn't sure if the baby was mine. I was sure that I didn't want her to fuck up the great thing I had going on in my life right now.

I slid the key in the lock just as the door opened, and Dionne stood there in a skimpy French maid's uniform with a sheer black bra and lacy stockings. On her feet were a pair of red bottoms I'd just copped her. "Come on in, sir. Dinner is already done."

I bit my lip as I walked in and closed the door. Then I grabbed a handful of her thick ass hanging out the bottom of her uniform. "Come here, baby."

She turned around and grinned as she wrapped her arms around my neck. "I missed you," she murmured.

I cupped her ass. "Show me," I challenged her.

She didn't need to be asked twice. Without another word, she slid to her knees, pulled my pants and boxer briefs down, then placed my dick in her mouth.

I kept my hand on the back of her head as she kept a steady rhythm. I loved the way she licked and sucked all over it like it was the best thing she had ever tasted in her life. I loved how she didn't forget to massage my balls as she deep-throated me, and I couldn't get enough of the way that she moaned. Dionne was one of those females who came when she was giving head, and as her moans got louder and longer, I knew that's where she was headed.

I wanted to feel her cum, though, so I backed away from her.

"Baby, what's the matter? Why you stop me?" she asked in a voice that sounded more like a whine.

I didn't answer her as I gently pushed her back onto the floor and ripped her lace stockings off before I lifted her skirt. She watched as I kicked my shoes off, then my pants and boxers, before lying on top and entering her.

I had been with plenty of women. Most of them, I couldn't even remember their names or what they did for a living if you paid me. And yet none of them, not one of them, had ever gripped the soul out of my dick the way Dionne did. She would squeeze her walls around my dick and release, then squeeze again even longer. Fucking her felt like I had been granted access to tight pussy heaven. She could have taught a class on how to properly do Kegels 'cause her shit sucked me in and never wanted to let me loose.

"Baby, I love you," she moaned as she matched me thrust for thrust.

I looked down at her cute face as she said those words. Dionne was a mere eighteen years old and Kenya's best friend. I had no business crossing the line and fucking her, and I knew it. At first it was supposed to be fun, just something to do, but she had me feeling so good that I moved her out of her grandmother's house and into the condo I'd purchased years ago. I upgraded her, took care of her, but never made promises of commitment or professed my love for her. So, to hear her throw those words out there made me realize what I was doing with her. I wasn't shit, and I knew that. I didn't deserve to have a sweet young girl like her falling for me. I would fuck up her life.

Still, she felt so good to me, clenching her walls down on my dick and matching me stroke for stroke, that I couldn't stop the lie that flew out of my mouth to her. "I love you too, baby," I told her as I stroked her as deeply as I could.

Hearing those words seemed to make her pussy even tighter and wetter. We went at it for what seemed like hours right there on floor. When we were done, we lay there in silence for a moment before she got up went to the bathroom. When she came back, she had a warm rag in her hand and began to wipe my dick and balls down. I lay back with my eyes closed. She was a fucking keeper for real.

"Keon, how long do I have to keep us a secret from Kenya? She keeps asking me where I'm getting all this new stuff from and who my man is. I feel funny lying to her."

I opened one eye and looked at her. "I understand that, baby. Let me be the one to tell her."

Dionne looked at me doubtfully but said nothing else as she finished cleaning me off.

I got up and put my boxer briefs and pants back on. Then I sat at the dining room table and pulled out a small baggie of coke. I made two neat lines on the table just as Dionne returned. I saw her from the corner of my eye as I leaned down and snorted the first line. The rush hit me almost instantly.

"I wanna try some," she said.

I looked at her like she was crazy. I indulged every now and then, nothing too serious. I had a few little habits I dabbled in that kept me buzzing but not addicted. A blast of cocaine every now and then was one of them. However, I didn't feel comfortable turning Dionne on to it. She was a young girl who had her whole life ahead of her. I didn't want her to develop a habit trying to keep up with me.

"Drugs are bad for you," I told her sarcastically as I leaned down and did another line.

"Some people might say you are bad for me too, but here we are," she shot back.

I laughed. "You ain't ready to take this trip, baby girl. Trust me on this."

"I know what I'm ready for. Wouldn't you rather me try it with you than somebody else? At least I can trust you."

I looked at her. Dionne was a cute girl, and while she didn't have much up top, she was beyond blessed in the hips, thighs, and ass department. I didn't want to see her start using coke and begin to lose her looks. However, she was right about one thing. If she did it with me, I could moderate her use. Plus, high sex was out of this fucking world. I could only imagine the freaky shit we would get into if we were both high off it.

"A'ight. Don't do this if you ain't with me," I warned her as I laid a line out for her. "Do it slowly."

She bent over the table and snorted, then leaned her head back and started fanning her face rapidly. I knew her nose was burning like crazy since she was feeling the first-time effects of using it. I looked at her face and watched as a smile spread across it after a few minutes. "Wow," she said with a grin.

Watching her made my dick hard as hell. I was ready to go again. "Bring your sexy ass here, girl," I said as I grabbed her and placed her on my lap. I was more than ready for round two.

Chapter Nine

Rallo

"Raymond . . . Raymond, wake up!"

I rubbed my eyes slowly and looked at Shaterra, my woman. She stood by my bed with one hand on her hip, the other on her very pregnant belly, calling my government name with a big frown on her face.

"What's up, baby?" I asked her as I yawned.

"Did you get that money I needed for the light bill?"

I got up slowly. "Naw, but I'ma get it."

She rolled her eyes. "It was a ten-day notice. I was 'bout to leave for work and got one for seventy-two hours in the mail." She tossed an open envelope on my chest. "I'll just pay the shit by myself *again*."

"You ain't got to do that," I protested as I walked over to her. "I told you I got it."

"Apparently, I do! I can't let us be in here with no lights," she replied with a roll of her eyes before walking out of the room.

"Shit," I mumbled as I went after her.

I entered the living room just as she grabbed her purse. "Babe, I said I got it," I told her.

She ignored me and went over to our five-year-old daughter, Raymiah. She knelt in front of her and signed that it was time for her to go. Raymiah stood up and grabbed her small backpack, but when she saw me, she ran over to me. I scooped her up in my arms and held her tightly. "Daddy loves you," I told her as I stared directly at her.

She grinned and signed back that she loved me too before getting down and running back over to her mother.

"I'm going over my mother's after work," Shaterra said with her back still toward me. "I'll see you later, I guess."

I went to open the door for her before walking outside with them to her car.

"You didn't have to walk out here with us," she said as she opened the door for Raymiah.

After she made sure Raymiah was strapped in and secure, she slammed the door shut then turned to look at me. I hated what I saw in her eyes. She looked disappointed, upset, and tired.

I bit my lip as I rubbed her stomach to ease some of the anger I felt building up inside of me. I wanted nothing more than to make this pregnancy easy for her, especially since she was giving me the boy I always wanted. I felt that when my son got here, we would be complete. I didn't want to stress her out at all. Raymiah had been born partially deaf, and although the doctors said there was nothing that we could have done during her pregnancy to prevent that, I felt differently. Back when Shaterra was pregnant with her, I had cheated on her a lot. I took her through a bunch of bullshit that could have been avoided. I felt like Raymiah's handicap was my fault as a result of everything I put her mother through, and I wanted to make sure I did everything right this time.

Yet here I was, fucking up again. She might not have had to worry about other women anymore, but she should never have to be the one to keep our lights on. As her man, I should have been able to provide a better life for her. I didn't even want her to work while she was pregnant, but I couldn't tell her that when she was the main breadwinner and the one keeping the roof over our heads. I felt lower than shit, like less than a man.

"I'ma get up us outta this, Shaterra. I promise, baby."

She nodded her head slowly, but I could tell she didn't believe me. It felt like a sucker punch to the gut.

I opened her door for her, then waved as she pulled off with her car making a loud noise. Shaterra drove a blue 2008 Malibu with over one hundred thousand miles on it, and the wear on the car was starting to show. Something was always wrong with it.

I went back into the crib and grabbed my phone to call Rick. It was time to ride out on them Kings. If he wasn't gone do it with me, then I would do it on my own.

Just as I dialed his number, a text message from him came through. It looked like a picture.

"The fuck is this nigga sending me pics for?" I mumbled.

I found out as soon as I opened it. My little brother, Armani, had posted a pic of a bad bitch with the caption "mine" on his Instagram account. As I focused on the woman in the picture, I realized exactly who the bitch was. "Kenya King," I said as my lips formed into a smile. Armani being with the baby sister of the King family was the best news that I had gotten in months.

Maybe there was light at the end of the tunnel after all.

Chapter Ten

Khalia

"Why did we come all the way out here to this mall?" Drew asked as we pulled into the parking lot of Pittsburgh Mills Mall out in Natrona Heights.

I didn't want to tell him that the only reason we were here was because I needed to grab some gifts for my nephew but couldn't risk being seen with him at any of the more popular malls where someone might recognize me. Pittsburgh Mills was in the cut. It was the mall that people went to when they were trying to be low. I wasn't trying to hide Drew, but since he didn't know who I was, I couldn't just be out there with him like that either.

So instead, I stroked his face softly before turning it slightly to look at me. "Does it matter where we go as long as we're together?" I asked him before kissing him deeply. Our tongues did a nice, slow dance as they intertwined. Drew snaked his hand around my waist and practically lifted me onto his lap as he deepened the kiss.

"Mmm," I murmured when we broke apart. I wiped the side of his mouth with my thumb and bit my lip. "Keep kissing me like that and we won't make it inside."

He looked at me intensely. "Maybe that's the point." He kissed me again and leaned his seat all the way back to the back row, then lifted me onto his lap. I felt his rock-hard dick underneath me immediately. I gazed at him lustfully.

He lifted my oversized Moschino T-shirt dress and palmed my ass. "Oh, you wearing underwear today?" he asked with a smirk as he slid his hand beneath the lace Fenty panties.

"We shopping, baby. I gotta have 'em on to try on clothes," I responded.

He gripped my ass with both hands and pulled me down onto him. "You can take 'em off in here, though," he murmured before kissing and sucking on my neck.

I backed away from him and raised an eyebrow. I had to admit I was turned the fuck on to the fullest. I had never fucked in any of my cars and damn sure never in a mall parking lot. Somehow, that added to the thrill of it all. Plus, all the windows to my Mercedes G-Wagon were heavily tinted, so nobody could really see us unless they walked right up to the windshield and stared into it.

Slowly, I slid my panties down and slid my foot out one side. Then I made a show of sliding them off the other before unbuckling his pants and pulling his boxers down. His dick stood straight up like it was saluting me. As I slid down on it, I balled my panties up and stuffed them in his mouth. I thought he would protest, but instead, his half-open eyes gazed at me lovingly. As I rode his dick, I had to bite my lip to keep from crying out. Drew always felt so good, but I knew that the real reason I was enjoying him so much was because of how I felt about him. It was something that I knew was dangerous, but I couldn't stop myself from falling from him even if I wanted to. But I didn't want to.

I was cumming all over him in no time, and he was right behind me, busting a nut the size of a walnut inside of me. I hopped off him and grabbed the baby wipes I kept in the console. I grabbed a few to clean myself off before handing them to him.

"I gotta get you back for that," he told me with a smile, showing off those blinding white teeth.

"Oh, yeah? I'm looking forward to it," I responded with a grin as I finished cleaning myself. I slid my panties back on, picked up my Chanel bag, and hopped out of the truck.

As we walked hand in hand through the mall, I let him tell me about his day. He complained about his supervisor down at the post office and how he had been picking up extra shifts so he could save more money. The whole time he talked, I nodded and made comments like I understood where he was coming from, when I didn't get none of that shit. I had never worked a nine-to-five job and wasn't close to anyone who did.

When we entered Foot Locker, Drew looked at me. "You want sneaks?" he asked doubtfully as he looked down at the thigh-high Monika Chiang gladiator heeled sandals I had on my feet.

I laughed. "I can't want to dress down?"

He shrugged. "I seen you rock a pair here and there, but you're usually always in heels." He grinned again. "Not that I don't like it."

I chuckled because he was right. I was a boss bitch, and I dressed the part every time I stepped out the door. There was never a hair out of place on my head, only the best clothes graced my body, and I always had on six-inch stilettos.

"The shoes are for my nephew," I told him. "His birthday party is coming up soon, and he's a sneaker head."

"Oh, that's dope. Can I come to the party with you?" he asked me as we walked over to the shoes on display. "I would love to meet your family."

I paused before answering, although I already knew the answer would be no. I couldn't take Drew around the Kings. He would never understand our world. He was a blue-collar man, a working man. Hell, he didn't even know who I was. I couldn't take him around a family full of kingpins and expect him to just fit in.

He chuckled slightly at my silence. "You know what? My bad, Kyra. I'm sorry for asking. I thought we were trying to build something here, but guess I was wrong." He walked away.

I wanted to call after him, tell him to come back and explain that we were building something that I treasured. I had never had anything even remotely close to this with any other man, and I valued him so much. Yet as much as I wanted to tell him those things, I didn't. I had never seen my mother go after my father, and he had stayed around for years. I just didn't have it in me to chase a man.

I picked the shoes I wanted for Nahim and was about to let a young salesman help me when I saw one of the female workers all in Drew's face as he checked out the sweat suits. I saw nothing but red as I marched over and stood directly between them.

"You need to back the fuck up," I told the female bluntly.

She was taller than me, but since I stood at five feet, almost everyone was. She was fair-skinned and had long, wavy hair falling down her back, which I pictured wrapping around my fist as I flung her around the store.

"Excuse me?" she asked in a shocked tone.

"Back the fuck up out his face!" I yelled at her, drawing the eyes of the other shoppers in the store. Ask me if I cared.

"Kyra, what are you doing?" Drew hissed.

I ignored him and placed my hand on my hip as I glared at her. "Why are you still here?" I asked her seriously. It would be nothing for me to reach in my Chanel bag and grab the pistol I kept there to show her who she was fucking with, but I knew that I wouldn't even need it for her. One smack would probably do the trick with her, and I was ready to lay hands on her if she didn't get up out of my man's face.

She didn't say another word as she walked away.

Drew shook his head and walked out of the store. This time, I followed behind him. I had lost my cool and showed a glimpse of the real Khalia King, which scared him off.

"Drew," I started, but he cut me off.

"Kyra, what the fuck was that?" he snapped at me. "How can you refuse to invite me to meet your family one minute but get jealous of a female talking to me the next?"

"It's complicated, okay?" I responded as I tried to keep up with his long strides. When I couldn't, I grabbed his hand to make him stop.

He stopped but didn't turn to face me. So, I went to stand in front of him. "Listen, I don't have a regular family. I don't want them to embarrass me. But please know that you're important to me. I wouldn't even waste my time with you if you weren't."

He looked down at me doubtfully.

"Look, let's just get a room out here, and I'll show you just how much you really mean to me," I suggested. There was a Marriott right up the block from the mall, and although I never stayed at anything less than a five-star hotel, I was willing to go there to please him.

His face softened slightly. "Girl, I don't know what the hell you doing to me."

I reached up to touch his face. "I don't know what you doing to *me*," I said honestly. He had me feeling things that were foreign to me. I didn't know what I was doing when it came to him. I just knew I didn't want it to end.

Chapter Eleven

Khalid

The last couple of weeks had been draining. Working to get back up in the polls was not an easy feat. I was back out there doing interviews, showing up at schools and rallies, shaking hands, and kissing babies. Anytime I got exhausted, I remembered what the end goal was: making it to Capitol Hill and taking over the drug trade there. Who knows? Maybe one day I could even make it to the White House. It wasn't like we didn't have a history of drug-dealing presidents that sat in the Oval Office. Ronald Reagan was the biggest drug dealer to ever live in this country to this day, in my opinion.

I walked into my penthouse condo and loosened my tie. Nisa was walking toward me, dressed in nothing but a short black silk robe and stilettos. Her hair was curled and flowing down her back. She looked gorgeous as usual, but how did that saying go? Show me a beautiful woman, and I'll show you a man who is tired of fucking her. That was basically how I felt about Nisa. Our relationship had pretty much run its course. The more I worked, the more I got sick of her shallow ways and the fact that she had absolutely nothing going on for herself besides who her family was and the prestige of being with me.

To keep it a hundred, her shallowness was nothing new. In the beginning it had meant nothing to me. Our families had grown up close, and I had always known that Nisa was a high-maintenance female. When I decided to fuck with her, I overlooked it because she was so smart, plus she could handle a pistol.

Lately, that hadn't been enough though. For as smart as she was, she wasn't applying it to anything but me, and that was a turn-off. She needed a life outside of me. Instead, she was pressuring me to marry her. I felt the noose getting tighter and tighter around my neck, and I didn't like it.

"How was your day, handsome?" she asked me as she approached me and kissed me.

I barely kissed her back. "Long," I said flatly as I walked to the bedroom. "Is my pops here?"

"He came past this morning. Said he had to go see a property and would be back later."

I nodded as I walked into the bedroom. Pops had been staying with me since Vincent Morelli dropped the bomb that he was Keon's father. I didn't mind having him there at all, even when it came out that he had been the one who tried to sabotage us. Keon wanted to kill him and was pissed at me that I didn't feel the same. I wasn't sure what Khalia wanted to do, since she was hard to track down these days, but what I did know was that if she wanted Pops dead, he'd already be stinking somewhere.

"There was something else I wanted to talk to you about," she started as my phone rang. I saw it was Larry and held my finger up to stop her. She folded her arms across her chest and rolled her eyes but didn't say anything else.

"What's up?" I answered.

"Khalid, your boy's sister is a genius," Larry said excitedly.

I frowned. "My boy who?"

"Your boy Tommy! His sister Toni just saved us a bunch of fucking money."

I perked up at hearing that. "Oh, yeah? How?" I asked as I took off my shoes.

"She was here waiting on her brother and heard me complaining about the campaign budget. You know it was almost nonexistent until you came back. Then, once you started rising in the polls again, the Democratic party decided to pour funds back into your campaign."

I chuckled as Nisa began to unbutton on my shirt. "Of course."

"So, here I am trying to figure out just how we're going to spend the money and where, and she asks me if she could look over the budget. No lie, less than twenty minutes later, she had everything figured out *and* saved us thousands of dollars, which she suggested we donate to the recovery for the rest of the victims."

I couldn't stop the smile that spread across my face. "Toni is very smart. You know she's in school for finance and works at PNC Bank."

Nisa stopped unbuttoning my shirt and glared at me angrily.

"Well, she needs to come fucking work for us. Do you know how many points that fund will score us with both the Democratic party and the voters? Everyone will be on our side. It's like a win-win for you all, thanks to her!"

"Yeah, that was a great idea," I admitted. "I gotta call and thank her."

"You do that. I have a feeling that thanks to her, we will definitely be calling you Senator King."

I smiled again at the sound of that as we ended the call. I started to call Toni but decided I would do something nice for her, just the two of us. We were always around each other, but it usually involved Tommy in some way. I wanted this to be personal.

"I hope you don't think you calling that bitch while I'm standing right here." Nisa's voice brought me back to the present.

"First of all, if I wanted to call my friend and thank her for saving me money, then that's what I'll do. You don't control who I talk to or when I talk to them."

"I do when it comes to her. You keep passing her off as a friend, but I know better, Khalid." She folded her arms across her chest and glared at me. "I've seen how you look at her. It's the same way you used to look at Amber."

Usually, my heart plunged at the mention of the only woman I had ever loved. I had never really gotten over the way she was brutally murdered by a bullet that was never meant for her. Nisa knew that. But at the moment, I knew Nisa was just throwing her name out there to get a reaction out of me, same as she always did.

"I haven't fucked that girl or anything. She is just a friend."

"But you want to."

"No, what I want to do is learn from her. She just saved me a bunch of fucking money and figured out a way to get everyone on my side despite what just happened. I didn't even have to ask her to help me."

Nisa snaked her neck. "And you have to ask me?"

"I don't, but it's different. You aren't teaching me things that I can't learn out in the streets. I'm trying to move beyond that shit, Nisa."

She laughed hysterically. "Khalid, who are you trying to fool, baby? Sitting up here tryna be somebody you're not. It's like you forgot that the only reason you're even running for senator in the first place is to keep selling the drugs that your uncle Jamar supplied them politicians with. You don't really give a fuck about helping the people or making a difference. If you did, you wouldn't keep supplying them with narcotics. Get the fuck outta here with that bullshit."

I can't even lie, her words stung. She had thrown a few verbal daggers, and they had caused more harm than she could ever imagine. Yes, I wanted to keep the Kings' unlimited power going by continuing to move our weight through our very corrupt political system. Uncle Jamar, my pops' brother, had started it but was forced to stop when he was sent to prison for sexually abusing numerous young girls. When he got to prison, he took the coward's way out and committed suicide, but he didn't take the names of the people he dealt with to the grave with him. Instead, he sent them in a letter to Pops. My mom had already decided I would be groomed to be his successor once she learned of my interest in politics. I was already in the perfect position to take his place anyway, since I was a congressman. It may have been family tradition to keep the drugs flowing to Washington, but I actually did want to make a difference for people. I was more than just a drug dealer, and I thought that the woman I lay next to every night would have known that.

"The fact that you said that just shows that you don't know me at all," I said to her in a calm tone.

Her eyes widened. "Oh, so I'm wrong? You're not a drug dealer?" she asked sarcastically.

"I'm more than that. Way more." I looked at her seriously. "You want me to marry you, but you don't even know who I am. You don't know about my dreams or who I aspire to be."

"Who else can you aspire to be but a drug dealer, Khalid? You're a fucking King! Y'all move weight. It's in your DNA." She laughed again. "You don't see me sitting up here trying to be anything different than who I am."

"And maybe that's the problem." I shook my head. "I have dreams and goals, baby. I told you all about them. But I guess you were too busy trying to rush me down that aisle to listen to them or even care about what I want to do with my life."

"I listened—"

I held my hand up and cut her off. "Naw, you didn't, baby, and that's cool. I'm trying to force you to be somebody that you're not, the same way you're rushing me to be your husband."

"I don't call asking you for a wedding date 'rushing you,'" she retorted, using her fingers to make air quotes. "We're engaged, and we should at least know when we're tying the knot."

"Or you should know, so you can plan a big, fancy-ass wedding full of people who don't care about us anyway."

"If you think I'm letting my wedding day go by without throwing a big party, you snorting that shit you're supposed to be selling."

I nodded my head. The more she spoke, the deeper she dug her own grave. It was amazing that we had lasted this long. "And I've told you over and over that I don't want all that shit. Marriage isn't about the wedding. It's about two people working to become one. I don't need all that fancy shit to love you the rest of my life."

"Well, I do!"

"I know you do," I agreed. "We want separate things. And that's why we should just end this shit now."

She looked at me with wide eyes, surprised. "What?" she asked in disbelief.

"You want me to be somebody that I'm not," I went on like she hadn't said a word. "You want the violent drug kingpin. That's Keon; that ain't me. You want the flashy nigga. That's Keon too; that ain't me. Shit, I let you pick out this penthouse, and this ain't even my style for real. I don't need all of this. It's way too fancy for me," I confessed.

"Khalid, you don't know what you're saying," she said as she came to me and wrapped her arms around my neck. "Just because I want a big wedding doesn't make me a bad person. That's just what I want."

I removed her arms from around me. "Did you hear everything else I said? I'm not content to just be a drug dealer my whole fucking life. I have bigger plans and goals for myself. You don't believe in me, so it's time to let you go."

"I never said I didn't believe in you."

"That's exactly what you said." I grabbed a few suits from my closet, put them in a garment bag along with some underclothes, and headed toward the front door.

"Where are you going?" she yelled as she chased after me.

I turned to face her. "I'm leaving. Something I should have done a long time ago. You can have the penthouse and all this fancy shit I never wanted anyway. But me and you, we're done." I opened the door and walked away from her, feeling like a new man.

Chapter Twelve

Rallo

"Damn, Rallo, you stopped again?"

I panted, out of breath, as I leaned over and put my hands on my knees. "Fuck you, nigga," I said in between breaths.

Armani, my younger brother, stopped jogging and stood beside me with a smirk. "Come on now. You hit me up tryna get in shape, old man. I told you that you wasn't ready for me to train you. Come on. Let's sit down so ya old ass can get it together," he said with a laugh as he led me to park benches right across from us.

I sat down and immediately felt relieved.

Armani passed me a water bottle. "What you tryna get in shape for anyway? You probably the unhealthiest nigga I know. From shootouts to fucking mad bitches raw, all you do is engage in unhealthy behavior," he joked.

I chuckled at that. "I'm tryna change. You know Shaterra having the baby in a few months, and I wanna show her I'm living a better lifestyle. She ain't really fucking with me too heavy right now."

Armani sipped from his water bottle and nodded his head. "You buy her something nice?"

"Everybody ain't got it like you, Mr. Football Star," I told him, only half joking.

Me and Armani weren't biological brothers, but that shit meant nothing to me. My stepfather, Leo, was his real father. Armani's mom, Marilyn, was the complete opposite of mine. She was a dentist and was able to afford to give Armani the life that I dreamed of having all on her own. Her downfall had been fucking with a street nigga like Leo when she was fresh out of college, but when she realized he wasn't going to change and square up, she moved on from him real quick. Meanwhile my mother, Rita, was an old fling of Leo's. They had always had an on-off relationship, but when Marilyn pushed Leo to the curb and my pops ran out on us, it seemed that they came back together for good.

Leo made sure that I knew who his only son was and brought Armani around all the time. Armani grew up in a life of privilege, so he was always excited when he got to come to the hood. It was like an adventure for him. However, Leo didn't teach him the rules about surviving on the streets like he had with me. It was like he sensed I was destined for the gutter, while Armani would go on to become one of the greatest wide receivers in the history of college football. I never had any malice against him for that, either. Rita wasn't interested in making sure I played sports or stayed active, and honestly speaking, being an athlete wasn't my thing. I watched sports all day but didn't like to play them. So, when Leo placed a gun in my hand and a football in Armani's, it just made sense to me.

Armani shook his head. "I ain't a football star. Just playing the game I love."

"Save that shit for the press," I told him. "I ain't gone hold you. I hit you to work out, but there's something else I need from you."

"Get the fuck outta here," Armani said sarcastically.

I chose to ignore the sarcasm in his voice. "I need to know everything you know about her family," I said as I held my phone out and showed him the picture of Kenya that Rick had sent me.

He looked at it, smiled, then looked back at me. "What you need to know about my girl?"

"I need to know about her family," I repeated. "How she moves, how they move, where they do drop offs, pickups, all that."

Armani frowned. "Why you need to know that? And how would I know how they run all those funeral homes? I don't care about none of that shit."

I laughed at his naïve attitude. "Don't tell me you think they got all that fucking money from them funeral homes."

He shrugged. "I know they have other businesses and shit, but yeah, I figured they made it from those. If you didn't notice, there's a few King Funeral Homes in every major city up and down the East Coast."

"Nigga, the money they make from them homes can't even pay their bills for a month," I said. "They're drug dealers. They sell weight. And I need to know who the top players are in their organization and where they keep that shit."

Armani looked at me with a shocked expression. "You sure about that? I met them, and they don't seem like—"

"Look, the whole family some hustlers." I cut him off again. "I don't know what your girl does, or if she does anything, but she's a King, so I wouldn't put it past her. I need to know what they're doing at all times. Shit, maybe we can even kidnap your girl for some ransom money," I joked.

"You ain't kidnapping Kenya," he snapped at me.

"If I don't come into some money soon, ain't no telling what I might do," I shot back at him. "I wouldn't give a fuck about snatching that bitch and dropping her body parts on their doorstep just to make a point. Now, you be around them niggas enough. I need you to act as my inside man."

Armani stood up and shook his head. "Naw. I can't do that for you, bro."

I stood up too. "Fuck you mean you can't do this for me? I know you ain't 'bout to pick that bitch over your family."

"First of all, my lady ain't nobody's bitch," he snapped at me with way more bass in his voice than I ever heard him use. "Second, I can't be caught up in none of that bullshit you tryna pull. I got too much going on in my life to risk it all for some street shit that has nothing to do with me."

"Too much going on." I laughed. "Sorry, superstar, everybody don't get a chance to play college ball and get offered a chance in the NFL."

"I wasn't offered a damn thing. Anything I got, I worked hard for it," he said seriously.

"And you saying I don't?"

"I'm saying you go about getting it the wrong way," he said flatly. "Listen, I love you. Blood couldn't make us no closer. I don't want to see you end up like my pops, Ray. He taught you everything he knew, and look, none of that saved him. Your kids need you, and if the Kings are doing it as big as you say they are, then going after them is a suicide mission."

I was tired of hearing that. "I will never be scared of any nigga that bleeds like me," I told him seriously. "Now, I hate that you can't get down with me on this because if you were to help me, it would save a lot of lives. But since you can't, or rather you *won't*, then any blood shed will be on your hands. Can you live with that, superstar?"

"Ain't a damn thing gone be on my hands 'cause this has nothing to do with me." Armani placed his hand on my shoulder. "Listen, you don't gotta do nothing crazy. If everything goes right, this time next year, I'll be in the NFL. I can bring you on as my assistant or my security guard and pay you a great salary, bro. You don't gotta go out here and do whatever it is you tryin' to do."

I brushed his hand off my shoulder like it stank. "I'm a man. I don't take no muthafuckin' handouts. I'm sick of waiting on other niggas for my chance to eat. I offered to do this the peaceful way, but since you don't wanna help, I gotta do what I gotta do. Don't say I ain't warn you."

I walked away after that. There was nothing left to be said. I had done enough homework on the Kings to know enough of their capos. I would have rather cut the head so the body would follow, but I had no problem putting in work to get what I felt was long overdue to me.

Chapter Thirteen

Kenya

"Ms. King. Good to see you as always," the Democratic presidential candidate, Rod Collins, greeted me as I stepped into his office.

"Likewise," I said with a smile as I laid my briefcase on the table. I set my oversized Gucci hobo bag beside it as well. "I come bearing gifts."

"Gifts?" he asked in surprise with a raised eyebrow.

I nodded and pulled a large bag full of Xanax out of my bag. "We just got plugged with these, and as a gift to our most loyal customers, we're throwing in a few as samples. These are the highest dosage of Xannys out right now, and very, very hard to get."

"But of course, the Kings have them."

I smirked. "Of course."

Rod accepted the bag as we switched our briefcases. "And I made the list as one of your most loyal customers? That's a first."

I chuckled. "Well, let's just say that this time around, you earned it." I winked at him and picked up the briefcase, prepared to walk out of his office, when he called my name and stopped me in my tracks.

"Kenya."

I turned to face him. "Yes, Mr. Collins?"

"Have you given any thought to what your future may hold?"

The question caught me off guard, so I shrugged. "Sometimes. Figured I'd stay in the family business."

He looked at me doubtfully. "Now, why would you do that?"

My phone vibrated in my bag. I reached down to grab it, saw that it was Armani, and silenced it. He had been calling since I got to the capitol building in Harrisburg. I couldn't afford to talk to him and be thrown off guard.

"It's tradition," I said with another shrug.

He snorted. "I wouldn't advise you to do that."

"And why not? It seemed to work out well for you," I pointed out. Rod Collins had grown up on a meth farm. He still sold the meth his family made and was very rich because of it.

He walked toward me and stopped right in front of me. "I want you to listen to me and hear the words that I'm about to say to you, all right?"

I nodded.

"Staying in the family business worked out well for me because I am *me,* Kenya. It doesn't matter what I did or what my family does. As a white man in America, I have privileges that an African American man doesn't have, and as far as an African American woman? Forget about it. Most white people would like to ignore our privilege, but I acknowledge it. It would be plain ignorant of me to act as if it didn't exist."

I didn't see where he was going with this. "Well, I don't want a political career, so I'll be fine."

"It's not about wanting a career in politics. It's about being who you were destined to be. You walk through these doors, and I see so much potential in you. You're young and smart. That's why I make sure I give you a little bonus every time we meet. I want you to realize that you need to make a way to get out. I did, but you're going to have to work twice as hard. You're a double minority in a world designed for white men to win." This time, he shrugged and walked back over to his desk. "The next time you come here, I want to see you with a business plan."

I scrunched up my face. "A business plan?"

"Yes. You need goals outside of your family if you want to succeed." He picked up the bag of Xanax. "I think I'll sample the merchandise on these. Have a good day, Ms. King. I'll be talking to you soon."

"Likewise," I told him before walking out of his office.

As I followed behind Carlos, one of my family's soldiers whose main duties were to drive me throughout the tristate area to deliver drugs to all the top politicians and chiefs of police, I couldn't help but think over his words. No one had ever talked to me like that before. I graduated from high school a few months back and had no idea what I wanted to do. I was into clothes and fashion but didn't know the first thing about sketching any clothing and never wanted to go to any design school. I was lost on what I was supposed to do with my life. At least working for my family gave me some sort of direction.

When I got into the back seat of the Lincoln Navigator, I popped open the briefcase. Rows and rows of money stared back at me, with the usual manila envelope resting on top of it. Out of all the politicians I saw, Rod was the only one who consistently gave me a large amount of money separate from what I was already making. I put his money in the stash. For some reason, this very successful white man seemed determined to look after me, and I didn't understand why. I didn't fight it, though. Rod could very well be the next President of the United States, and to be close to him was something money couldn't buy.

As Carlos drove off, I finally pulled my phone out to call Armani back. I grimaced at the sight of all the missed calls from him. Lately, he had been tripping and overreacting if he couldn't get in touch with me. I wasn't sure why, but I decided to dead whatever had made him so insecure in the first place.

I loosened my hair from the bun I wore and shook it free. Then I unbuttoned the top couple of buttons of the plain white blouse I had on underneath the blue fitted blazer I wore. Each time I came to Harrisburg, I dressed the part of a young politician so that I could fit in. I even had a strand of pearls around my neck.

I FaceTimed him, and he answered before the first ring went through.

"Kenya, where are you?" he asked shortly.

"Just leaving a board of directors meeting for the funeral homes, baby." I pouted my lips and poked my chest out a little more as I angled my phone better so that he could see everything I was showing.

Either he was uninterested or supremely annoyed because he didn't seem to notice. "Meet me at McCormick and Schmick's in a half hour so we can grab something to eat."

A half hour? Harrisburg was five hours away from Pittsburgh on a good day. I bit my lip, almost forgetting that we were on FaceTime.

"What's wrong? You ain't hungry?" he asked in a knowing tone.

"I am. It's just that it might take me a while to get there because—"

"Because there was no board of directors meeting. Right?"

I wanted to keep lying, but I was so tired of doing that. I knew I wasn't supposed to let Armani know who I really was or what I really did, but I also didn't want to risk losing him. Being with him made me happier than I had been in a long time. But could I betray my family's trust for that happiness?

"There was, but I gotta go help Dionne move, babe. Her grandma put her out, and she has nowhere else to go."

He still looked skeptical but didn't protest right away. He knew how close Dionne and I were. I would drop everything and help her if she needed it, and he couldn't be mad that I would.

"Kenya." He said my name slowly. "You know you can tell me anything, right?"

"Yes."

"A'ight. It's my job to protect you. If you're doing some shit I know nothing about, then I can't do my job. You understand that, baby?"

"I do."

"Good." He smiled and finally seemed to notice what I had on. "Damn, baby. You was in the meeting dressed like that?"

I laughed. "No! I just did this when I called you. I wanted to remind you of what you were missing."

He gave that sexy smile that turned me the fuck on. "I'm always missing you, babe. I'll show you." He lowered the camera slowly so that I could take in his muscular chest and six-pack abs before moving it down even farther. He pulled his dick out slowly and deliberately so that I could get a good look at it. My mouth watered at the sight of it. It was long, thick, and just as beautiful as the rest of him. And I took all of it faithfully. My clit thumped a little in anticipation, as if my kitty knew I was staring at her owner.

"Mmm," I moaned involuntarily like he was right there touching me.

"Hurry up and finish with Dionne, baby. Then come straight over here."

I promised him that I would before we hung up. After we did, I laid my head against the soft leather of the truck and closed my eyes with a smile on my lips. Meeting Armani Collins was unexpected, but I was so glad that I had. I hadn't had a boyfriend since I caught my high school boyfriend cheating on me the year before we graduated. Armani was showing me that Chris had been child's play. He was the real deal, and I was lucky to have him. I knew a million bitches were waiting to take my spot.

Yet, I wondered if he would leave me if he ever found out what I was doing. The conversation we'd just had was different, like he was on to me. We were so new that I wasn't sure how he would react. I decided to cross that bridge when I came to it.

Chapter Fourteen

Toni

I rushed into Muddy Waters, an oyster bar right up the block from my job at PNC Bank. Khalid had been asking me to let him take me to lunch for weeks, and I had finally given in.

I was about five minutes late because my business had been booming quite unexpectedly. Although the anniversary dinner for Khalid's parents had ended in a disaster, I had made out pretty well. I got plenty of business cards from people who wanted to discuss their portfolios. That following Monday, I had followed up with them, and before I knew it, I was being paid to advise them on how to spend their money, how to save it, and where to put it. Plus, since I looked over the budget for Khalid's campaign, his campaign manager, Larry, had been begging me to work for them.

"Hey, beautiful," he greeted me when I reached the table where he was sitting. He stood up to hug me, and I got lost in his embrace the same way I always did. Something about being in his arms soothed the hell out of me, so much so that I never wanted to leave them. Plus, he always smelled great and looked even better.

"Hey," I said warmly, pulling back slightly to look in his eyes.

Khalid was the finest man I had ever seen. He had the smoothest chocolate skin that made me just want to taste him, long dreads that I yearned to pull on while making love to him, and warm, dark eyes that pierced my soul every time I stared into them. But my very favorite part about him was his smile. He had perfect white teeth and deep dimples. God had taken His time when He made him for sure.

But my attraction to him wasn't only because of the way he looked. Khalid had a heart of gold. When all those young lives were taken, he'd made sure each one had gotten a burial fit for a king at their funeral homes. He had also visited each and every injury victim and taken care of their hospital bills. And when it came to my brother Tommy, his insistence on me transferring him to a private facility run by top-notch physicians was literally the difference between life and death for him. He had broken down my barriers, forcing me to trust him. And I did.

Yeah, he was perfect in every way, which was why it made perfect sense for him to be engaged. A man like him would never be single.

He stroked my back softly, still looking into my eyes. "How is work?"

"Busy as ever. That's why I'm late."

He shrugged. "It didn't matter how late you were. I would have waited for you."

I wasn't really sure how to take his words. Our friendship definitely had flirtatious undertones, but for the most part, we'd kept it platonic. At first, I didn't believe that someone like him would be interested in a woman like me. I wasn't really his type. I was pretty in the face with a size sixteen waist, and while that never mattered to me or any other guy I dealt with, I knew that men like Khalid usually attracted the model type of females, the ones like Nisa who were always drop dead gorgeous and never had a hair out of place. I wasn't one of them and figured he was out of my league. Yet, over the last few months, he made it clear that he was interested, and while I was flattered, I refused to become a side chick to him.

"Is that right?" I asked him with a smile.

"You know it is." He pulled away from me and went to pull out my chair. I sat down, and he pushed me in gently before going back to his own seat.

"I'm surprised to see you're free for lunch," I told him. "I figured we'd talk later at the office."

He reached across the table and took my hands in his. "I'm tired of using business as a way to see you," he said bluntly.

I raised my eyebrow. I wasn't expecting that. "Oh, really?"

"Yes, really." He was about to continue, but the waitress came and took our order. I ordered the Louisiana lobster roll while he opted for the seafood gumbo. He also requested a bottle of Krug rosé champagne.

I looked at him in shock when she walked away. "Khalid, you know I can't drink like that right now. I gotta get back to work."

He rubbed his thumb along the back of my hand, making my whole body tingle. "I want you to work for me."

I snatched my hand back quickly. I should have known that he wouldn't really call me here for no reason. "So, that's what all this is about?" I snapped, a little more angrily than I should have. I couldn't help it. I had thought that he wanted to actually see me. I felt foolish.

He looked confused. "Huh? Why would this be about you working for me? I been asking you to have lunch with me before you helped Larry."

I calmed down once I realized he did have a good point. He had been persistent about getting some of my time for a while now. I was the one always using work as an excuse. I didn't want to fall for him—more than I already was.

"You're right, I just—"

He held his hand up to cut me off. "You're so stubborn, Toni. I get that it's hard for you to trust people, but damn. Haven't I proved to you by now that I'm worth it?"

I felt bad upon hearing his words. He had done nothing but be generous since he met me, and all I'd given him in return was bullshit. "You have. I know I can be difficult—"

"As hell." He grabbed my hands again. "But you're worth it, too. You see I'm still here."

I nodded.

"I think it should be obvious by now that I'm tryna fuck wit' you," he went on. "I'm tired of beating around the bush about this shit. I been wanting you for a while now, ever since the first time I saw you in Tommy's hospital room. And I think you feeling me too, even though you be tryin' to fight it every chance you get."

I laughed slightly because he was right. I did try to deny that I wanted him, but it was only to protect my heart. I knew that he had the power to break it. I couldn't allow that to happen.

"I fought it because you're engaged to someone. And much as I like you, I don't want to become anyone's side chick or mistress."

He smiled that smile I loved so much. "What if I told you that I wasn't engaged anymore? Would you fuck with me then?"

I looked at him with wide eyes. I knew good and got damn well that Nisa hadn't walked away from him. "Are you serious?"

"As a heart attack. I left her, Toni. I should have done it a long time ago, but I guess I was just . . . used to her. Our families have always been close, and after Amber, it just seemed like the right move to make. I didn't want anyone that wasn't familiar with me to get caught up in my life and my bullshit. Nisa was familiar territory to me, and even though I was never in love with her, she seemed to be the safe choice." He stared at me seriously. "And then I met you. And you make me feel . . . alive again. Meeting you felt like completing a puzzle that I didn't even know was incomplete. Whenever I'm around you, I just feel . . . man, I don't know, just good as hell. I want to return the favor to you, give you what you've given me."

"You've done so much for me and Tommy, Khalid. You don't have to give us anything else," I assured him.

The waitress came with champagne, an ice bucket, and two champagne flutes. She popped it open, poured each of us a glass, and walked away just as fast as she had come.

"What if I just want to make you feel good?" he asked genuinely. "Why can't you just accept that? Quit fighting me on everything and let me do what I want to do for you."

I bit my lip before asking, "Why me? You can have anyone you want. What is it about me? I'm boring, I'm basic. I go to work and come home. I'm not out here like that. I'm not a diva."

"First of all, there's nothing boring about you, and you're far from basic. It's everything about you. It's your independence, even though it drives me fucking crazy 'cause you won't let me do anything for you," he said as he shook his head.

We both had to laugh at that one. We had definitely gone back and forth about everything. Khalid was so giving, and I was so reluctant to take.

"It's your energy, your vibe. They're just unmatched. You have a good soul, love. I love how good it feels to just be around you in your aura. You're genuine in a world full of fake. You're a good person, which is why I never stepped to you the way I wanted to when I was with Nisa. Bad as I wanted you, I knew you deserved more than half a man. I would never even try to give you that."

I raised my eyebrow slightly. "And now?"

"Now you can have all of me." He looked at me seriously again. "Listen, there's a lot going on for me right now. They saying I should pretty much win the election for senator. I need someone smart and who has my best interests at heart by my side when that happens. You trimming the budget like that without me even having to ask lets me know that you're the right one. I want you to be the Michelle to my Barack, baby," he said with a goofy grin.

I chuckled. "Oh, really? You think I can be her?"

"*We* can be *them*," he corrected me. "As good a leader as Obama was, he always reminds us that he wouldn't have been shit without Michelle. And as great as my journey has been to this point, it can only get better with you, baby."

I bit my lip as I thought over what he was really saying to me. It all sounded good, but a part of me was scared to death to fully let him inside. Growing up with no parents, it had always been my brother and me against the world until my grandmother took us in. The feeling of abandonment I'd had since childhood had only intensified when she passed away. Everyone I had loved, with the exception of Tommy, had always broken my heart and let me down.

I hadn't even dated much. I mean, yeah, I'd had a few guys I kicked it with when the mood hit, but I was too scared of getting too close to any of them, so none of them ever went too far, and that was the way I preferred it. Now, here was this man, asking me to let him in. By all accounts, he had shown me that he cared about me. I was scared of the depth of my feelings for him without actually dealing with him in a romantic way. The intense chemistry between us scared me. It had been there since day one, and I had successfully managed to act like it didn't exist.

"Why are you even acting like this is something to think about?" Khalid said, sounding exasperated. "This is us. You and me. Now that Nisa is out the way, we can quit pretending like shit ain't what it has been with us from day one." He smiled and leaned over the table. "Come here," he commanded gently.

I leaned over the table, too. We were so close I could smell the mint he'd eaten on his breath. He kissed my lips gently, and when I didn't pull away, he did it again, with a little more force. Then he cupped my face in his hands and kissed me one final time before stroking my cheek and leaning back in his chair. He picked up his champagne flute and looked at me. I was so turned on by that gesture of affection that it took me a minute to sit back in my seat. When I did, I picked up my champagne flute as well.

"I think you need more convincing, and I get it," he said as he took a sip.

I shook my head. After all he had done, I didn't want to seem ungrateful, but I couldn't act like I wasn't worried that he really wasn't over Nisa. "I don't want to be your rebound," I said honestly.

He smirked. "She was the rebound. You are a new beginning."

I took a deep breath. Khalid was every woman's dream, and here I was consistently turning him down. Something had to be wrong with me. "Well, okay. Let's give it a shot."

He smiled, and my panties got moist. "It's 'bout time you agreed. Quit fighting me on everything," he repeated with a laugh. "I will never steer you wrong."

"I already know that."

"Good. Now, take the rest of the day off. I'll give you double what you would have made for today. I want us to spend the day together, just you and me. No campaign, no work, no Tommy as an excuse to be around each other. Just me and you. Can we do that?"

I started to say that no, we couldn't, but I couldn't act like that didn't sound intriguing. We used everything else as an excuse to be around each other when all we really wanted to do was spend time together.

I nodded and sipped my champagne again. "Okay. We can do that. Now I know why you got that Krug in the middle of the day. You knew exactly what you were doing."

He chuckled. "It was time for me to celebrate getting out of something and pursuing something new. I just know what I want."

This time, it was me who smirked. "And that's me?"

He bit his lip and looked at me intensely. "It's always been you."

I didn't have anything else left to say. And for once, I was okay with that. It was time for me to scoot over to the passenger seat for a change. I had found a driver who I could trust.

Chapter Fifteen

Khalia

"Took, you know you don't have to drive me to this party," I told him as I hopped into his truck. He had volunteered to take me to my parents' place in North Huntington. Keon had convinced my mother that Nahim's birthday party should be held at the mansion. I honestly don't know how he talked her into it. When we were younger, our birthday parties were always planned by my father. Since he loved to cook, he would cater them on his own. Whenever we didn't have big parties, we would go on big trips. My favorite was on Khalid's and my thirteenth birthday. My parents took us to Montego Bay, Jamaica, for a week of nothing but beach, sand, palm trees, excursions, and jerk chicken. Ever since then, no matter where I went, Jamaica was always my favorite place in the world.

"I did. I hardly get to see you anymore, Boss Lady," he said with a grin as he drove.

I smiled slightly. "Been a little busy lately. My fault, Took."

He paused for a moment. "Can I say something to you, Boss Lady?"

I frowned at the fact that he felt he even had to ask. Although Tookie had been my driver and bodyguard for years, he was more like family than an employee. "You can say anything to me. You know that."

"This new man in your life, does he make you happy?"

I blushed slightly that I had been so transparent. I thought I had been low with Drew, but I guess not. "How you know about him?"

"I was born at night, but not last night," he joked as a smile stretched across his otherwise stoic face. "For as tough as you are, you're still a woman. And every woman wants to be loved. The reason I'm asking is because I know if you're fucking with a nigga, he don't know who you are. You too scared a man that knows you will lose respect for you if you cross that line."

I nodded. "We both know that's the truth, though. Why should a nigga listen to me if he can fuck me?"

"You are untouchable, Boss Lady. Ain't no denying that. But if he makes you happy, you should let him get to know all of you. If he run, fuck him."

I took a deep breath and looked out the window. "He ain't part of the life, Took. He's a civilian. Works a nine-to-five and all that. What I look like bringing a civilian into this life? You see what happened when Khalid did that with Amber. He lost her and their baby." I shook my head. I always felt responsible for the loss of Amber and my unborn nephew. A bullet that had been meant for me had taken her life, and although I shot back immediately, it had done nothing to save her or the baby. It was something I would always carry with me.

"I know, and that was fucked up. I remember what that did to you. But if you tell him and he run, he ain't the nigga for you. And if he don't, then—"

Tookie was cut off by a hail of gunfire. I watched in horror as a bullet pierced his neck. Blood spurted everywhere as he slumped to the side, losing control of the Range Rover. They were still shooting, so I couldn't hop into the front to take over. The truck steered onto a sidewalk and hit a fire hydrant before stopping completely.

Holding Down a Cartel King: Part 2

"Fuck!" I roared in anger as I pulled a pistol from my waist. I remained low as more shots were fired into the truck. It was a miracle that not one bullet hit me. Once they stopped, I heard footsteps approaching us, just as I expected them to. I hurriedly grabbed Took's gun from his waist, kicked the door open with my Jimmy Choo stilettos like they were Timberland boots, and started firing. The first two men were dead before they knew what hit them. The other door behind me flung open, and I fired on him just as fast. My bullet met its mark right in the middle of his forehead. I took a second to take a breath before getting out of the car and crouching as low as I could on the ground. I heard sirens in the background and knew I needed to get the hell out of dodge, but not before I knew that whoever had killed Tookie was joining him in the afterlife.

"That bitch killed Rick!" I heard a man's voice yell out in agony.

I had no idea which one of the three dead niggas on the ground was Rick, and I didn't give a fuck. I moved slowly around the side of the truck toward the voices.

"We gotta get the fuck outta here, Rallo!" another voice yelled.

Rallo? The name sounded familiar, but I couldn't place it immediately. It didn't matter. I shot the closest one to me and watched in satisfaction as his head split like a watermelon. The other took off running and hopped into blue Malibu, but not before I put hot lead in the back of his leg. It was the best I could do. I was pissed that one had gotten away.

I stood and surveyed the damage that was done. Four niggas lay with their faces blown halfway off, and while I would usually be proud of my handiwork, I felt nothing but overwhelming rage at what they had taken from me. All those bitch niggas combined would never equal one Tookie.

I grabbed my bag and any personal belongings out of the back of Tookie's truck, and then looked at him again. His eyes were still wide open in surprise as he lay there lifeless. It was the saddest thing I had ever seen, and it made my anger triple. "I'ma get them niggas, Took. I promise," I swore as I left the scene quickly. For a second, I was lost on who to contact. I went to Tookie for absolutely everything.

I called Grimm, another trusted lieutenant for my family, and gave him my location. Then I stood in the shadows and shed tears for the first time in years. I couldn't remember the last time I let myself cry, but the loss of Tookie was devastating. And just like Amber, it was all my fault.

Chapter Sixteen

Kelvin

I hadn't been around my family much since the anniversary party, and I had to admit I missed them all. I missed Kenya's innocent smile, Khalia's determined attitude, Khalid's suave personality, and Keon's no-nonsense ways. I didn't care whose blood ran through Keon's veins. I had been there for him since Dutchess told me she was pregnant with him. He was my son, and nobody could ever tell me any differently.

It was my grandson's birthday party, and although I knew it could be dangerous for me to show my face, I had never missed a moment in my grandchildren's lives, and I wasn't about to start now.

I was about to walk out the penthouse door when Nisa came walking down the hallway, her feet slapping against the marble floor. For the first time since I'd known her, she looked less than perfect. She wore baggy black sweatpants and an old Pitt college T-shirt of Khalid's. Her hair was all over her head, and bags appeared under her eyes.

"Nisa, are you sick?" I asked her, concerned.

She shook her head and held her arms across her stomach. "Mr. Kelvin, have you talked to Khalid?"

I hesitated before answering. Khalid had texted me that he had left Nisa and was moving out just the other day. I'd been so busy trying to get The King's Palace up and running and looking for a place of my own that I'd barely had time to respond back to him.

"Yeah, I have," I told her.

"Well, did he say when he was coming home?" she asked desperately.

"We talked business, Nisa."

"Oh." She looked away like a lost little girl, and I almost felt sorry for her, seeing her in such a vulnerable state. I knew that she loved my son, but I also knew she wasn't right for him.

I left without another word. The closer I got to the estate I shared with Dutchess, the more nervous I became. The last time I saw Khalia and Keon, they had been ready to kill me. Dutchess was in love with another man, and I couldn't control how angry I got whenever I thought of how she had betrayed me. Kenya and Khalid were my only saving graces in this situation.

Still, I had as much right to attend this birthday party as anyone else. We were still a family, no matter what we were going through, and I had put just as much work into getting this house as Dutchess did. It was still mine.

I pulled into the circular driveway and parked. There were many cars there, but that was to be expected. Dutchess didn't entertain much, but when she did, she liked to show out. I grabbed my grandson's birthday card and walked through the home's double doors that I loved so much.

From the first step inside, I looked around and realized how much I missed my home. I decided then and there that I wasn't staying another night at Khalid's. I was coming home until I found something I loved just as much as this house. Shit, he wasn't even there.

Dutchess was coming from the back, and for a moment, we just stared at each other. Dutchess had always been a beautiful woman, and that day, she wore a royal blue and yellow sundress that hugged her in all the right places, making her more beautiful than ever. It was what attracted me to her all those years ago and a part of what kept me with her.

"Kelvin. I knew you would come," she said with a warm smile. "All the guests are out back."

"I'm not a guest in my own home, Dutchess."

"Your home?" she asked with a raised eyebrow. "You left me and this house, remember?"

"I left you so that you could be with Vincent," I corrected her.

She looked away for a second. "I never wanted to be with Vincent," she lied.

"Yes, you did. You always did. It was just that with street politics being what they are, there was no place for you in that white man's world. He couldn't take you home to La Cosa Nostra. So, you decided to marry the only man dumb enough to look past who you really were. I understand."

She shook her head. "I really do love you, whether you believe it or not. I may not have shown it the right way, but it was always there. You gotta believe me."

I held my hand up. "I don't have to believe a damn thing you say to me, and I don't. I still want the divorce, but I will be coming back home till I find a place."

She folded her arms and looked at me. "And how are we going to divorce if you're still under this roof? I didn't sign those fucking papers, Kelvin. And I'm not signing any other papers that you send. We can get through this."

"You love another man and lied to me about my son, Dutchess. Why the fuck would I want to get through anything with you?" I shot back. I was shocked by her audacity, but I shouldn't have been.

"Kelvin, just listen to me."

I backed away from her like she had the coronavirus as she walked closer to me. "Is my grandson out back?"

Before she could answer, the front door opened, and Khalia strutted in. Usually, her walk alone could command a room, but it wasn't her stride that drew my eyes to my eldest daughter. As always, she was dressed to impressed, but I noticed that her one-piece light pink outfit had specks of blood all over it. Her nude Jimmy Choo heels were also splattered with blood.

"Baby girl, what happened?" I asked, my voice full of concern.

At the same time, one of the workers from out back ran into the house. "Ms. Dutchess, you might want to come out here. Nahim's mother is causing a big scene."

Dutchess frowned. "What? Keon gave strict orders that she's not even allowed on the premises. Who let her in here?"

The worker shrugged her shoulders.

Dutchess sighed, then looked back at us. "Make sure she's okay, Kelvin. I'll be back."

I frowned and was about to call out that I didn't need her assistance to look after my daughter, but one more look at Khalia made me swallow those words. She appeared visibly shaken, and for her, that spoke volumes. Nothing rattled her.

"Let's go get you cleaned up, baby girl," I said to her.

She looked at me, her eyes big and sad as I took her hand. As l led her up the stairs, I didn't see the feared murderer that everyone knew her as. I didn't see the queenpin Dutchess had made her out to be. I only saw my baby girl, my first daughter, who had stolen my heart from the very first moment I laid eyes on her.

Khalia went to her old bedroom. All the kids' rooms were the same as they had been when they lived at home. Their closets still had shoes and clothes in them.

"I need you to strip out of everything you have on. You know the routine," I told her as I grabbed an old laundry bag from the side of her dresser.

She stepped out of her six-inch heels and appeared even smaller before me. "Can I trust you to get rid of all this?" she asked me in a low voice.

I understood why she had asked the question, but it still broke my heart nonetheless. "Baby girl, you have to know that I would never turn you or anyone in this family over to the feds. You gotta trust me on that."

"I don't know what to trust or believe anymore, Daddy. The FBI burst in, and then you were gone . . ."

I bit my lip. "Your Uncle Keith told me that the FBI has been following Vincent Morelli around for months," I lied. I couldn't tell them the truth, that I was the one who insisted on throwing the Mob boss in jail. Keith had just wanted to kill him when he found out the truth.

"I didn't know he was going to be there," I continued. At least that part was the truth. "I came to meet your brother, and when I saw him and Prime there, I couldn't believe it."

"I killed Prime," she said flatly.

I felt bad that the young man had been killed, but I knew it was coming when I saw him there. It had been his involvement with me that caused his senseless murder, among others. I sighed and wiped my hands down my face before looking at Khalia again.

She stood before me, beautiful as ever with her curly hair pulled in a bun, still wearing her pretty pink outfit, stained with blood. It was ironic to me, since that was the way our family was. We appeared to be beautiful and perfect to the world, but we'd built a fortune from blood money, and it also stained our souls.

I went to stand closer to her. "Remember when we used to cook together all the time?" I asked her.

She grinned. Out of all the kids, it was Khalia who had picked up on my love of cooking. It was the one thing we both enjoyed doing together.

"I loved teaching you my recipes, how to present any meal just right. You copied my every move but always had to add your own touch to it. I would just watch you and think of how original you were. How you would always move to the beat of your own drum. Those were my favorite moments with you."

She looked at me fondly. "Mine too."

"One year, we made a big brunch for the whole family for Dutchess's birthday. You and Khalid couldn't have been more than ten years old. Anyway, when we were setting the table, you asked me why I liked to cook so much and why Dutchess never cooked. You even told me that it was the woman's job to cook. You were very bold like that, even then."

She chuckled. "I remember asking you that. And you told me that people take care of the people they love in different ways. You said that everyone has a role to play and a job to do."

"That's right." I nodded. "And later on, when you cut yourself trying to slice that mango that I told you to save for me . . ."

We both laughed at that one. Khalia had insisted on slicing the fruit, although I told her she couldn't use such a sharp knife just yet. She had done it anyway while I loaded the waffles in a serving pan, and she cut herself pretty deeply.

"Anyway, that day when I cleaned you up and bandaged your wound, you told me that you were glad that my job was taking care of you." I looked at her lovingly. "I never stopped taking care of you, baby girl. Ever. The things I did were never to harm you. I just don't want us to be involved in this life anymore. I don't want there to be any more bloodshed or any unnecessary people getting hurt. I want us to be able to walk away from this unscathed with none of us dead or in jail. So yeah, maybe I went about it the wrong way. Maybe I didn't have to take such drastic measures. But I had been asking Dutchess to scale back and move to the legit side of the business for years. I wanted us to live happily ever after. I always wanted what's best for you, and living like this isn't it. I know you're tough enough to handle whatever comes your way, but whatever happened today has you shook. Maybe it's the wake-up call you need."

Khalia looked down at the floor before looking back at me. Then, without warning, she burst into tears. I embraced her while she sobbed, and for a moment, it felt like I had my little girl back. I couldn't remember the last time Khalia had shed a tear, not even when she cut herself. Now, she was too feared to show any signs of weakness, yet the woman in my arms was not the woman the streets knew. She was my baby girl, who Dutchess had forced to grow up too fast.

When she was done, she pulled away and looked at me. "Tookie got killed today," she told me softly.

Now it all made sense. Her dazed expression, the blood on her clothes. "And you were there. That's his blood," I said.

She shook her head. "No, it's not his blood. It's the niggas' that killed him." She stood by the full-length mirror that was right next to us and stared at herself. "I got four of them, but one got away. I gotta get him for what he did to Tookie, but . . ." More tears fell from her eyes. "None of it will bring him back, Daddy. It's like no matter how many niggas I murk for this, nothing will bring him back to me. I feel the same way I felt when them niggas killed Amber but worse because—" She stopped, and I could see that she was choking on her words as more tears spilled from her eyes like they were broken faucets.

"This is *Tookie*, Daddy," she whispered.

I heard the pain in her voice and embraced her again. When I let her go this time, she stared straight at me. "I think I finally get what you've been trying to tell us about this life. Losing Took, it's crushing me. It feels like I can't breathe. I can't handle feeling like this and never wanna feel like this again." She grabbed the laundry bag out of my hands. "I'll put my clothes in here and set them outside the door while I take a shower."

I nodded. I would take the soiled clothes and shoes to one of the funeral homes and toss them in the crematory to get rid of the evidence forever. I already knew that she had gotten rid of the gun.

Before I left the room, I looked at her once more. I had never seen her look so lost, so sad, so defeated. I knew there were no words I could use to comfort her in this time of need. Tookie had been so much more than an employee to her. He was her right hand. Khalia hardly ever made a move without him right there next to her. I knew that this loss would devastate her, and understandably so. I prayed it would be the turning point she needed to get her life together.

"I'm so sorry for your loss, baby girl," I told her sincerely.

She nodded and wiped her eyes.

"I love you," I said seriously. Ever since Dutchess had decided that Khalia would be the main enforcer of our family, it had damaged our relationship. We weren't nearly as close as we used to be. But she would always be my little girl.

She smiled, and it warmed my heart. "I love you too, Daddy," she said warmly.

Her words tugged at my heart. I hoped it was the beginning of mending our relationship and getting her out of the game for good.

Chapter Seventeen

Kenya

I sat with Dionne and Armani around a table in my back yard at my nephew Nahim's birthday party. Keon got along with his other kids' mothers with no problem, but Stacey was always a problem, so this year, my brother had decided to give him a thirteenth birthday party on his own. Nahim loved the fact that he got two different parties, although he already told me he liked this one better.

"So, bro, I have to tell you I ain't seen my girl smile like this in forever," Dionne said to Armani, a little louder than she needed to, since we were all sitting so close.

Armani grinned. "It's my job to keep her happy," he responded as he scooted his chair closer to mine.

I smiled and kissed him on the lips before looking back at Dionne. I noticed she was a lot more fidgety than usual. She was twirling her fingers, playing with the place setting in front of her, messing with napkins. She just couldn't sit still, and it was so unlike her. I couldn't put my finger on what was wrong with her for the life of me, but I knew it wasn't all good.

"My man does the same thing," Dionne sang. "I can respect a nigga that knows his job is to take care of home."

Armani nodded but glanced sideways, indicating that he, too, had noticed Dionne's odd behavior.

"Speaking of your man, when are we ever gonna be able to meet him?" I asked. Dionne had been going on and on for months about this guy, but no one had yet to lay eyes on him.

Dionne sucked her teeth. "I told you already, Kenya. I'm keeping it low."

I wanted to press her harder but would never do that in front of Armani. So, instead, I pulled my phone out as Armani and Dionne engaged in small talk.

The top news stories were on the front of my phone screen. I had alerts from all of the top new publications come to my phone simply because I liked to know what was going on with all the politicians we did business with. Usually, one of them was caught with their pants down or in some other scandal. Knowing what they were doing kept me one step ahead of them at all times.

Any other day, I could just scan them and keep it moving, but one headline from *USA Today* caught my eye. I saw it and couldn't believe my eyes.

U.S. SENATOR ROD COLLINS FOUND DEAD FROM APPARENT DRUG OVERDOSE.

"What the fuck?" I mumbled in disbelief as I clicked on the story to read it. I couldn't help but wonder if he had OD'd on our drugs and what that meant for me if he did. Before I got a chance to read, I heard Stacey's loud voice interrupting the tranquility of the party.

"Where the hell is Keon?" she yelled so loudly that the whole neighborhood could hear her.

Stacey was brown-skinned with a very pretty face and a petite build. The thing about her being so small was that whenever she gained a few pounds, it was always noticeable right away. Usually, any weight gain looked great on her, but today, her round, protruding belly caught the stares of everyone in attendance.

Dionne spoke on it first. "Is that bitch pregnant?" she said incredulously.

I looked at her curiously because of the animosity in her voice. "Looks like it. So what?"

Dionne was on her feet and marching toward Stacey before I knew it.

I stood up to chase after her and heard Armani mutter, "Shit," as he came after me.

"Stacey, you need to leave," Khalid told her in a low voice.

She looked him up and down like he wasn't shit. "I'll leave when I talk to Keon. Now, where the fuck is he?"

"Bitch, why are you even here?" Dionne snapped as she walked up on her before Khalid got a chance to respond.

Stacey looked at her and smirked. "Oh, he finally let you outside to play?" she said sarcastically. "I thought your little young, dumb ass would forever be his little secret. He got you laying up in my place, playing my role." She rubbed her stomach dramatically then looked back at Dionne with a devilish smile. "Did he tell you about his *other* little secret?"

Dionne was speechless. She looked at Stacey like she hated her.

Meanwhile, I was speechless as well. I couldn't believe what I was hearing. Was *Keon* Stacey's man? If he was, it would make sense why she would never tell me who the mystery guy was.

"Get ya young ass outta here," Stacey went on as she gloated in Dionne's face. "Go back to playing outside with Kenya. You ain't ready for this shit."

Dionne went to lunge at Stacey, but Keon came from nowhere and stepped in between them. "Chill," he warned Dionne. Then he looked at Stacey with disdain.

"The fuck are you doing here?" he yelled at her angrily.

"Nigga, this is *my* son's party. I have every fucking right to be here," she snapped at him as she got in his face.

The vein in Keon's neck throbbed, letting me know he was about to snap out something vicious. "Stacey, you need to leave before I drag you the fuck out of here," he warned her.

"Touch me, nigga, and see if I don't press charges against ya ass," she said with another smirk.

"You fucking love trying me, don't you?" he yelled at her. Before I or anyone else could stop him, he lifted her up and started to carry her out. Stacey kicked and screamed the whole time, knocking decorations and balloons everywhere before landing a good kick in his nuts. He howled in pain and let her go.

Stacey laughed like a crazy maniac before pulling a .22 out of her bag. Everyone at the party gasped. I couldn't believe my eyes. Stacey was so out of it that she really pulled a gun out on her son's father at her son's party.

"Stacey, put that shit down," I heard my mother snap as she made her way to the front of the crowd.

"Move, Ms. Dutchess," Stacey said. "This has nothing to do with you."

"You're at my muthafucking house ruining my grandson's party," my mom said in return. "Your ass shouldn't even be here. Now, put the gun down and get the fuck out of here."

"He's my son," Stacey shot back. "And your good-for-nothing-ass son just wants to keep him from me."

"Stacey, no one wants to keep Nahim away—" my mom started, but Keon cut her off.

"Don't explain shit to her. We been giving Nahim separate parties for years, and she knows it. She's just mad I moved on and don't want her no more."

"Does *this* look like he don't want me no more?" Stacey said with another crazy laugh as she rubbed her pregnant belly.

My mom looked at Keon and shook her head. "*Please* tell me you didn't knock her up again."

"That can be anybody's baby," Keon told her, but I heard the uncertainty in his voice.

He redirected his attention back to Stacey. "Put that little-ass gun away and get the fuck outta here *now,* or this time I *will* drag your ass outta here. I won't be so nice."

She smiled a crazy smile, and I noticed that she really seemed off. She raised her gun and fired, not at Keon, but at my mother. The bullets met their mark, and my mom fell back, bleeding profusely.

Armani tried to cover me and shoved me to the ground, but not before I pulled my own gun from my waist. I didn't hesitate to shoot her right in her leg, and she fell to the ground, but not before letting off a few rounds and hitting both Dionne and Keon as well. The back yard was a fucking mess as kids and adults ran around screaming. I tried to break free from Armani and go to my mother, but I was no match against his superior strength. Still, I could see my mother continuing to bleed out, and I knew that this did not look good at all.

Chapter Eighteen

Keon

I sat at my mother's bedside in the hospital and looked at all of the tubes and machines that she was hooked up to in amazement. Dutchess King had never been a weak woman, but she looked so helpless now. I held her hand with my good hand as guilt racked my body. I was ready to *kill* that bitch Stacey for what she'd done. She'd shot me in the arm, and a bullet had grazed Dionne's leg as I pushed her to the ground. I had a sling on, and Dionne had a bandage on her leg, but my mother was not so lucky.

I'd been with Stacey for many years. I'd made my other two sons on her. My last child, my only daughter, Keonna, was the only kid I had when we weren't together. So, she'd put up with a lot of heartache and bullshit from me. Our relationship was extremely volatile, and we'd had a couple of physical altercations. My temper was red hot, and Stacey didn't back down from anything. We were doomed from the start. But for her to do some crazy shit like this was unfathomable.

I'd taught Stacey everything she knew about handling a gun. She was damn near as good as I was with the hammer. So, it was no surprise to me that each of her bullets had hit their mark in my mother. Every single bullet had damaged a vital organ. Now my mom lay here on life support, lingering in that area between life and death.

"I'm sorry, Ma," I said quietly. "I never meant for any of this to happen."

"She knows you didn't, son."

I turned at the sound of Vincent Morelli's voice. He stepped into the room, wearing his usual tailored suit and expensive Italian leather shoes. His presence wasn't exactly a welcome one.

"What are you doing here?" I couldn't imagine my pops or my siblings allowing him to walk past them in the waiting room to come see my mother.

"Everyone heard about the shooting at the house," he said as he strolled closer to the bed. "I had to find a way to see her without letting your family know that I was here. One of the nurses on a different unit here is my niece. She let me know your mother was here and let me come in the elevators that are just for employees, so no one would spot me."

"And what if they come in and find you here?"

He shook his head. "I already know this ICU only allows one visitor at a time, so I'll be here while you're here and leave the same way I came when you leave. It'll work because no one ever saw me come in here."

I already knew that trying to talk him out of it would get me nowhere. I'd definitely inherited my stubborn streak from him. I couldn't help but be amazed by how he always seemed to know everything that went on with us

As he looked at my mother, he said softly, "I love Dutchess, more than you will ever know. She's the love of my life."

"I have a hard time believing that, considering how you tossed her out your life."

He chuckled at that as he stood on the other side of her bed and gently held her hand. "I never tossed her out of my life. She left me when my wife got pregnant. Not that I blame her."

"Neither do I."

He looked me straight in the eye. "I would have never left her, son. Ever. If I could have been with her the way I wanted to, I would have."

"So, what stopped you then?" I asked.

"Business and family politics being what they were. The same reason you never told anyone that you're fucking with that jailbait."

I glared at him. Vincent never missed a beat when it came to me. I didn't even bother asking him how he knew about Dionne. He knew everything. It didn't matter now that the word was out anyway. "She's eighteen," I said defensively.

"And still too young for you and the drama you're dragging her through."

I laughed harshly. "So, what you call yourself doing right now, giving me some fatherly advice?"

"No, just some man-to-man advice. That girl is not ready for you and everything you come with. And by trying to keep up with you, she's gonna lose who she really is. Then you won't even recognize her." He shrugged and looked back at my mother.

I thought of Dionne's insistence on snorting coke with me and knew that he was right. That wasn't even her. Or at least, it used to not be her. She got zooted with me on the regular now.

"I always hid how I felt about you from the rest of the world," he said to my mom as if she could hear him as he leaned down and stroked her cheek. "You deserved better than that. You're the one true love of my life, and with God as my witness, if he lets you wake up, I will spend the rest of my life showing you. I don't care what anyone has to say anymore."

I watched as he struggled to hold back the tears in his eyes and felt like I was interrupting a private moment that should not have been witnessed by anyone outside of the two of them.

"You've left me twice before. Don't leave me again, Dutchess. Please don't. We have the rest of our lives to spend together. We're supposed to grow old and watch our grandkids together." His voice sounded shaky. "I love you, Dutchess. Come back to me, baby." He gave her one more kiss before looking back at me. "I'd prefer to hear about her condition from you rather than my niece. Okay?" He made it seem like he was asking me, but I already knew I didn't have a choice in the matter.

I nodded my head in agreement.

He left just as silently as he came. I looked at my mom again and wondered if she could truly hear us as she hung in the space between life and death. Would she choose to wake up or leave us? I prayed that she woke up. My guilt was already eating me alive for this. It would bury me if she didn't make it.

Chapter Nineteen

Dutchess

They say when you're about to die, your whole life flashes before your eyes. I never believed it when I heard that saying, but I figured I must be on my way to Hell's door because I saw myself in different stages of my life like a fucking slideshow.

I was about eight the first time I saw a dead body. The victim was an unknown john of my mother's. My mother had turned tricks for as long as I could remember. It seemed to be her favorite way to put food on the table. But that night changed everything. She claimed that the john had tried to lunge at her when she wouldn't perform extra sex acts that he hadn't already paid for. She kept a straight razor under her tongue and sliced the man from ear to ear when he lunged at her. Then she went into his pockets before calling her brothers to come dispose of the body. My uncles arrived and tried to shield the man from my view, but I still saw him. Instead of being scared, I was intrigued.

The first time I ever sold a drug was when I was fifteen years old. I wasn't even sure if I could call it a drug since I started off selling dime bags of marijuana. I had watched my boyfriend, Nate, sell it to high school and college students at the time. He was in high school like me, but he had fancy clothes, shoes, and jewelry. I wanted those things too and didn't want to wait around for him or my mother to buy them. So, one time when he was bagging up his product, I swiped a few bags when he wasn't looking. I continued to do so until I had sold enough to buy my own to sell. The rest was history.

Kelvin King's fine ass walked into my life with a purpose in my early twenties. By then I had been hustling for a while but was nowhere near where I wanted to be. Kelvin wasn't the kind of guy I would normally deal with. He was very fair-skinned with a pretty-boy look to him. I preferred my men dark and rugged. He also wasn't knee-deep in the streets, but he was slightly rough around the edges, just enough so people knew not to fuck with him. Then, when I found out he was the legendary Big Vic's son, I figured I could learn from him. And I did, but not about the game. He had told me Big Vic kept him shielded from all of that, so I didn't learn any street lessons from him at all. Instead, he taught me how it felt to be loved by a man who would always put you first. He pulled no punches when it came to showing me how he felt about me. Then there was the fact that he was also very good with numbers.

When I met him, he worked for some big company downtown and sold weed on the side so he could get the things he wanted. He had plans to work for himself eventually. I tried to tell him that working a regular job would take too long to achieve his dreams, but he didn't want to hear it. Losing his father the way that he had made him wary of diving into the drug game, no matter how profitable it was. Since he refused to see my vision, I decided I had to make it happen on my own. And that's when Vincent Morelli came into the picture.

I grew up with Vinny's driver. He still came to the hood and was one of my most loyal customers, so pressing him to get a chance to meet the legendary Mob boss was easy. Vinny took me under his wing and taught me the ins and outs of the game. He upgraded my product from pounds of weed to kilos of cocaine. He taught me how to properly kill a man, how to cut him so he would bleed out and not make a sound, and how to weigh product just by eyeballing it. I would not be the woman I am today without that man.

He also taught me about passion. I loved Kelvin, and our sex was heated, but I had fallen in love with Vincent, and that was a big damn difference. Whenever he touched me, my whole body seemed to ignite with flames. I couldn't get enough of the fine-ass Italian who was packing meat like he was a brotha. We did it any and everywhere that we could. He spoiled me rotten and plugged me with his connect, so that I was able to make my own fortune. Our love affair was one for the books. There wasn't a story like ours.

The birth of Keon changed my life once more. I had prayed that he was Kelvin's since Vinny already had a wife who was also pregnant, but when he came out, I saw Vinny's features right away. Kelvin was so light-skinned that I was able to pass Keon off as his with no problem. Not too long after that, we had the twins, Khalid and Khalia, and then finally, my baby girl, Kenya. I had a special bond with all of my children, but it was Khalia whom I chose to carry my torch. She was the most like me in every way. She even looked just like me and had my fiery temperament. Watching her was like watching myself. It was scary, but I loved it.

Our empire grew so much that Kelvin convinced me we needed to open something big to hide all the money. We'd bought properties, but that just wasn't enough anymore. So, he convinced me that opening King Funeral Home was a good idea. Soon, business was so good that we opened another location, and another after that.

Pretty soon, we had the largest chain of funeral homes in the entire Northeast, which was no easy feat at all. I owed that to Kelvin, since his brain for numbers and business made it grow. Over the years, he'd begged and pleaded with me to get out of the game, but I didn't listen. He was convinced that we would end up dead or in jail. So far, we'd proven him wrong. So far . . .

"She's coding! We're losing her!" I heard someone scream faintly in the background.

All my life, I'd won every fight I'd ever been in. Physically, no one could beat my ass. And when it came to getting my way, especially with men, I won that game too. Only the last year or so of my life had been a total fucking mess. I had to admit I was surprised that my husband had gone to such lengths to be free from making money in the fast lane. I knew he'd never hurt our kids, but the fact that he'd tried to destroy everything we built spoke volumes. Kelvin wasn't even the type to initiate any type of violence. He had to be provoked, but when you started with him, watch out!

"Bring the cart! Now!" the same voice yelled, but they sounded even lower now.

I'd wanted the best for my family. I really did. I know it may have seemed harsh, the way I came across to them, but I couldn't help it. I'd risen to the top in a game that was designed for men only, and I'd won. I'd put my family on. My great-grandkids were already rich because of what I'd done, and I had no regrets about any of it. The drugs, the countless murders, grooming each of my kids for a role in our empire, Kelvin, Vincent . . . I regretted none of it. Even now, when my family was in shreds because of my affair with Vincent, I wasn't ashamed that I'd slept with him or that he was Keon's father. He was the great love of my life. Had it not been for him, we'd still be selling weed.

"Again!"

This time, the voice sounded like a whisper.

I had fought all my life to come out on top, but I always knew, in the back of my mind, that I'd have to pay for all the wrong I'd done, all the lives I took and ruined on my way to the top. Even now, as I watched the slideshow of my life, it seemed to stop at my grandson's birthday party. It seemed ironic to me that with all the dirt I'd done over the years, my story would end at the hand of some crazy woman and not a drug war. On the other hand, it also made sense. I was one of the coldest, baddest bitches to ever step into a pair of stilettos. Many had tried to end my life. I'd survived shootouts and numerous attempts on my life. The only way to get me would have to be like this: totally out of the blue and from the person I never saw coming.

"We lost her," were the very last words I heard before my fight with life ended.

The one time I'd needed to win, when it mattered the most, I lost.

Chapter Twenty

Khalid

I always prided myself on being prepared to handle any situation life threw my way, but nothing could have prepared me for all of this. My mother was dead. Stacey had killed her, while also managing to shoot Keon and graze Dionne. Kenya had shot Stacey. My niece and nephews had witnessed the entire thing.

My rivals for the seat in the senate went to the Internet and offered me condolences in one breath, then said with all the tragedies that kept happening in my life, I was not fit to be a senator in the next. According to them, I had too many other things going on in my personal life, and those things would be a distraction.

"Don't listen to them, baby," Toni said as she soothed me night after night. "They're just jealous that even with you having to deal with your mother's passing, you're still passing them in the polls right now."

It was true. My ratings had never been higher. Still, I didn't have time to think about that. I had to get everything prepared for my mother. The responsibility of burying her fell into my lap. Kenya didn't really know too much about the funeral business, Khalia was too grief-stricken and guilt-ridden to do much of anything, and Keon was too busy blaming himself and consoling his kids to be any help. Each time I thought of my niece and nephews, I felt so horrible for them. A tragedy of this magnitude was hard enough for adults to accept, but for the kids to witness it all was just awful.

Stacey had been arrested right at the scene. It wasn't like she could go anywhere with a hole in her leg. Plus, my family home was in fancy North Huntington. The cops were on their way as soon as the first gunshot rang out. She claimed the bullets had been meant for Dionne and Keon, but I knew better. She was pregnant and hurt that he had apparently moved on. Everyone knew that Keon was a mama's boy. I figured she wanted him to live with the pain of not having Mom around and the guilt that it was his fault she was gone.

All of that was irrelevant, though. I had a funeral to plan and knew it had to top any of the others King Funeral Homes had ever given.

My mom's favorite color was purple. She claimed it fit her since purple was the color of royalty, and with a name like Dutchess King, I couldn't agree more. I got her a gold casket with a plush, violet interior. I arranged for dozens upon dozens of violets and white lilies to be at the funeral. Toni helped me find her a beautiful purple silk dress to wear. I made sure that everyone was to wear white with a purple accent. No black was allowed. I also had small purple flowers to be pinned on close family and friends. I went through her room and found massive pictures of her when she was young. Her resemblance to Khalia was striking. I had certain pictures blown up to put on easels at the funeral home.

Toni was by my side during all this, always willing to lend a helping hand. I was so grateful to her and knew I had had made the right decision to be with her. If anything, this incident taught me that life was too short to waste time.

The day of the funeral, I rode in the limo with Kenya and Khalia. No one had been able to get in touch with Keon. For the first time, I noticed just how strong my mother's presence really was. There was a big gap without her.

"Before we pull up to the home, I want to thank Khalid for putting everything together," Pops said quietly. He looked like he'd aged in the week since Mom was killed.

"You left no stone unturned, son. I saw most of what you and Toni have done."

I smiled slightly. "Needed to make sure it was fit for a queen."

"That it is," Pop said with a nod. Then he looked around at all four of us. "Lately, we've been at odds with each other. I know a few of you weren't even speaking to Dutchess before she died."

Khalia lowered her gaze slightly. Everyone in the limo knew that it was her resistance to talk to Mom after the anniversary party that had hurt her the most. Khalia and my mom were like two peas in a pod.

"Myself included," Pops went on. "I know none of you all know this, but I had served Dutchess with divorce papers. I just couldn't see past working on everything that had happened between us. There was a lot more damage done to our relationship besides the thing with Vincent. That was just the straw that broke the camel's back."

I thought of all the times I'd seen my mother emasculate him and had to agree. I never understood how he put up with a woman who would say such scathing things to him and talk to him as if he were nothing.

"I'm not saying this to say that I would have changed my mind if she were still here," Pops continued. "Our love affair had run its course. I got four kids and a lifetime of experience out of it. However, I can't help but feel bad at the way that I treated her during her last few days on Earth. I know some of you feel that way too. So, I'm saying this to say that make sure that the people you love know that you love them. Say it to them. Show it to them. The last few months, Dutchess probably thought that I hated her. I sure as hell acted like I did out of all the anger I felt toward her. But no matter how mad I was at her, I never stopped loving her. And now she will never know that because she's no longer here for me to tell."

I thought about Pops' words as the limo cruised to a stop in front of the funeral home. He was definitely dropping gems and giving free game. Tomorrow wasn't promised to any of us. My mom being taken away from us like this proved that to me.

There were plenty of people already outside. I noticed a lot of soldiers from Khalia's team and knew that she had hired them for extra security. I was glad that she had. I had been so busy pulling everything else together that I had slacked on that part.

Once we got out of the limo to enter the funeral home, I was surprised to see Nisa standing out front, although I shouldn't have been. Our families had always been close. She was dressed in a fitted white pantsuit and purple high heels, with a purple Chanel clutch under her arm. Her hair was long and flowing, and her makeup was perfect. She looked just as good as she always did.

Pops shot me a look when he saw her. He'd never really cared for her. Kenya and Khalia greeted her warmly before walking into the home.

"What are you doing out here?" I asked in between clenched teeth as I looked around. Toni was due to pull up any second.

"I came to show my respects to my mother-in-law." Nisa glared at me. "You know I was pissed that my mom had to be the one to tell me about Ms. Dutchess. Why didn't you call and tell me?"

"That's not my job," I replied simply. I moved to go around her, but she stepped in front of me again.

"Khalid, why you acting like you don't miss me? Like we didn't have a good thing going? You really left because I want to get married, and I just don't understand."

"Nisa, I told you the real reason we won't work. Everything has to be about you. Even today, at my *mother's funeral,* you're still talking about you. Leave me the fuck alone, man. I don't want you," I said harshly as I stepped around her.

"Khalid, I didn't mean it like that," Nisa pleaded, but then I heard Toni's voice cut her off.

"Didn't my man say for you to leave him alone?" Toni asked in a calm voice.

She stepped into my view, and I had to stop myself from gripping her up. She was wearing a white linen dress that hugged her just right and showed just a hint of cleavage. A colorful purple scarf was tied around her waist like a belt. Her hair was straight as hell as it hit her shoulders, and her makeup was done in subtle shades of purple. On her feet were a pair of white heeled sandals, and I noticed her toes were painted lavender. She looked amazing.

"You look gorgeous, baby," I greeted her happily, Nisa all but forgotten.

"Yes, you do look nice. Did Lane Bryant have a sale or something?" Nisa asked smartly.

Toni smirked. "See, that's strike three for you. And by now, I would have kicked your ass, but it ain't the time or place. But don't worry where I got my clothes from, boo. My man likes it."

"I sure do, baby," I assured her as I offered her my arm and kissed her cheek as she looped her arm through mine. We walked past Nisa like she wasn't even there, and once we reached the inside, I stopped and looked at her.

"Thanks for not going off on Nisa. I know she's a lot to deal with."

Toni held her hand up to cut me off. "Let's not make this more about her than we already have. Today is about you, your family, and your mother. Fuck her. She's already a distant memory."

I stroked her cheek. "How did I get so lucky?"

She smiled at me and melted a piece of my heart. "God knew what He was doing when He sent us each other. Now, come on."

I walked through the double doors of our biggest parlor and realized that even with the extra seats I'd put in, there still wouldn't be enough seats for everyone. I had tried to keep the services nice and simple, but word spread. Everyone knew that the queen of the Kings had passed, and anyone who was everyone wanted to pay their respects. The problem with that was it would be impossible to fit everyone in. It looked like there would be standing room only soon. I sighed and decided that my mom would have liked it like that anyway. She loved being the center of attention.

Holding Toni's hand the whole time, I made my way up to her casket. Khalia was already standing there with some guy I never saw before right by her side. I let Toni's hand go to hug my sister. Khalia was barely five feet tall, but her presence always spoke volumes. Even today, she was dressed to kill in a white dress with her curly hair pressed straight and flowing down her back. There was not a stitch of makeup on her face, but Khalia rarely, if ever, needed any.

Still, for as fierce as she was, she looked so lost. She had lost my mom and Tookie all on the same day, and I knew that couldn't have been easy for her.

"I saw the guys out front. Thanks, sis," I told her with a smile.

"It's the least I could do," she said softly, never taking her eyes off Mom's body. "I will not be burying another one of us." Her tone was soft, but I knew that she meant every word that she said.

"We won't have to, long as we got you. The best shooter in PA," I joked, trying to make light of the mood.

Khalia still didn't crack a smile. "And where did that even get me? I couldn't save Tookie. I couldn't save Mom. I don't know, man. Maybe it's time for me to hang my guns up for good. They're worthless."

I had never heard her talk like this before. I was surprised to hear her think about quitting the game. She was deeper in it than anyone I knew. However, I couldn't blame her either.

"Whatever you decide to do, you already know I'm here. If you're really ready to quit the game, Dad been thinking about opening a new business with nothing but clean money. I'll put you down with the details later, but it might be something to interest you."

She nodded and then looked at Mom again. "She looks like she's at peace. You did such a great job. She's beautiful."

I looked down at her too. She looked peaceful, angelic even, as her head rested on a purple silk pillow that matched the interior of the coffin. Her makeup and her hair were impeccable. "She does," I said quietly as I gazed at her. Never had I seen her so quiet and still. She looked like an angel lying there. Briefly, I wondered if her soul had made it into heaven, then felt ashamed for having such thoughts. It was almost as if I was judging her, and I was no saint either.

Still, looking down at her, I knew that everything she had done, all the lengths she had gone to, were because she loved us unconditionally. I was just glad that I had still been speaking to her before she passed. I knew that being on bad terms with her before she died was a burden that Keon and Khalia would have to carry with them for the rest of their lives.

Loud murmurs and voices in the crowd made me and Khalia turn around. When we did, we couldn't believe our eyes. Keon was coming up the aisle with Dionne hanging on his arm. She was dressed in a white dress that was slightly baggy on her, stilettos she kept stumbling in, and her hair was in a sloppy ponytail on top of her head. That was bad enough, but Keon looked ten times worse. His eyes were bloodshot red, his hair hadn't been cut, his white shirt was buttoned wrong and had stains on it, and his white pants had a small hole on the knee.

"These mafuckas really came up in here high as a kite," Khalia muttered beside me in disbelief.

"What the fuck," I snapped as I marched toward them.

"Khalid! Wassup, baby bro!" he exclaimed loudly as he moved to hug me. I could see that his pupils were dilated.

"Let's go get you cleaned up, man," I said with a fake smile as I dodged his hug.

He scowled at me. "Fuck is you talking 'bout? I'm clean in this bitch. Now, I'm 'bout to shoulder lean in this bitch!" he joked with a laugh as he quoted "Shoulder Lean," an old hit song from rapper Young Dro.

I saw Toni looking at me with concern. Aware of the other eyes on us, I tried to reason with him again. "You know Mom would want you to look your best. This ain't your best. But we got clothes in the back to get you in before the services start."

"Fuck that! I look good, don't I, baby?" he said as he looked at Dionne.

"Of course you do, boo," she told him.

I noticed Kenya walking back in with Armani and prayed she could talk some sense into her friend.

"Oh my God, Ms. Dutchess looks so pretty!" Dionne squealed as she rushed toward the casket. Keon was right behind her. They stood in front of her casket, talking about how good she looked, looking like a fake-ass Bobby and Whitney. I wanted to move them but figured he had the right to look at her just as we did. When the pastor came to the podium, everyone cleared the front by the casket but those two.

"Y'all need to come on and sit down so he can start," Khalia snapped at them.

"We'll sit down when the fuck we feel like it!" Keon snapped back at her. "I'm sick of you always acting like you run shit. You ain't the oldest. I am!"

"He can't be serious right now," I muttered under my breath as I stood up.

"Oh, yeah? You're the oldest? Well, you need to fucking act like it," Khalia shot back.

I noticed the man next to her pat her hand as if trying to calm her down, and once again, I wondered who he was.

"Maybe I will when you quit acting like a fucking man!"

The low murmurs were back.

"Baby, you have to stop them," Toni said anxiously.

I nodded at her and moved out toward the center of the aisle. "Can y'all chill, please, so we can start?"

"Well, we all know you don't know a damn thing about acting like a man," Khalia retorted like I hadn't said a word. "You come up in here like R. Kelly with some jailbait on your arm but still got coke on your nose, so you look more like Bobby."

The crowd gasped as Keon automatically wiped his nose with the back of his hand. But Khalia still wasn't done. I knew before she even opened her mouth that there was more to come. We were twins, after all.

"How dare you come up in here tryna talk bad to me like *you* run shit, when at the end of the day, we wouldn't even be here if it wasn't for you," she yelled at him. "You can't control your bitches, and that's the reason my mother is laying up there in that casket."

All hell broke loose before I could stop it. Keon lunged toward Khalia, and I jumped in between them right before he could grab her. The crowd lost it, and my father ran back in from where he had been greeting guests out front. He saw me struggling to contain Keon, who was a good five inches taller and twenty pounds heavier than I was, and rushed to help me out.

"You need to cut it out!" he snapped at Keon. "You can't come in here causing all sorts of trouble like this. It's your *mother's funeral*, and you're in here ready to fight your *sister*." He looked at him in disgust before shaking his head.

Keon hung his head low in shame.

I looked back at Khalia. She was standing now, too, and I didn't miss the gun in her hand. Shit had gone from bad to worse quickly. I knew she wouldn't have hesitated to shoot Keon if he'd succeeded in putting his hands on her.

I waited until our gazes met before looking down at her gun and then back at her. We were twins. I didn't have to verbalize what I wanted to say to her. She got it right away and tucked her piece. I noticed the man sitting next to her looked at her with a shocked expression but didn't say anything.

I stepped to the pastor. "Give us about ten minutes, Pastor Wilson, so we can clean my brother up. My mother's death was so unexpected that it's bringing out the worst in all of us."

Pastor Wilson looked at me with a raised eyebrow. "Ten minutes?" he asked doubtfully.

"Ten minutes," I repeated. After I assured Pops that I could handle him, I escorted Keon back to the main office of the home. Once we got back there, I gave him a clean shirt and pair of slacks. Then I straightened his purple blazer. He still looked high as a kite, so I found some Visine and put the drops in his eyes.

"Thanks, Khalid," he said gratefully. "You did a great job putting all this together. I'm sorry I kinda fucked it all up."

I shook my head. "It didn't even start. Let's just forget this even happened and go back out here to start this service, a'ight?"

Keon gave me a small smile. "No one wants me out there after the way I came up in here."

"You damn sure didn't have to come up in here high as fuck with *Dionne* hanging on your arm, just as zooted as you," I agreed. "But that's for another time. Right now, we have to bury our mother. Can we please do that in peace?"

He nodded.

We walked back out to the service, and I gave the pastor a signal that he could start the funeral. Then I sat down and picked Toni's hand up and kissed it.

She looked over at Keon, who was sitting on the other side of me, and stroked my cheek affectionately. "You really fix everything all the time. You're like Superman."

I kissed her hand again and smiled slightly at her words. Even though this was the saddest day of my life, she had still found a way to make my heart smile. I was so happy she was by my side.

Chapter Twenty-one

Rallo

"It's time for more pictures, Rallo!" Shaterra called out to me with a smile.

I got up from my seat at the table where we had just been eating and limped over to Shaterra, who was standing by the huge cake and presents. The gunshot to my leg had affected my walk slightly, but I still managed to make it work.

None of that mattered to Shaterra, though. She was glowing happily as I approached her, and she looked so pretty to me that I couldn't help but smile back. I kissed her cheek, wrapped my arms around her, and rubbed her belly. We posed for the pictures with her smile a mile wide. For once, I didn't have a scowl on my face. That's because, although we had lost a few men, things had finally started to look up for me.

It had been a week since we killed Tookie. I tried my hardest to send that bitch Khalia straight to hell with him, but she surprised me by taking out four niggas all on her own, including my favorite cousin Rick. I was still sick over that one. I was closer to him than I was to Armani. We did everything together. To make matters worse, his mom, my Aunt Dot, didn't let us have a funeral for him. She insisted on cremating him, stating that funerals were a waste of money. I felt that the real reason was that she wanted to keep the majority of his life insurance policy to herself. Right after the small memorial service she had for him, she took a plane to Jamaica and still hadn't come back.

Losing Rick hurt, but it gave me the fuel to go extra hard in memory. I would not let his death be in vain. So, I got my toughest soldiers together, and we rode out on all the mid-level workers for the King family. The timing couldn't have been more perfect. Dutchess King getting killed had put them at a standstill, at least until they buried her. While they were mourning, I took full advantage and raided all the spots Tookie had been in charge of. He and Khalia were their muscle, and it showed. They had other shooters, but they were easy pickings. I was able to take over with no problem and, best of all, with their drugs. The addicts didn't give a fuck who died. They still wanted to get high.

Things were going so well financially in such a short period of time that I decided to throw Shaterra the baby shower she had always dreamed about. I saw her constantly going to other people's baby showers that looked more like wedding receptions. I personally thought it was a waste of money to spend all that for one day, but I wanted to make her happy. I couldn't get everything that I knew she would want because it was so last minute, but I was able to get enough. I couldn't remember the last time I had seen her so happy, and I was proud that I could finally treat her the way she deserved.

After we took the pictures, I noticed a few of my soldiers waiting off to the side for me. I hadn't invited them, so I knew they were there on business.

"Baby, I'll be right back," I told Shaterra before kissing her on the cheek and walking over to them.

She looked at them, then back at me with a disapproving look, but didn't say anything else.

"What's up wit' it?" I greeted them. "If y'all niggas here, you must have bad news or great news."

"We got excellent news," Blackie, the most reckless one out of all of them, said with a grin.

"Give it to me."

"It's Dutchess King's funeral today. We know which one of their funeral homes they're having it at." He looked at me with a glint of danger sparkling in his eyes.

I knew what he was thinking because I was already there. There wouldn't be a better time than now to take out the Kings. They would never see us coming.

"Let's go," I told them with no hesitation.

Chapter Twenty-two

Khalia

My mother's funeral services were all a blur to me. I tried to pay attention to the good things that everyone was saying about her, but I couldn't take my eyes off her in the casket in front of the room. She had meant so much to so many people. She was feared by grown men just like me. She had always been the life of the party, never still, and now she was dead. It blew my mind.

Drew stroked my hand as he sat next to me. I looked over at him and smiled, grateful that he hadn't run off when I revealed the truth about who I really was. If it weren't for Tookie, I probably would have never told him, but his last words to me had been, "If he makes you happy, you should let him get to know all of you. If he run, fuck him." I decided to take his advice and do just that.

Usually, I was so guarded with my heart and my feelings, but losing my mother and Tookie on the same day made me more vulnerable than I normally would have been. I needed someone to help me through the pain of what I was experiencing. I had my family, but I needed more. I wanted someone to hold me at night when I couldn't sleep. I needed to let Drew in so he could understand and comfort me.

That night, when I got home, I realized I couldn't be there alone. Visions of Tookie and my mom danced around in my head. I invited Drew over and explained what had taken place that day and why losing Tookie had hurt me so very much, almost as much as losing my mother. I gave him a short version of who I was and an even shorter version of what I did for a living. I let him know just enough to know I wasn't the one to be fucked with, while leaving out anything he could run back and tell anyone.

When I was finished, he just stared at me in shock. I understood he was surprised by what I had laid on him, but I also wasn't in the mood to keep explaining myself. "Now that you know who I am, are you gonna keep fucking with me or not?" I asked bluntly. "I would love to have you here to help me get through this, but not if you gonna keep looking at me like I'm crazy."

He laughed slightly and pulled me into his arms, a gesture that easily soothed me. "I ain't goin' nowhere. I just can't believe my mail-carrying ass pulled you, that's all."

I laughed a little too, grateful for my decision and his reaction to it.

He accompanied me to the funeral for Tookie and rubbed my back as I apologized profusely to his mother and girlfriend. I promised them I would always look out for his two small kids, and it was a promise I intended to keep. Tookie's services had been hard enough, but my mother's was a whole new world of pain that I thought I was prepared for. I wasn't at all. Add Keon's high ass starting his usual bullshit, and I was just over it all. The sight of him pissed me off. My sadness mixed with my anger was not a good combination. I was glad that Khalid grabbed him when he did because I would have no problem putting a few holes in Keon if he put his hands on me, brother or not. He deserved it anyway. He was the reason Mom was gone, and nobody could ever tell me any differently.

We were walking outside of the funeral home, right behind my brothers and the rest of the pallbearers carrying the casket, when the unthinkable happened. Two blacked-out Tahoes pulled up, lowered their windows, and started spraying the crowd. Bullets ripped into my mom's casket, and her stiff body fell out.

I pulled my gun out and aimed the second truck, hitting the driver directly in his forehead and the backseat shooter as well, before Drew knocked me to the ground roughly. I struggled against him with all my might as bullets flew around us, but I was no match for his strength. By the time the truck sped off and he hopped up off of me, I was pissed.

"Why the fuck would you do that?" I yelled at him angrily.

He looked at me, confused. "What you mean, why would I do that? Why would I push you out of the line of fire?"

"Yes!" I exclaimed. I looked over at the damage that had been done. One truck had gotten away, but the other had crashed into a pole with the two men I'd killed hanging out the front and back windows.

"It's my job as your man to protect you," Drew said in a low voice.

"And it's *my job* to protect this family!" I screamed back. "I could have killed all those niggas! And now, because of you, some of them got away!"

"Because of me," he repeated in disbelief. "Baby, there are other people with guns out here. They could have taken care of that. It was my place to make sure none of those bullets hit you. And you're mad at me because of that?"

I closed my eyes impatiently. I knew bringing him here was a mistake, letting him into my world. What he didn't understand was that it didn't matter how many other niggas were out there, my brothers included. None of them were as nice as I was when it came to gunplay. If I had been able to do what I do, we would have both trucks turned into Swiss cheese instead of just one.

"I don't need you to protect me," I said between clenched teeth when I opened my eyes again. "I've been doing a damn good job of it over the years on my own. What I needed was to get those niggas who shot up my mom's funeral and her casket. Do you not see this disrespectful shit?" I exclaimed as I pointed at my mom's already dead body, riddled with more bullets. Daddy and Khalid moved her body away from the steps and put her back into what remained of her casket.

"I see it, and I'm sorry it happened, but it would be even worse if it were you."

"It wasn't going to *be* me! I didn't need you getting in the way of how I do shit!"

A hurt expression came over Drew's face as he nodded his head slowly. "A'ight. Maybe it's just best that I go then."

"You think?" I snapped sarcastically as I walked away from him. I noticed Daddy shaking his head at me, and I knew that he had probably heard our argument, but I didn't give a fuck. I walked over to the truck to see the damage that had been done. The truck had been loaded with shooters, but only one survived. He was on the concrete, bleeding out from so many bullet holes that I knew he didn't have long.

I kicked him in his face. He winced in pain. "Who the fuck do you work for?" I asked him point blank.

"The devil," he spat, his mouth full of blood.

"Wrong answer, nigga. I'm the devil," I responded as I stood on the bullet wound on his bleeding hand with my stiletto. He howled in pain.

"You got one more time, and I suggest you don't strike out. Who the fuck do you work for?" I asked as I twisted my heel back and forth in his wound.

"Agghh! Rallo! I work for Rallo!"

I gave him my best smile. "See? Was that so hard?" I asked before blowing his brains out. His blood splattered all over my clothes, but I didn't give a fuck.

I tucked my gun back in my waist and looked at the remaining soldiers standing there. "This is the second time I heard this nigga Rallo's name. Find out who the fuck he is ASAP," I ordered them. I walked away to go back into the funeral home to get rid of my clothes and change. As soon as I was about to enter, my eyes met Drew's. He was in his Denali truck, but his gaze told me he had seen everything. I shrugged and walked through the doors. I didn't have time to babysit his feelings. I had one more soul to send to hell.

Chapter Twenty-three

Kenya

Armani paced back and forth in his off-campus apartment as I sat on his bed and watched him as if he were losing his mind.

"You'll be fine, baby. I promise no one knew you were there," I assured him.

He looked at me in disbelief. "Do you think that's the only thing I'm worried about?"

"Yeah," I responded with a shrug of my shoulders. "I know you have to keep a clean record, or you fall to low rounds in the draft, and you've worked so hard to get here."

"Fuck the draft!" Armani exploded angrily. "I don't care about that more than I care about keeping you safe."

I looked at him in surprise. "What?"

He kept going like I hadn't said a word. "Look, I don't say shit about what you do, but now I'm starting to see my mistake in that. If we're gone be together, we need to always be honest with each other."

"Okay," I said slowly, not sure I liked where this was going.

"It should be obvious to you that I know about your family."

I frowned. "What are you talking about?"

"Cut the bullshit, Kenya, a'ight? The night I met you at your parents' anniversary party, there was a fight between your father and Vincent Morelli. Then the shooting at your nephew's birthday party, where that woman shot your mom. You even ended up shooting her!"

"I had to!" I snapped at him as visions of Stacey holding that gun flashed through my mind. "She would have kept shooting."

"I didn't even know you had a gun, Kenya. And then today . . ." His voice trailed off.

I bit my lip as tears welled in my eyes. The incident with Keon notwithstanding, the funeral had been absolutely beautiful. Khalid had pulled out all the stops to make sure it was a success. I was so proud of him, and so sad that all his hard work had gone to nothing the second we walked out of the funeral home.

The shots ringing out had caught me by surprise, but I was no longer hesitant in what I had to do. I shot at those trucks along with everyone else, and while I wasn't sure if my bullets had met their mark, I knew I looked different in Armani's eyes.

"This was the second time I saw you shoot a gun in a week, Kenya. You can't lie to me anymore. I know you're into the same shit as your family. And if you are, you gotta choose between me or that life."

I stood up, shocked he would even consider giving me an ultimatum. "Are you serious? You would really make me choose between you and my family? I would never do that to you."

"I'm not asking you to choose between me or your family. That's your family. But you do have to choose between me and being legit." He took my hand in his. "I don't know the extent to which you're involved, but you go outta town so often that I know it's deep. I can't risk losing you to that life. My brother is knee-deep in it, and it has gotten him nowhere."

I looked at him in surprise. "You have a brother?" I asked. I had met his mom and his aunt but never heard him mention a brother before.

"Yeah. Well, he's really my stepbrother because my dad was with his mom before he died, but that shit doesn't matter. What matters is us." He looked deep into my eyes. "I don't really fuck with my brother like that no more 'cause he's letting that street shit take over his brain. That's all he cares about, all he wants to care about. It fucked up his priorities. I don't want to see that happen with you, Kenya. You're beautiful, you're smart. Why don't you put the guns down? At least for me? I promise you won't have to worry about a damn thing if you do. The streets can't do what I can do for you."

I thought over his words carefully. It wasn't like I was so invested that there was no way out for me. No one really knew who I was besides the politicians we dealt with, and Khalid could easily slip back into that role if he chose to do so.

"I might have to do that anyway," I told him slowly as I thought about Rod Collins. It had been confirmed that he had died from overdosing on the pills I'd given him combined with meth. I didn't know if they were going to research where he got the pills from or if they were more interested in the meth found in his system. All I knew was that it was a close enough call for me. Rod had also warned me to get out while I could.

I decided right then and there that I was done. I had money put away, but even if I didn't it wasn't as if I were broke. Plus, I didn't want to make the same mistake as Khalia. It had been a few days since the funeral, and she was back to looking miserable again. We had been cleaning out Mom's room, and I noticed she kept checking her phone every other minute. I knew without a doubt that she was hoping to see if that fine-ass chocolate man she'd had at the funeral with her had hit her up. Each time she slid her phone back in her pocket, it looked like she was ready to cry again.

I had heard the way she blew up at him after the shooting, and I thought that she was dead-ass wrong for that. I was glad that Armani was there to protect me, and I would have been offended if he hadn't pushed me to the ground.

"I don't even wanna know what you were doing or how you were doing it, baby. Just as long as you give me your word that you're done, we're good," he said seriously as he continued to stare deep into my eyes.

"I promise we are."

"A'ight cool." He hugged me and kissed me before looking back at me again. "I got one more thing I need you to do for me."

"Damn, niggas want a lot of favors today," I joked with a laugh, already knowing that I would do anything that he asked.

He laughed, too, before pulling away slightly so his gaze met mine. "Dionne. You can't fuck with her no more."

I pulled away completely and snaked my neck. "What you mean I can't fuck with her no more? That's my best friend, Armani."

"She's getting high," he said bluntly. "That's your best friend, so I know you noticed that shit. I suspected she was at your nephew's birthday party but didn't want to believe it. But the funeral confirmed it. She's over there doing coke with your brother. You don't want to be in the middle of that."

I bit my lip because I knew there was honesty in his words. As close as Keon and I were, it broke my heart that he would do my friend the way that he was. In a way, it made sense for him to make sure she told nobody. He had her living the part of his girlfriend, dressing the part, but was slowly turning her into a cokehead. My heart felt so cold toward him for that. Still, I couldn't abandon my friend because she had made a few bad choices. What if I had gotten pinched all those times I smuggled drugs across state lines? I would be pissed if she left me out to dry.

"I can make her get clean," I told him.

He looked at me doubtfully. "Baby, an addict won't get clean until they're ready. You see the way she came up in there. She clearly ain't ready, and I can't have my girl around none of that."

"Well, what if I tried to get her clean first? Took her to rehab and all that. Then, if she refuses, I'll back off."

"You mean when." He still looked doubtful but pulled me back into his arms again. "If she gets clean, you can be around her. But that's a big if. If she doesn't, you can't fuck with her, Kenya. She's going down the wrong path. I can't have you caught up in none of that. You got your whole future ahead of you."

"Doing what?" I said with a deep frown. I still had no idea where my life was headed.

"Being a stylist to the stars," he said with a grin. "Style me and some of my teammates on and off the field, when we have ESPN and bowl games. Watch that shit take off for you."

I was quiet for a second. I had never thought of that before, but now that he mentioned it, the idea stuck. With my love for fashion, it made so much sense to try to be a stylist. He had planted the seed; all I had to do was water it.

"You with me, right?" he asked as he kissed my forehead.

"Of course," I replied with no hesitation.

"Then trust ya man. You got me, I got you, we got us."

I looked into his eyes and knew that, without a doubt, I was starting to fall in love with him. I used to fear it, but now I welcomed it with open arms. No one had ever made me feel the way he had. Even in my darkest days, he had given me light. I knew there was nothing I wouldn't do for Armani Collins. I was so glad that he was mine.

As we laid back on his bed, my mind drifted to Dionne once more. I couldn't just leave her out in the world with a monkey on her back and no one who really cared about her. I made up my mind that I would go see her soon.

Chapter Twenty-four

Keon

The new school year had been back in for about three weeks, and man, was I happy about that. Nahim had come to live with me since Stacey was still in jail and probably would be for the rest of her life. Since Nahim was staying with me, my other kids came around a lot more than usual. I started to feel like a single dad, and my appreciation for single mothers skyrocketed as they ate me out of the house and home and still expected me to entertain them.

It was only up to me to entertain them anyway. My sweet young thing, Dionne, who had been on her way to having my nose wide open, had completely turned me the fuck off. She was snorting way more coke than was needed and was turning out to have a true habit. I used myself, but it was always recreational. I had decided to distance myself from her and left her at the spot at The Washington and retreated back to my own deluxe condo, complete with all my gym equipment and my faithful chef/housekeeper, Marisol. I used the excuse that the kids were always with me now, and my place had more space. At first, she complained, but then she bought it when I left her an eight ball of cocaine. After that, I heard no more complaints.

After my mother's funeral, I had decided it was time to fly straight. No coke, no pills, none of that. I got back on my daily routine of working out and running my miles, trying to get back to the man I used to be. I knew that my family was ashamed of me. Hell, I was ashamed of myself. That was why I was trying to eliminate all the toxic things in my life and focus on being a better man.

I grew closer to Vincent, too. No matter how much I pushed him away, he only pressed harder. In a way, I was glad that he did. It was like he sensed that I was constantly blaming myself for my mother's murder, so much so that I hadn't fully allowed myself to grieve. He came through with positive memories for me. My pops said polite things about my mom, but I could tell his heart wasn't really in it. They hadn't been in love for years, whereas Vincent had loved my mother until she took her last breath.

Today, we were sitting in my family room, enjoying a delicious lunch of chicken fajitas that Marisol had cooked and watching ESPN. Eating and watching sports were our favorite pastimes.

"So, what's your next move?" he asked me.

I was confused. "As far as what?"

"Well, I see you getting back in shape, getting clean and all that. So, I wanna know what you're preparing yourself for. What moves are you about to make?"

I shook my head. "None so far. Just had to get my mind right, you know? I got Nahim full-time now, and I can't let him see me on no bullshit."

"True indeed. But a man should always have a plan." He sat back in the recliner and looked at me.

I shrugged. "We business as usual, but you know how that goes. I barely touch the shit anymore."

"Exactly. So why sit around and be idle? Do something you enjoy."

"Something like what? The only other thing I ever liked to do was hoop. You know that. I'm great at this game. It's the only thing I know."

He looked at me thoughtfully. "I know that. You're the son of a Dutchess and a Mob boss. You didn't have a choice but to be knee-deep in this shit. You're street royalty, for crying out loud."

I laughed at the truth in his statement. "A'ight, so what do you suggest I do, old man?"

Marisol came in and cleared the table. "Is there anything else I can get you, sir?" she asked as she stared directly at me.

I returned the stare boldly, knowing that it would never go anywhere. Years ago, a housekeeper had flipped the switch on me and accused me of rape after she willingly gave me the pussy. The charges were dropped, but the shame and anger were something I would never forget. So, even though Marisol looked good as hell, I would never take it any further than a flirtation here and there.

"A couple of beers, sweetie," Vincent said from behind me, breaking our stare.

She turned and smiled at him. "Sure thing," she said as she left the room.

I watched as his eyes followed her before looking back at me. "How long you been fucking her?"

"I don't fuck her," I replied simply.

"Well, you should."

We both laughed.

"Anyway, back to business. I've always had my own dealings outside of what the family does. It was the way to build my nest egg to retire," he explained. "I'm ready to do just that, but first, I want to pass my operation on to someone I can trust."

I looked at him, wide-eyed. "You wanna pass a Mob operation on to me? Will they even accept me?"

"Hell no," he said with a laugh. "That's why this is separate from what I do with them. I can never fully retire from them, just scale back. My little thing is completely separate. It's something I hoped to pass down one day before I even had kids. Then Dutchess had you but wouldn't allow me to be around, which I fully understood. Angie gave me all girls, but none of them have balls of steel like your sister Khalia does."

Another wave of guilt washed over me as I remembered lunging at my own sister. Her words hurt me, but it was no reason to put my hands on her.

"Anyway, if you're looking for the next phase of your career, this is it," he said. "I'm talking a full-scale distribution network from Boston to Miami, son. The entire East Coast. Very little work to do for you, but millions to be made." He grinned at me.

I didn't even have to think about it. "Teach me the muthafuckin' game, Vincent."

His grin widened. "I thought you would never ask."

Chapter Twenty-five

Toni

I sat on Khalid's bed in his loft with my laptop open, going over each one of my clients' portfolios before sending out their monthly updates. Then, I shut the laptop with a sigh of relief before placing it on the nightstand next to me.

"About time," Khalid murmured from the edge of the bed. "I didn't think you would ever get done."

I laughed as he pulled the comforter off me in one slick move. "I don't complain when you're working," I pointed out.

"I know. You don't complain about shit. That's why you my baby." He took my foot in his hand and began to massage it. I leaned my head back and closed my eyes.

"That feels so good," I murmured, my eyes halfway closed.

"I know," he responded cockily. Then he placed my big toe in his mouth, gently sucking on it before kissing and licking up my leg, then my thigh. Then he finally pulled me to the edge of the bed so he could bury his face in my pussy.

I moaned low and slow as he took his time and ate me like I was the best thing he had ever tasted in his life. I was exploding in his mouth in no time, and while I usually let him keep going, I pushed his head away.

He looked at me, slightly confused, but said nothing as I threw my T-shirt over my head, got off the bed, and kneeled in front of him. I loved being at eye level with his dick. It was ten inches long, thick, was the color of dark chocolate, and tasted better than any piece of chocolate I had ever eaten in my life.

I licked all over it like it was my favorite popsicle, sucked, and kissed on the head of that pretty muthafucka before sliding it in my mouth and massaging his balls at the same time.

"Toni," he moaned, turning me the fuck on even more. Khalid brought out a freaky side of me that I didn't even know existed. I loved hearing my name flow from his mouth like poetry. My pussy was already dripping with honey, but I still played with myself as I sucked on my favorite treat.

When I felt he was close to busting, I stopped and pushed him back on the bed. He gazed up at me passionately as I sat on his dick, then he reached up and grabbed my hair to kiss me. Our tongues did my favorite dance as I savored the taste of myself on him.

He smacked my ass with his other hand as I rode him like I had a point to prove. He smacked my ass again and grabbed my waist, slowing me down. Our frantic pace slowed down as he pulled me down to him again. This time, our kiss was slow, meaningful, and passionate.

"Toni," he murmured as we took a break from kissing. "Baby, I love you."

It was the first time he had ever said the L word to me. I already knew I felt it toward him. Even with all the drama surrounding his family, the shootouts, all that shit, there was no one else I'd rather give my heart to.

My eyes welled with tears, and one fell on him. This was the first time I had ever shed tears of joy and happiness. "Oh, baby. I love you too."

"Y'all love each other. Ain't that shit cute."

Khalid pushed me off him. I recognized the voice immediately. It belonged to Nisa.

"Nisa, what the fuck are you doing here?" Khalid asked angrily as he stood up and slid his boxers on. I hurried and threw my T-shirt back over my head.

She came into view then, the moonlight shining on her through the large windows. She was wearing all black, with her hair pulled back into a tight bun.

"What you mean, what the fuck am I doing here? I came to see you, baby," she replied condescendingly. "You won't talk to me any other time. I call and text, but you don't answer. So, I said to myself, 'Where can I find him?'" She tapped her temple and looked at both of us.

"I knew you wouldn't be at her raggedy-ass crib," she went on. "It ain't good enough for you, but knowing you, I bet you played it off like you didn't want her brother to see y'all there like that."

My eyes widened at her words because that's exactly what he had said to me.

Khalid looked at me and shook his head. "Don't listen to her, baby. She's just mad because I left her ass."

"Damn right, I'm mad!" she exclaimed. "All the years I stood by your side and supported you, and you just let this fat *bitch* come take my fucking spot like I was nothing."

I'd had enough of her. I jumped off the bed and started pounding on her. "I told you about disrespecting me," I yelled as I landed blow after blow on her face.

Khalid pulled me off her, and she leaped to her feet, brandishing a gun as she did so.

"Nisa, put that gun down," Khalid said in a calm voice.

"Fuck you!" she screamed at him.

"You know you don't want to do this," he said in that low voice.

Nisa laughed a crazy laugh then. "You wanna know something, Khalid? For as smart as you are, or claim to be, you're still dumb as shit. I've done *this* before when it comes to you, and I'll gladly *do it* again."

Khalid looked at her, confused.

"You still don't know what I'm talking about? How about your *dear, sweet* Amber?"

Khalid's confused expression changed to one of complete disbelief.

"Yeah. *Amber*. I had to hear you go on and on about her. She was perfect to you. How much you loved her." She laughed again but kept her gun trained on me. "You know how hard it is loving a man you've known since you were kids? And then never have him look at you the same way because there was always this bitch or that one in the way? I could take the rest of them, but *Amber* . . ." She shook her head. "No, she had to go. And then, when she got pregnant, that sealed the deal. It was so easy to get her while she was out shopping with Khalia 'cause—let's be honest—who ain't tryna kill her?"

Khalid started to march toward her, but Nisa cocked her gun back. "Aht aht aht, I don't think you wanna do that. Not unless you want your new bitch to meet your old bitch."

She continued, "I was there for you after she died. I comforted you. I got you through it. And because I want what was owed to me, you left me like I never meant shit to you."

This bitch was crazy. She was really talking about how she had helped him get through a problem that she had created herself!

"I loved you," she said with tears streaming down her face rapidly. She wiped them away and raised her gun back to me. "I would have done anything for you. But I can't sit back and watch you love another woman, Khalid. Not again."

She fired her gun just as Khalid pushed me out of the way. The bullet struck the wall right behind where I had been standing. Khalid wrestled her to the floor and took the gun away from her easily. When he stood up, he looked down at her.

"Get the fuck outta here before I blow your brains out myself," he hissed at her.

I looked at him in shock. "You just gone let her go?"

"I am." He looked back at me. "She's not worth the trouble."

Nisa laughed from the floor. "I'm not?"

He turned back to her. "Naw, you're not. Look at you. You're miserable as fuck. You have no life, no nothing outside of me. And while I should kill you right now for what you did to Amber, a part of me feels bad for you. So I'ma let you go now, but I swear to God, if you pop back up to bother me or my girl again, I'll kill you myself."

She stood to her feet, still laughing. "Why wait?" she asked sweetly, and before either one of us could stop her, she pulled a smaller gun from her waist, held it to her temple, and pulled the trigger.

The sight would remain with me for the rest of my life.

Chapter Twenty-six

Khalia

I sat in the exam room at the doctor's office and scrolled the pictures on my phone as I waited for my OB/GYN to come back into the room. I had just had my yearly exam and was ready to go. I looked at each picture of me and Drew with a small smile on my face. I longed for the days when he only knew me as Kyra James. I knew that when he found out about Khalia King, everything would be different.

He had yet to answer a phone call or text message from me in the weeks that followed the funeral. I understood that he had seen me kill a man, and maybe that was the reason he was avoiding me. I got it. But ever since then, I had seriously thought about hanging my guns up for real. My soldiers had tracked down the occupants of the other Tahoe and murdered them as well. The only person we had yet to catch up with was Rallo. I figured he would pop out sooner or later. His murder would be the last one on my hands. After that, I was done.

Times like this, I really missed my mother. She would more than likely tell me to stay in the game, but I didn't want to go to her about that for once. I wanted to talk to her about matters of the heart. I had never been in love before and wasn't sure how to handle it. Was I supposed to let Drew go? Was I supposed to confront him? He didn't seem to appreciate how aggressive I could be. Was I supposed to tone it down to appease him? What was I supposed to do?

Dr. Miller walked back in and grinned at me. "Okay, Ms. King, everything looks good to go, and the labs looked great."

"Cool." I stood up and grabbed my Birkin bag.

"Oh, one more thing," he said as he looked down at the paper in his hand and back at me. "Looks like you're pregnant."

I sat back down quickly. "Me? Pregnant? Are you sure?"

"Positive, Ms. King. Do you remember when you had your last period?"

I stared at him blankly. I couldn't remember at all. So much had happened in such a short period of time.

"Well, we need to make your first prenatal appointment. We'll get a sonogram and see just how far along you are then. If you choose to exercise other options, we can discuss that as well."

"I'm keeping it," flew out of my mouth. There was no way I would ever consider getting rid of Drew's baby.

I left the office and drove straight to Drew's. My pride had stopped me from going to his house, but now that was out of the window. We needed to talk.

I was glad when I saw his car parked in front of his townhouse in Forest Hills. I pulled right behind it and parked. Then I hopped out of my truck and rang his doorbell anxiously. After a few minutes, no one came to the door.

"Aye, Drew, I know you in there! Come open this door!" I started to bang loudly, and finally, the door opened.

Drew stood there in hoop shorts and a white tank top, his arms folded across his chest. He had a fresh haircut and lineup, and I could smell the cologne he wore from where I stood on the porch. "What's up?" he said dryly.

"What's up?" I repeated. "That's all you have to say to me?"

"I don't want you thinking I'm trying to run you or something. Gotta watch what I say to you."

I chuckled slightly. "I guess I deserved that. Now, let me in. We need to talk."

He looked over his shoulder before glancing back at me. "Now is not a good time."

I looked at him like he was crazy. Just from that gesture alone I knew what it was. A sane person would have left, but I had stopped being sane a long time ago. Without warning, I shoved past him and walked into the house. Standing on the steps, wearing a long T-shirt and nothing else, was the young, light-skinned girl I'd had to check months ago who worked at the Foot Locker out the Pittsburgh Mills Mall.

I looked back at Drew. "Really, nigga?" I spat.

Drew looked at me apologetically. "Khalia, it's not what you think."

His words pissed me off even more. I snapped. One minute, I was standing at the bottom of the steps, and the next thing I knew, I had grabbed the girl by her long hair and dragged her down half a flight of stairs. I punched her in her face over and over, until Drew finally pulled me off of her.

"Get the fuck off of me!" I yelled as I struggled against him.

"Not until you promise that you won't lay another hand on her," he said as he tightened his grip around my stomach. His iron grip around my waist reminded me of the real reason I'd come to see him.

"Get off me," I repeated in a calmer voice. "I swear I'm done."

He reluctantly let go of me but still stepped in between us as the light-skinned woman stood to her feet. "Asha, I'm sorry about this," he apologized to her.

I snorted but held my tongue.

"Oh my God, Drew, we have to call the police on her," Asha exclaimed as she held her swollen lips.

"You might wanna tell your little girlfriend why that's not such a great idea," I warned him seriously.

"She's not my girlfriend. You are," he said as he looked back at me, and I swear my heart fucking melted.

He looked back at Asha. "I'll get you an Uber, but you gotta go, sweetheart."

"She ain't catching no fucking Uber from here," I interrupted him.

"She can wait outside for the Uber. It's the least I can do," Drew said as he gestured toward her face.

I surveyed the damage done and didn't say a word.

"How can you do this to me? What about my clothes? My bag? My phone? You can't do me like this, Drew!" she screeched.

I marched upstairs and found her clothes in a heap at the end of his bed. Her raggedy bag was right next to it. I controlled the fit of anger that threatened to overtake me as I tossed her shit downstairs.

She started to put her clothes on, but I stopped that right away. I opened the door and looked at her. "Get dressed outside."

She looked at Drew, pleading with her eyes for him to be on her side. I looked at him, too, daring him to side against me.

He shrugged his shoulders. "Wait outside, Asha. I got your Uber already. She's driving a red truck."

She looked at him in disbelief. "You really gone do me like this?"

He shrugged again. "I told you my girl was crazy and to wait upstairs. Nobody told you to be nosey and come down here."

"But, Drew . . ."

"Get the fuck out of here before I finish what I started," I snapped, growing tired of hearing her beg.

She left without another word. I slammed the door shut as she was walking, hitting her heels on the way out.

Then I turned to look at Drew. "Really, nigga? You wasn't answering your phone 'cause you wanted to be laid up with that bitch?"

"She has nothing to do with it," he responded as he sat on his love seat. "You are the reason we aren't speaking, and you know it. You don't know how to talk to me like a man."

"What do you mean?" I snapped. "I don't talk to you like you're not a man."

"No, you talk to me like *you're* a man," he shot back.

I bit my lip at hearing his words. I heard my father say the same exact thing to my mother countless times. In the end, he had left her alone. I didn't want the same thing to happen to me.

"I'm not trying to run you or force you to be someone that you're not, but I can't have my woman talking down to me when I'm trying to be her protector. That shit ain't cool."

"I wasn't talking down to you. I just wanted you to be aware of my job in our family—"

He held his hand up and cut me off. "I did my research on the Kings. I know exactly who you are and what you're about. And I don't give a fuck about none of that, Khalia. When I'm around, I don't need you to be on ya shit like that. You got me. I might not have the street resume you have, but I'll never let anything harm you or come your way."

For once, I was speechless.

"I was reacting off natural instinct, and you emasculated me," he went on. "And then I saw you put that bullet in that man's head, and I had to really think if I wanted to get in deep with someone like you, someone who kills people like it's nothing."

I tilted my head to the side. "Well?"

"Well, you here, ain't you?"

I nodded. "I am."

"Listen, I ain't never been with a woman like you, but even as I tried to get my mind off you, I don't know, I just couldn't. No one or nothing could make me stop thinking about you or wishing I was with you."

I smiled, glad to hear that I had been on his mind, but still mad that he had even felt the need to be with other women to forget about me.

"But I can't be disrespected like that," he went on. "I may not do what you do, but I'm an honest man. I make an honest living, and I'm not ashamed of who I am or what I do. That doesn't make me any less of a man than those guys you come in contact with."

I sat down next to him. "I get it. I do. I've never had a man before. All this shit is new to me. I watched my mom do it to my daddy, and I guess I thought it was normal. I have to be taught how to let you lead, but I promise you, I will still be right in the driver's seat beside you. You can be the head; I'll be the neck. It's the only way that this will work."

"Oh, yeah?" He smiled at me, showing me those dimples that I loved. "And you gone beat up any bitch you catch near me?"

"That or worse," I said seriously. "So, it's best for these hoes out here if you just don't cheat at all."

He burst out laughing. "I feel that shit."

"And that bitch. Did you get her number that day at the mall?"

"What?" He frowned. "Naw. She found me on IG and slid in my DMs. I recognized her, one thing led to another, and you know . . ." He shrugged.

I snorted. "Yeah, I do."

"She ain't you. But I ain't know what to do with you, so she filled the time till I figured that shit out. You back now, so she's gone." He spread his arms wide. "Now, come here. Daddy missed you."

I sat on his lap and gave him a deep kiss. "Next time you fuck around, I'ma fuck you up," I warned him. "You get a pass this time."

He laughed. "This time don't count. We was on a little break. I'll never cheat on you, baby. I promise."

"You better not." I looked deep in his eyes. "And the real reason I came over here was to tell you that I'm pregnant."

His eyes lit up. "Pregnant? How far along are you? When are you due?"

I laughed. "I don't know any of that yet. I just found out today. So, congratulations, Daddy."

He rubbed my still-flat stomach and kissed my cheek. "Thank you, baby. I'm gonna be the best father ever. You'll see."

Chapter Twenty-seven

Kelvin

I walked into Buffalo Wild Wings and headed straight toward the bar in the back. I didn't frequent this restaurant too often anymore. When Dutchess and I first started out, we liked to come every now and then. When we made a little more money, our taste upgraded to restaurants with linen tablecloths, but this spot was perfect for the young man I was coming to meet.

I saw Armani sitting at the bar and greeted him warmly. I had known Armani's mother, Marilyn, for years from attending some of the same charity events, which was the reason they had been invited to our anniversary party. "What's going on, son?"

"Hey, Mr. King," he said with a smile. "What you drinking?"

I knew they didn't have Louis XIII here. "I'll take a Long Island."

Armani ordered the same and then looked back at me. "So, I know you're wondering why I wanted to meet you here."

"Inquiring minds do want to know."

Armani looked at me in silence for a moment. "What if I told you I know who is responsible for what happened at Mrs. King's funeral?"

I damn near fell out of my chair. "What?"

Armani nodded slowly before looking back at me. "I been debating if I want to tell you, but he put all our lives in danger that day. I can't have that, especially when it comes to Kenya. I would lose my mind if anything happened to her."

Although I had already approved of him being with my daughter, he now had my full respect. "So, you want to protect her. That's very noble of you."

"She's my heart," he replied simply. "Listen, I know how y'all take care of things, which is why I came to you instead of any of your kids. This man is very close to me. I was hoping you would handle it with kid gloves."

I raised my eyebrow. "Who is it?"

He took a deep breath as the bartender set our drinks down in front of us. "My brother Rallo."

I frowned. "Your older brother? Leo's stepson?" I asked, just to be sure.

He nodded. "Yeah. He's just tired of not having shit, and I get it. But he's gone too far."

"Does Kenya know you know he's behind this?"

He shook his head. "Naw, I ain't tell her. I didn't want her to try to handle it herself, or worse, tell her sister and brothers."

"Good call." I sipped my drink as the wheels turned in my head. For what he had done, Rallo deserved nothing short of death. I didn't want to be the one who pulled the trigger, since Armani trusted me with this information, but I also knew there would be no other ending for him. Still, I assured Armani that I would handle things differently. Then, I texted Keith to meet up with him.

Chapter Twenty-eight

Rallo

"When are you gonna tell me what you're into?" Shaterra asked as she helped to prop my leg up on a few pillows on our bed.

"Why are you worried about it? Ain't the money been flowing?" I asked her as I scooted back.

"It has, but all money ain't good money, Raymond. You been shot twice in the last couple weeks."

"Wrong. I was grazed the last time," I corrected her as I touched the small bandage on my shoulder. When we lit up Dutchess King's funeral, I just knew we had the rest of them. I had sorely underestimated the amount of security they would have there and Khalia King's viciousness. She shot it out with us like a true pro. I was in the first truck, and we were lucky to get away with flesh wounds and one dead body, who we pushed out of the truck a block away. The second truck wasn't so lucky, but I didn't have time to worry about them. One by one, all of the traps we had just overtaken were ran in, and the workers were killed. I was losing a crazy amount of men each day as the Kings regained their power over the city. I had been preparing to fight a war, but they left me with no one to fight it with. As fast as I had gained all that territory, I was losing it. I didn't know what to do or who to turn to. Rick was gone. Armani was so far up his girl's ass that trying to go to him with a kidnapping scheme was out of the question. I still had some money, but with Shaterra about to have the baby, that money would dry up quick.

"Oh, my bad. *Grazed*," she repeated sarcastically.

"It is a big difference."

She rolled her eyes. "If you say so. Whatever you're into out there in those streets isn't worth it, Raymond. I don't want to bury you, baby. I want our kids to have a father."

"They will. I promise I ain't going nowhere, a'ight?"

She looked at me, uncertainty shining through her eyes.

"Shaterra. I'm gone always be here. Me and you forever. Nothing will ever change that. This family we've made together means everything to me, baby. I'll never leave it."

She still looked unsure but smiled a little anyway. "I believe you."

"Come here." I waved her over to the bed.

As soon as she began to walk toward me, the unmistakable sound of our door being kicked in rang out, followed by, "Police! Get down!"

No fucking way.

Shaterra looked at me as I reached under our mattress. "Raymond, *no*. Baby, please don't," she pleaded.

Her cries fell on deaf ears. I had gone to jail for a year after Raymiah was born, and I had sworn that I would never go back to a cage again. I meant that shit with my whole heart, too. There was nothing that would make me even consider being locked up like an animal again.

I looked at her with so much love in my eyes. Then I gazed at her stomach, carrying a son I would never know. I thought of Raymiah, who was safe at her grandmother's house, since Shaterra had to work a night shift and I was in no condition to watch her on my own with my leg.

"Get in the closet, Shaterra," I told her calmly, even as tears spilled down my face. I knew what I was about to do.

She shook her head. "I won't leave you."

"You have to, before they come in here. First one that hits the door, I'm spraying," I promised. "I don't need you caught up in that shit. Now, go get in the fucking closet."

She sobbed harder than I had ever heard her cry before. "I love you so much, Raymond."

"I love you too, baby." I heard their footsteps approaching. "Now go!"

She went to the closet and pulled the door shut just as my door burst open. I didn't even get a chance to lift my gun from my hiding spot. As soon as these cops came through the door, they lit me up with bullets.

As I lay out bleeding on my bed, I thought of Shaterra, Leo, and my kids. Had I made one right turn instead of the left, maybe I would have been able to have the family I always wanted. But I was Leo's son. Live by the gun; die by the gun.

One cop walked over to me with a shit-eating grin on his face. "Look at this, boys. He got a gun in his hands already. Guess he really was supposed to be one tough muthafucka, huh?"

The rest of them laughed heartily.

The cop leaned down and whispered in my ear, "This is for the Kings, muthafucka."

If I could have laughed, I would have. Those damn Kings. They had still managed to beat me at my own game and had even sent dirty cops to do their work for them. The shit was brilliant.

The cop smirked before standing back and firing a single shot at my head.

Everything faded to black.

Chapter Twenty-nine

Kenya

I could hear the music blasting from behind the closed doors of the condo where Keon had Dionne staying. I was so nervous about what I might see that I debated turning around and going back home. Still, I knew I couldn't do that. I hadn't come all the way over here just to back out like a punk. Plus, she needed me. Keon had already warned me that Dionne's drug use had far surpassed recreational and was a full-blown habit now. He told me not to be surprised if she no longer looked or acted like the best friend I had been so close to all these years. He had so much advice about how she would look and act that I started to cuss him out. How was it that he was walking around looking like the picture of health, and Dionne was strung out on a drug that he introduced her to?

Still, I reserved judgment for when I saw her myself. Keon had given me the key to the condo, certain that Dionne would either be too high and in her own world to hear me, or coming down from her high and feeling down. Either way, he was sure she wouldn't let me in on her own. I took a deep breath, inserted the key in the lock, and walked through the door. Even though Keon had warned me, I still wasn't prepared for what I saw.

Dionne was dancing around to Chris Brown's old song, "Poppin'," all off-beat and singing alone. She was sweating profusely and smiling like she was in her own little world. When she finally opened her eyes, she leaned down to take a hit of one of the white lines laid out on a small mirror on the coffee table. When she looked up, she finally noticed me standing there, my mouth wide open in shock.

"Kenya!" she yelled much louder than she needed to. "Girl, what are you doing here? How long you been standing there?"

I walked over to the loud Bluetooth speaker and snatched the cord out. "Long enough," I said quietly.

"Oh, shit. Remember the dances we made up to that song?" She attempted to do a dance step that we had done years ago and failed miserably. Knowing she fucked up, she started laughing hysterically before looking back at me.

"So, I guess you saw me, huh? You figured out my little secret." She laughed as she wiped her nose with the back of her hand.

My heart broke as I looked at her. She had lost weight since the last time I saw her at my mom's funeral, and even then, she was too thin for her frame. She looked sick now. Her hair, which was usually styled so nice and neat, was barely combed. Yet, she still danced around as her clothes hung off of her.

At that moment, I hated Keon for doing this to her.

"Yeah, I saw you," I murmured. "That's why I'm here. You need help, and—"

She waved her hand. "Oh, my goodness. Who told you I needed help? Keon? The nigga that introduced me to this shit? Now all of a sudden he too good to have fun with me."

"He got his kids now, Dionne. He can't be doing all this shit in front of them."

"Miss me with that bullshit. How old is Nahim now, thirteen? He *been* doing this shit. Now he wanna be a saint 'cause he got custody of him and the others are around more? Please. If he really gave a fuck about those kids, he would have cleaned up his act a long time ago."

She had a good point, but I still couldn't agree with her. "It's never too late to do what's right. I hate to see you like this. Please get some help, and I promise I'll be by your side every step of the way."

"You?" she screeched, then burst into laughter again. "Kenya, you don't give a fuck about nothing but that nigga and those trips you make out of town that you think nobody notices. You don't give a fuck about me."

I looked at her, confused. "What are you talking about I don't give a fuck about you? I'm here, ain't I? I came here to help *you*! Your family ain't here, even though they gotta know by looking at you that something's wrong. Your man ain't here. He left you to go get clean on his own. You ain't even seen that nigga. All you got is me, and you talking 'bout I don't care about you?"

She sighed dramatically. "What, you feel sorry for me or something? Or let me guess. Your brother said the only way I could stay here is if I get clean? Is that it?"

I couldn't believe what she was saying and didn't understand why she didn't want to get back to herself. Couldn't she see how bad she looked?

"My brother hasn't said one word about you. He hardly uses this place, so I truly don't think he gives a fuck if you're here or not."

She shrugged, bent down, and sniffed another line. I went over to the table and knocked that mirror off of it. The rest of her coke flew everywhere.

"Bitch!" she screeched, and the next thing I knew she charged at me. I threw her off me with no problem, but she came at me again, swinging madly and leaving me no choice but to do her like a bitch in the street. I might have been hesitant at times when it came to shooting my gun, but never when it was time to fight. I ducked all her swings and came back with quick, hard punches to her face. It slowed her down but didn't completely stop her. She came at me again with her hands out like she wanted to scratch my face up or some shit. I grabbed her wrist, bent it backward, and tossed her on the floor.

She howled in pain as she curled into a ball, holding her wrist. I stood over her and tried to feel bad about what I had just done, but the truth was that I just didn't. I had gone light on her. She was lucky I ain't dog-walk her like I wanted to.

"You really tried to fight me over that shit," I said as I shook my head. "Me! The only person who ever had your back. Over some fucking drugs!"

"Shut up," she spat me. "I'm tired of your fucking whining when you ain't never had shit to whine about in the first place. You get *everything*, Kenya. And you're mad that I won't kiss your ass?"

"Kiss my ass? When did I ask you to do that?"

"You keep saying that you're the only person I got. Well, I didn't ask you to be here for me. I didn't ask you to come here trying to fucking *save* me. I don't want to be saved, and I don't *need* your fucking help."

If possible, my heart shattered even more with her words. I wished I had listened to Armani and kept my distance from her. Never in a million years would I have imagined that she would come at me like this. Our friendship had always been one of the most important things in my life. I treasured it more than any piece of jewelry I owned, any car that I drove, or clothes that I wore. But looking at her now, I could see that she was too far gone for my love to help her. I decided right then and there to throw the towel in.

"You know what? You're right, sis. You didn't have to ask me to be here for you. You've *never* had to ask me to be here for you because real friends know when you need them. Being there for your friends is not a chore. It's not a task, nor is it a job. When you love someone, everything you do for them is from the heart 'cause it comes from a place of love.

"Now, I'm here because, regardless of what you may think or how you feel, you do have a problem, and you need help. I can't give you that. Keon never tried to give you that. And now I see only you can give yourself that. I'm here even though you haven't extended the same to me. My mother died, and you didn't even call me to check on me. Barely spoke to me at the funeral."

She finally met my gaze, letting me know that I struck a nerve.

"I would have *never* even thought of not being there for you day and night if something like that happened to you. But see, we ain't the same no more. So, I get it. I tried to excuse you being absent when I needed you the most on the fact that you had to be there for Keon too. But that was bullshit. And now, I'm done with you. I hope you find everything you need and want in those white lines, sis. I ain't got shit else to say you."

With that, I turned and walked out of the condo. A small part of me hoped that she would call after me, apologize, and admit she needed help. But a bigger part of me knew that she wouldn't. That monkey on her back was just too big. She couldn't even admit that she had a problem.

I did know one thing, though. I was done selling any kind of drugs. Seeing the effects they had on a person so close to my heart devastated me. There had to be another way to get money for me outside of destroying people with poison. I was determined to make something shake.

Epilogue

Two Years Later...

Kelvin held a glass of Louis XIII and smiled as he looked around the table at his children and their significant others. He had never been prouder of any of them and wouldn't have dreamed of celebrating such a huge night with anyone but them.

"I just want to say thanks for all the hard work you all have put in the last couple years to make this dream come to fruition," he told them. "It was a lot of work, a lot of blood, sweat, and tears."

"And a lot of money!" Keon cut him off, making everyone around the table burst into fits of laughter.

"A lot of money," Kelvin acknowledged. "But what we have here is something special. Something grand. No one has been able to do this, and no one will be able to duplicate it. So, before we go greet everyone, I just want to say that I love and appreciate each and every one of you. None of your hard work has gone unnoticed." He looked around the table again before raising his glass for a toast.

"To Dutchess Palace!" he said.

"Dutchess Palace!" everyone repeated.

Kelvin grinned. "Now, let's go make some muthafuckin' money."

Everyone laughed and followed him out to the front.

Epilogue

A line was wrapped around the block for the grand opening of Dutchess Palace. The lounge was medium-sized, not too big and not too small, so patrons would not feel like they were on top of each other. The key that was sure to be the success of Dutchess Palace was the exclusivity that surrounded it. Only the very rich and very famous would be allowed to enter. Once inside, they could listen to various bands or the hottest DJ in the country, depending on the night, and have a selection of the finest foods and wines to sample.

Kenya had gone all out to make sure the décor was up to par. Since the club had been named after her mother, she had decided to do the interior in all shades of purple, Dutchess's favorite color. There were purple couches, the cushions on the seats were purple, and even the dance floor was purple with a huge gold crown on it. She had managed to make the club look fit for royalty. She knew she had done a great job, but she was still nervous about opening the doors.

"You think everyone will like it?" she asked Armani anxiously as they made their way to the front.

"If they don't, they're some fools," he assured her.

She stopped and looked him over to make sure nothing on his outfit was out of place. He was, after all, the top wide receiver in the NFL. He'd broken all the rookie records for the team he played for, the Atlanta Falcons, and for the NFL as well. He was one of the most famous men in the world at the moment and had received both the Rookie of the Year and MVP awards for the league. He'd taken the Falcons back to the NFC Championship game, and while the team had lost, he still put on an amazing performance. His mission this year was to get them to the Super Bowl and win it all.

His and Kenya's relationship had not been without problems. They'd moved so fast in the beginning without truly getting a chance to get to know one another. After his second year at Pitt, Armani stayed true to his word and entered the NFL draft. He was immediately selected by the Atlanta Falcons, and Kenya followed him down there with no hesitation. It was the best move for her at the time.

Armani had kept his word and allowed her to style him. As the star of the team and a Heisman trophy winner, he was constantly in the news. His interviewers started to mention just how fashionable he always looked, and he didn't hesitate to mention that his girlfriend, Kenya King, was a stylist and did all of his looks. Pretty soon, Kenya's phone was ringing off the hook, and her emails were bombarded with requests from famous athletes for her to style them as well.

Kenya couldn't believe her good fortune. She knew that not many people were blessed with an opportunity to make a living doing something that they really loved, and she figured that it must have been her mother smiling down on her. Dutchess had forced her to take part in the family business, but she always knew that Kenya's heart was not in it at all.

Things had been looking great for the couple until Armani started playing in the NFL. Kenya thought that she was prepared for the lifestyle since Armani was already a household name due to his performance in college, but in no way was she ready for everything that came with Armani playing professional football. Up until that point, Armani had never cheated on her, but in his rookie year, he had been unable to help himself. He tried to sample damn near every piece of pussy that was thrown at him. It had gotten so bad that he'd even given her chlamydia once, and that was when Kenya left him. She loved Armani, but she didn't want to stick around and wait for him to give her something she couldn't get rid of. She moved out of the mansion he'd purchased with his huge contract and into her own luxury condo from the money she made on her own. It had taken Armani a good six months to finally convince her to come back home to him where she belonged. Since then, they had been tighter than ever. Armani took Kenya to every away game or any big event he had to do out of town without her even having to ask him to do so. Her trust meant everything to him.

"You're right," she told him as she straightened the collar on the lightweight red blazer he wore. Underneath the blazer, he had on a black short-sleeved button-up shirt with the top two buttons undone. She fixed the gold Cuban chain that lay against his bare chest so that it was straight, then tugged at her own little black dress.

"Relax. You look perfect," he assured her as he pulled her close and gave her a kiss. "Always the prettiest woman in the room."

Kenya blushed at his compliment.

"Get a room!" Khalia joked as she walked up to stand next to them. She was on Drew's arm, and the two of them looked as happy as could be.

It hadn't been easy for Khalia to learn how to let a man lead her, especially a man like Drew, who wasn't what she would call a boss. Still, she had learned that letting a man lead was easy when you trusted where that man was taking you. And aside from that mishap with Asha, which she didn't like to count since they were no longer together, Khalia wholeheartedly trusted Drew.

Her pregnancy hadn't been easy, but not due to complications or anything like that. Khalia was used to constantly being on the move and looking extremely sexy as she did. Watching her body change from curvaceous to round as she carried their son was something that she just was not prepared for. Giving up her body-hugging clothes almost broke her heart, but she managed to find ways to dress her bump so that she could still feel sexy.

They'd kept the baby's sex a surprise, wanting to find out at birth. The first time Khalia laid eyes upon her son, she felt a love that she never knew could exist. He was a beautiful baby, with her curly hair and Drew's chocolate complexion and dimples. They decided to name him Dutch after Dutchess.

Khalia took to motherhood. She surprised everyone with the new, softer side of her. She traded in her love of murder, torture, and guns for changing diapers, cleaning bottles, and playing with her son, especially when she learned that Rallo had been killed by the police. She had no more beef left in the streets. Her transformation amazed everyone but really pleased Drew, who had always had doubts that she would be able to fully leave her queenpin life behind.

Yet, she did just that. She loved having a family so much that she wanted more kids, and Drew didn't hesitate to knock her up again. She was now six months pregnant with their second child and couldn't be happier.

She had done a complete change from the woman she used to be. Losing Tookie and her mother on the same day, two people that she was so close to, had proven to her that life was not promised, and no one was untouchable. Drew's love had turned her ice-cold heart warm, but that old Khalia still bubbled underneath the surface if anyone tried to fuck with her family.

Khalid peeped out the window as they lined up to open the front door. The windows were black-on-black so that lounge patrons could look out of them, but no one could look in. He saw the limos stretching down the block and knew that they were filled with famous people that both he and Armani had invited to the opening.

"You think we'll have enough room for all the VIPs?" he asked Toni with a hint of worry in his voice.

She rubbed his hand and immediately calmed him down, as only she could do. "You planned this to the T, baby. There's enough room for people who are supposed to be here."

He nodded and planted a kiss on her forehead. "You're right." He looked over at Kelvin and nodded. "Let's do this."

Kelvin opened the doors, and it seemed as if the celebrities began pouring in immediately. Being somewhat of a celebrity himself, Khalid was prepared to deal with them.

He had won the seat in the senate by a landslide, just as everyone had predicted he would, despite all the drama surrounding himself and his family, or maybe because of it. America loved a good story, and Khalid was one of the best. It also helped that he was gorgeous and had a woman on his arm that most people could relate to. His popularity was immediate and through the roof. He quickly became one of the most well-liked politicians since Barack Obama. He kept his promises, touched people, and assured them that he was there for them. He had the ability to make everyone feel as though he believed in them.

Khalid appeared on late-night talk shows, on early morning radio shows, and on podcasts. He was everywhere because he was truly for the people. The country couldn't get enough of him. He did so much that he had decided to step back from the drug game as his sisters had. Pumping cocaine and heroin through the political system just wasn't important to him anymore. He had only agreed to do so to appease Dutchess and still chase his dream at the same time, but now that she was gone, he didn't feel the pressure on him anymore. Besides that, he truly wanted to help people. He was great at what he did.

Epilogue

Nisa's confession about killing Amber had fucked his head up for a little while, though. He couldn't believe that all this time, he had been sleeping with the enemy. He had never known how Nisa felt about him over the years. She certainly had never shown signs that she was in love with him. He tried to feel sad that she had killed herself, but he honestly didn't care. Anyone who killed a pregnant woman and her unborn child would never get any sympathy from him.

Toni had been more shaken up than him, and rightfully so. She had never seen anyone blow their brains out before. Khalid was used to it, since he had done his fair share of bodying people. Still, he was there for her and understood the trauma she felt behind it.

After Toni graduated from college with her degree in finance, she planned to continue working for PNC Bank, but Khalid had bigger plans for her. As a graduation present, he gave her her own financial consulting firm, since she had already managed so many portfolios. She was extremely successful and was so glad that she had finally stopped fighting him about everything he wanted to do for her.

Khalid split his time between Washington, DC, and Pittsburgh. Toni and Tommy, his official aide, went with him whenever they could. They lived a life Toni had only dreamed about. But it wasn't a dream. It was real life, and she was so grateful every day that she had let her guard down to be with him.

Keon greeted the various professional athletes and superstars who came through the door with a smile. He was the only one of the Kings, besides Kelvin, who had come to the event without a date, and he was okay with that. After the disaster with Dionne and Stacey, Keon had sworn off relationships again. He simply didn't have the time for it. Stacey was still rotting away in jail on murder charges for Dutchess and attempted murder charges on him.

She'd had the baby, and a blood test confirmed that the baby was Keon's. He was distraught. In no way was he prepared to raise another kid on his own, and a newborn baby at that. His mother was no longer there to help him. Khalia had a new baby of her own, and Kenya barely spoke to him. Yet, he'd had no choice but to take the baby. Stacey had their daughter, a little girl she named Neveah, while she was in prison. If he didn't step up to claim the baby, she would become a ward of the state. As pissed as he was at Stacey and the situation, he couldn't allow that to happen. So, he stepped up and claimed her.

His actions had all but destroyed whatever he had left with Dionne. The fact that he'd made a baby on her had devastated her and sent her even deeper into her addiction. Keon felt badly for how he had treated her and even worse for the way he handled her heart, but he couldn't allow her self-destruction to continue on his watch. He refused to supply her with any more cocaine, and when she flipped out and destroyed his condo at The Washington, he had no choice but to put her out. Last he'd heard, she was back at her grandmother's, getting high with the rest of her family. That crushed him, but there was nothing he could do about it. Her addiction had already ruined their relationship, the one he had with his sister, and the one she had with his sister as well. He knew better than anyone that she wouldn't get the help she needed until she was ready to do so.

Yet, he still needed help with his kids. Marisol, his housekeeper, had surprisingly stepped up and filled the role that they so desperately needed. She was amazing with the baby, Nahim, and his other children whenever they came to visit. Whenever he needed to make business trips, he felt comfortable leaving them in her care. She was great to them, but even better to him. They'd finally slept together, and in her, Keon found a kindred spirit, a woman who had been through it all and was in no rush to settle down. They formed an unconventional relationship that worked for them. Marisol tended to him and the kids when she was there, which was ninety percent of the time, since she still took care of the house, and what she did on her own time was her own business. Keon didn't sweat her, and she didn't ask him about his business either.

Keon was seeing more money than he could spend, thanks to Vincent. He'd had no idea just how powerful the distribution network Vincent had set up really was. He was the boss of bosses and was even more respected. At this level of the game, he didn't know about any beefs, didn't have any street wars, or none of that. He was truly the boss of the East Coast, and no one even knew. While Khalid, Kenya, and Khalia had stepped away to focus on their own dreams, Keon had stepped up, all thanks to Vincent.

He was growing close to the Mob boss. He couldn't help it. He saw so much of himself in the man. His relationship with Kelvin had also improved. He no longer felt like what the man had done warranted death. Kelvin had wanted out and decided to take it. Keon couldn't help but respect that. Besides, he knew that Kelvin would never do anything to intentionally hurt any of them.

As Dutchess Palace filled up, Kelvin sat back and watched with a proud smile. He was so proud of how far he had come. The road to get here had been filled with so much heartache, death, and destruction that he knew he was one of the lucky ones to make it out alive and successful. The game had claimed plenty victims, whether directly or indirectly. He knew that he was blessed and highly favored.

He thought of his loved ones who weren't there. He would have loved to share a night like this with them: his father, Big Vic; his brother, Jamar; and his estranged wife, Dutchess. He wished they could see what he had managed to accomplish.

"So, you pulled it off, huh?" Keith asked as he came and stood by his side.

"I did," Kelvin agreed with a nod. He was grateful to have Keith there. Besides his kids and grandkids, Keith was the only family he had.

"I knew you would. From the day I met you, I knew that you were gone be something great." Keith looked at him. "I'm proud of you. I know your father would be too." Then he walked off to join the party.

Kelvin felt a little emotional about his words. For some reason, Keith had seen fit to rescue him time and time again. For a long time, Kelvin had never been able to understand it. Even when he called in that last favor to get rid of Rallo, Keith had done it, no questions asked. For years, Kelvin hadn't understood, but now he did. When you see someone has potential to be great, you don't distinguish the flames; you ignite the spark. That's what Keith had done every time he'd put a book in his hand. It was what he had done when he'd learned that his son Khalid had his same love for learning, and in a way, it was what Dutchess had done when she saw that Khalia had inherited her no-nonsense personality.

Kelvin sipped from his ever-present glass of Louis XIII and smiled slightly at the thought of his ex-wife. She had been such a fiery woman that even in the years that passed since her death, no one had come close to replacing her. Kelvin dated, but he wasn't looking for anything more serious than a casual fling.

"I hope you're proud of me too, Dutchess," he murmured before draining his glass and going to rejoin the party. His dream had come true, and he wanted to make sure he experienced every minute of it.

The End . . .